MISSED OPPORTUNITIES

~

H E ROFFEY

heroffeyauthor@gmail.com

Charlson Publishers

ISBN-10: 0-9550404-1-8
ISBN-13: 978-0-9550404-1-2

Cover design and layout by SpiffingCovers

DEDICATION

My wife, Sonja, has been understanding when I've been hidden away, supportive when I've shown signs of lethargy, patient when she's needed things done and critical when I've deserved it. Without her love this book along with many other things would not have come to fruition.

CONTENTS

PREFACE

The first of a series of novels exploring the actions of various characters as they face pertinent social and moral issues.

ACKNOWLEDGEMENTS

No person is an island. However, alone with a keyboard, a computer screen and varying degrees of imagination, that old adage falls away and the safe ground one glides over towards the edge of the cliff suddenly becomes an abyss and without support, a fall is inevitable. Therefore I thank my wife, Sonja, for her many rereads and corrections and to Ian Steadman for his unique friendship, valued comments and encouragement. Thanks to my two sons, Carl and Dorian for enabling me to look through different lenses at life. Thanks to James Willis and SpiffingCovers for their immediate and comprehensive approach to converting my manuscript to final book.

This book is a novel and, as a consequence, it is difficult to thank the hundreds, if not, thousands of people that, even in a fleeting moment, have left sufficient impression to warrant reflection: the man, in a remote homestead in South Africa, who opened his door to me after I'd walked five miles from my ailing car late one night, immediately comes to mind. It's even more difficult, but necessary, to thank the very few people who were not so friendly but also left that fleeting impression for they have enabled me to reflect on the circumstances and draw on the feelings.

CHAPTER 1

'If you want to be the quintessential grumpy old man just carry on, but remember I'm the only one who'll tell you,' said John, as they walked to the car in the dark.

'I can't help it when I'm faced with people who should know better,' replied Victor.

'For goodness sake Victor it's only a book club. Not everybody's an academic.'

'Sorry, but tonight's meeting touched a raw nerve. Sorry, I'm being ungracious. I should thank you for getting me out. I know you want me to meet new people.'

'It's been nearly three years since Anne passed away and apart from me and your very occasional outings with the loyal Sylvia, you're becoming a recluse. You're fifty-seven going on eighty and I'm the only one who's going to tell you; so unless you want to become clinically depressed, do something other than college work. Come on, I'll drive you home. It's bloody freezing.'

'Thanks all the same but I need the walk.'

'Understood, but remember, you're too old to be the angry young man you never were.'

The air, which earlier hung heavy with moisture, had freeze-dried leaving diamond dust on the parked cars. Victor stopped every now and then and looked up at the rare sight of a star-bright sky, cruelly reminding him of his developing stoop. He thought of Anne, and John's parting, words but quickly refocused on the book club. His anger had begun when Pamela started saying that the Palestinians deserved what they got for firing missiles in the first place. He'd looked around the room, and apart from John who'd given him a pleading look to be quiet, none of the others seemed perturbed. They knew him to be a university don but none knew that he was an active human rights lawyer, or that he'd spent an hour in Arafat's company soon after the Oslo Accord as part of the legal team.

Apart from the greeting he knew he'd get from his ten-year-old cat Pib, Victor had no wish to arrive home. He stared at his empty house from across the street, wishing he could avoid it, but a faint light behind a window curtain on the first floor captured his attention. It went out but then appeared with wavering intensity in another window.

Ignoring Anne's voice telling him to ring the police, Victor crept along a narrow lane to his back garden, nearly knocking over a bike leaning against his shed. Sweating, but confident within the darkness of the shed and having a clear view of the house, he gripped a rusty steel pipe; suddenly he panicked, knowing full well he couldn't hit somebody on the head with it. He imagined brain damage, a wheelchair, food dribbling out of a mouth and a woman catching it in a spoon. 'Oh, God!' he mumbled, fumbling through his pockets for his phone while looking at a lithe-looking man about his own height, all in black apart from his white trainers, leaving the house. *Oh, God! He's getting away* he thought, crouching down while listening to the bike being dragged around.

'I don't know how I got out of the shed or why I did it', he said later, but the bike crashed onto the concrete path as he brought the pipe down onto the man's shoulder. Victor remembered feeling shocked as he watched the man collapse, first onto his knees and then, as if in slow motion, fall across the bike; then complete silence and this overwhelming fear of having seriously injured someone.

Anne, he muttered, searching with the shaking light of his phone for the ball of twine he knew hung on a hook on the inside of the shed door. On one knee he listened to the man's breathing and tentatively moved his hands and tied his thumbs together behind his back, he then leapt back as he tried to roll the man over.

'What the fuck are you doing?' shouted Andy, trying to sit up. 'Yow!' he screamed, falling back. 'My neck.'

Struggling to sit up and see more than the silhouette of Victor's face as it came into focus, Andy shouted, 'My mates'll be here soon and fuck you up,' and then 'Aagh!' he screamed and fell back from the sting of a vicious slap across his face.

'Shush for Christ's sake,' said Victor shaking his stinging hand and prodding Andy's thick padded jacket with a long screwdriver. 'And keep still. Don't make a sound. We'll be here 'till I'm convinced the neighbours are not interested.'

'I could scream and bring-----------.'

Victor pushed and turned the screwdriver into Andy's chest tearing the material and penetrating the padding.

'I said don't make a sound,' said Victor putting his hand over Andy's mouth and pushing his head hard against the spokes of the front wheel.

'OK, get up slowly,' whispered Victor into Andy's ear. 'You, me and this screwdriver are going into the house.'

'Stop snivelling and sit in that chair,' said Victor pushing Andy into one of two dark brown leather chairs situated across a low table from a matching settee.

'Watch it. It's fucking painful.'

'I'm surprised you haven't got a broken collarbone. I hit you hard enough; not on the head I hope you noticed. And don't say watch it, you're in no position to threaten me.'

'What you're doing is fucking illegal. You'll get prison for this, you will.'

'What would you like me to do then?'

'Let me go. You can have all your stuff back. I won't tell.'

'Let you go so that you can rob some other law-abiding person who'll call the overstretched police while you get away? It's too late for that I'm afraid.'

Victor felt he was watching himself and wasn't the person who'd grabbed a roll of bin liners and a large kitchen knife while prodding Andy forward through the kitchen.

Why would a good-looking guy stoop to being a thief he thought? He's fit enough to have laid me flat if I hadn't got in first, and what is he? Twenty at most, smartly dressed and over six feet tall if he held his head up straight.

'Don't look so worried - I'm not going to strangle you,' said Victor, twisting the continuous length of plastic bags to form a rope. 'This will have to make do until I think of something substantial.'

Victor went behind the chair, put the rope over Andy's head and pulled it tight against his throat.

'Keep still, you'll hurt yourself if you struggle,' said Victor, crossing the rope behind the chair and securing the ends to the chair legs.

'Relax and lean over to one side without choking yourself to death while I try and get your hands free. And keep still while I cut through the string. This knife is extremely sharp and I don't want blood all over the chair.'

'Look I'm sorry, honest. Let me go. I'll say nothing.'

'I've told you. It's too late for that, but I'll be honest with you, I don't know how this will pan out. I don't think I'll be calling the police. But if it helps, I don't want to injure you unless I'm forced to. I've already pointed out I could have hit you on the head instead of your shoulder. So, you're alive. Count your blessings; stop snivelling and for god's sake pull your jacket up to stop the plastic biting into your neck. And don't try kicking while I'm tying your feet to the chair.'

'You're going to be sorry old man. If I'm not back soon, my mates really will be here for me.'

'I'm going to set some ground rules. Don't threaten me and I won't threaten you. If you want to scream the fucking place down, as you nearly put it earlier, or anything else for that matter, just do it, go ahead; and if I want to do something, whether in response to you or not, I'll do it, regardless of the effect on you, me or anyone else for that matter. You have no idea how close you are to being injured if things go wrong here, and as for me, I'll let you into a secret: I've been in foreign prisons and at this point in my life I don't care what happens to me. Besides, a couple of years in a British prison could be a reasonable price to pay. It could even be an adventure, and I could probably do some research.'

'What are you going to do?' asked Andy, wiping his face with one of the sheets of kitchen towelling Victor had given him.

'I don't know yet. I'm hoping we can discuss it. You see it's like this: the critical mass of public feeling is moving towards victims of crime, and if I reported it now I could possibly get off with a warning.'

'Not if you've been in prison you won't.'

'I've been locked up for telling the truth and the British government helped me out. Now let's pretend something bad happens and you die. I'd possibly get no more than ten years, which means I could be out in five. Well that's enough about me. I want to know about you. You're young, you don't look as if you live rough, you're obviously healthy, and apart from the dirt you picked up in my garden you look pretty smart. It's a great shame you couldn't have turned out to be a better person but then again, you're probably one of those people whose more intent on climbing through the ranks of your poorly selected peers than accepting love or advice from those who have your interest at heart. Tripped up by your own ego; such a pity. I'm making tea, would you like some or would you prefer coffee or water?'

'I want to get out of here,' scowled Andy, wincing as he lifted back the hood of his jacket revealing neatly cut dark hair, which matched his eyebrows and a suntanned boyish face.

'You're not going anywhere, at least not for the next few hours. I haven't got a plan. In fact I'm amazed it's got to this. I thought I'd hit you, grab the bag and defend myself. It's sheer luck it's turned out like this. Now I want you to tell me about yourself. So what would you like?'

Andy closed his lips tight and stared blankly across the room.

'I'll bring you some tea and with a bit of luck I may have some biscuits.'

Victor went to the small downstairs bathroom and looked at himself in the mirror while washing his hands. Feeling excited and alive, he splashed cold water over his face, dried it, combed his grey hair and went to the kitchen.

Victor returned with a loaded tray, ignoring the slight repositioning of the chair and the tiny pieces of plastic from the rope on Andy's lap.

'Neck's a bit red I see. I'll let you into a secret,' he said pushing magazines out of the way with the tray. 'Had my wife been alive she'd have been terrified, but you'd have got off lightly. She'd have let the police handle it and you'd be miles away with our things by now and I'd have been left with an intense feeling of violation. Now tell me about yourself and let's see where we go from there.'

Victor poured the tea into two mugs and handed one to Andy who forgot he was restrained, coughed as the rope caught his throat. Victor held Andy's mug until he'd recovered, moved a small table for him and sat on the settee.

'I'm sorry it has to be like this. I'd sooner we talked as equals. Please believe me I'm trying to reach out to understand you. So take your time. Begin anywhere you like.'

'What do you want me to say?'

'You have plenty of time. You could start with your name.'

'This is fucking stupid,' said Andy.

'As we're both in an unusual predicament I'll say something provocative and you counter it. I'll start. I think you're an example of vermin that should be eradicated. Now please defend that statement for all you're worth.'

'And what if I don't want to talk?'

Victor nodded slightly and pursed his lips. 'Perhaps that's not the easiest way for you to start, and it's probably unfair of me to give you such a blank sheet. Here's a sort of framework: who are you? What else do you do? Tell me about breaking into people's houses and stealing. Where do you live? Who lives with you? It's one in the morning so you have plenty of time to tell me about yourself while I remain silent, unless of course, you ask me questions, then I'll choose whether to answer or not. So, who are you?'

'I'm not telling you.'

'So, you're a common thief with no name, living within a cycle ride of here. You're reasonably well dressed. You have new trainers, you're about twenty and you look fit and too clear-eyed to be on drugs. I'll call you Archie for the time being. Archie the thief.'

'What's your name then?' mocked Andy.

'Victor.'

'That's an ol' fashioned name.'

'I've never thought of myself as old-fashioned but I agree about the name. Archie's also an old fashioned name normally short for Archibald: a strange name. Don't know where it comes from,' said Victor, relaxing against the back of the settee. 'I can think of a few Archibalds though; I think most died in the first half of the 20th century but if I remember correctly there's a link, by name only you understand, from Archibald Leitch who designed football grounds and Lindsey Archibald who was a football sports presenter of a sorts. I think she's also a TV reporter but I can't remember if I've ever seen her. There was a similar link with some actors in the same film if I'm not mistaken, Lindsay Duncan and somebody Lindsay. Oh yes, Robert Lindsay, opposite sex in both cases. Interesting. Well to me anyway, I let it all go around in my head, no significance in any of it.'

After a few minutes of silence Victor retrieved Andy's bag from the kitchen and carefully tipped its contents onto the settee next to him.

'I'm glad you found my card wallet. I was worried about that while I was out. My new laptop; that must be worth something to you and a lot more to me, and what the hell is in this plastic bag?' asked Victor, tearing it open and letting rings and brooches spill out. 'And my wife's old phone,' he said, standing up and grabbing the knife from the table. Andy grabbed the arms of the chair and pushed his feet hard against the floor. Victor walked past him to the kitchen and once there gripped his hair on either side of his head with his elbows touching in front and, near to tears of rage, breathed deeply for a few minutes.

'Let's have your phone please,' said Victor, holding out his hand.

'Get it yourself.'

'Sure,' replied Victor picking up the knife. 'Sorry about the jacket though.'

'OK, OK, OK,' said Andy, unzipping an inside pocket.

'Come on Archie. Switch it on. Don't play with me.'

Andy's face grew red as he watched Victor taking notes from the phone.

'That's another crime against you, you bastard.'

'So it's Andy. I wasn't too far out. I see you call her "Mom", not "Mum". What's she like, your mom?'

Andy stared at Victor with jaws tightly shut and hands gripping the chair.

'Come on Andy for god's sake, what's she like?' shouted Victor.

'What was your mum like?' asked Andy.

'Are you making an assumption I no longer have one?'

'She must be fucking old if you do.'

'Do you have grandmothers?'

'Yeah,' said Andy.

'How old are they?'

'They?'

'Yes, your mother's mother and your father's mother. Wake up for Christ's sake Andy,' shouted Victor. He then felt guilty and compassionate towards Andy when he saw the puzzled look on his face.

'Sorry Andy. That was insensitive and not how I wanted it to come out.'

'Leave my fucking phone alone you cunt.'

Ignoring Andy's growing anger, Victor carried on interrogating the phone.

'Is Lizzie older or younger than you? I'm only guessing. Did you go home last night? Lizzie wanted to know yesterday afternoon so that she could tell Mom?'

The veins on Andy's neck stood out and his eyes watered. Victor handed him another square of kitchen tissue.

'OK, if you aren't going to answer those questions, at least give me some information about the names. Who's Jackie?'

'She's my girlfriend.'

'I don't think so Andy.'

'She says she's from a shop that closes at five-thirty and she'll keep the jacket for you 'til then, otherwise it's going back on the rack. Sounds very abrupt for a girlfriend. She did use your first name though. I'll possibly reply to her when the shops open in the morning.'

'What are you going to ask her?'

'I'll think of something,' said Victor.

'What for?'

'I'm interested in you and I'm building a picture. I'm getting to know quite a lot about you and I'm sure your mother will tell me even more.'

'My mom'll fucking kill you when she finds out what you've been up to.'

'I must admit, getting between a lioness and its cub is not the best place to be. So, come on, tell me what she's like, your mum.'

'She's good, a lot fucking brighter than you, and she's got connections so you're for it when she finds out what you've been doing.'

'I hope she's brighter. I appreciate intellect even when I can't keep up. It's the feeling of being challenged that makes me feel alive. I haven't experienced that for some time. So, she's good. What do you mean by good?'

'What the fuck do you think I mean?'

'Well she could be good because she works with sick people, she could be good because she indulges you, she could be good because she's a laugh, she could be good because she goes to church. You think she's good, so it's your opinion, hence my question.'

'I don't want to talk about her to you.'

'OK then, tell me about Elly. I think she's also your sister. She sounds very young. I'm guessing about the relationships but she also passed on the message from mom about dinner being ready at seven and if you haven't phoned by six she assumes you won't be there. I don't know why but I imagined you'd be saying 'tea' for a meal at that time. Anyway, whoever wants you home says 'dinner'.' Andy remained silent.

'I'm irritated by these long silences. You've hardly touched your tea. Do you want a fresh one? I'll make you one. Anyway, I could do with another.'

Victor leapt up the stairs, two at a time, to his bedroom. Put his and Anne's things back in their respective drawers and returned to the kitchen. After scratching about at the back of the 'junk' cupboard in the utility room he found the roll of cord he'd intended to install on the windy-dry two years back.

'You've had a real good struggle. There's bits of plastic all over the place and the wheals on your neck look painful.'

'I'm glad,' said Andy. 'I'll tell them you tried to fucking hang me.'

'You're lucky the chair didn't go over. You might have choked to death.'

'You'd 'ave been for it then, old man.'

'For it? What are you talking about? I've already told you but I'll tell you again: my life is spent and if killing vermin is one of my last actions, then so be it; or do you think you, Andy, can change into being something useful? Perhaps our little chat should hinge on that subject. Here's your tea.'

Victor held the mug out. Andy hesitated then took it.

'You're right about my mother though. She died many years ago so we can talk about her in the past tense. She was also good. When I speak of good, I mean she was fearful of doing wrong, would never hurt anybody. She winced when she heard any injustice. Is your mother like that?'

'My mother's tough,' said Andy.

'How do you mean, tough? Tough, like she's big and hairy with bulging biceps?'

Andy's face relaxed slightly as he thought of his slim five foot eight mother in tight jeans, tucked-in white blouse and the trainers she wore about the house.

'No. When she sets out to do something, she does it.'

'So, she's determined,' said Victor. 'Is she tough on you?'

'Nope. I do as I like.'

'Your sisters don't get away with much though, do they? I assume they're your sisters?'

Andy didn't answer but the creases in his forehead became pronounced as the silence continued.

'You have other sisters or brothers? Come on Andy. Tell me. I'm genuinely interested. My wife would have been interested but she wouldn't have approved of what I'm doing.'

'I bet she fucking wouldn't,' said Andy.

'How do you know? You didn't know my wife. She died in this house over two years ago. You never know, my death may unite us again and taking you with me could be my eternal torment or my eternal happiness. You play with fire when you break into people's houses. Anne, that's my wife, she'd be afraid I'd made a mistake and be in deep trouble. She'd have sympathy for you. She'd look for reasons for your behaviour in the belief that something could be done to help you and society. She wouldn't understand your wantonness and thieving as a living, just as she wouldn't understand your death as being beneficial to your family.'

'You're talking crap.'

'Unless members of your family have given their blessing to your thieving, you'd be surprised what they really think about you. Of course, your death would give them the opportunity to wallow in their own misfortune and guilt, but in reality they would mourn the loss of part of themselves and their missed opportunities, but they wouldn't mourn the loss of you as a person. Oh yes! They'd fight for you like all people who defend their investments, regardless of whether they're flourishing or rotting, but the benefits of your demise are, more than likely, enormous to your family and certainly society. It'd probably allow your mom, as you call her, freedom to focus on something worthwhile. At first of course, your family would probably bask in the limelight of the terrible thing that happened to their dear, gentle and loving Andy but you and I know that's all bullshit.'

'I need a piss.'

'OK. I'll be back in a second,' said Victor.

'Hold your arms out in front and put your thumbs like this,' said Victor, demonstrating. Victor tied Andy's thumbs together with string, released him from the chair and holding the screwdriver with one hand, helped Andy to his feet.

'I can't fucking walk. My legs are tied together.'

'Do your best.'

Andy shuffled to the toilet and fumbled his way through jeans and underpants while Victor stood in the open door and operated the taps for Andy to wash his hands.

'You'll manage,' said Victor, holding a towel for him to finish.

'Please don't struggle with this or you may really behead yourself. It's a windy-dry cord and there's a wire running through the plastic cover,' said Victor, while re-securing Andy to the chair. 'Hold your thumbs out while I cut the string. Let's tuck your tee-shirt under the cord. There you are, that's much better.'

Victor went to the kitchen and cut two slices of bread pudding that were somewhat dry but more than palatable to Victor, whose diet, especially when there was no prospect of a visit from one of his daughters, was governed more by what was about to go off or what was trapped in the ice in the freezer, rather than any exploration of his wants.

Andy took the large plate with the bread pudding on and a glass of orange without a word, and Victor, with a similar plate, returned to the settee.

Andy would certainly have been a child in Anne's eyes thought Victor. After the police visit, there would have been Anne's verbal listing of possible reasons for the robbery. His upbringing, his drug abuse, his peer group pressure, his deprivation, his desperate need for money to feed himself and possibly his family, his background, right down to the imaginary father who walked out when he was three months old and his alcoholic mother who was awaiting his return. All these possibilities would have been considered to form an understanding of why such a crime could possibly have been perpetrated. However, a few minutes later, a fresh set of possibilities would have been brought to bear that would have culminated in the same end. None based upon simple and wilful gain as an alternative to working for a living.

He imagined what would happen if the police were informed now: being processed by authorities and the judiciary in ways similar to others who had gone out on a limb. He imagined being arrested, charged, bailed, tried, sentenced, fined and possibly imprisoned. Then sued, harassed by legalese, made to pay compensation and costs. Years would have been removed from his life during which part of his mind would have needed ring-fencing to enable some sort of defence to keep up an appearance and go about his university work, that is if he remained employed. He could forecast the constant nagging of thoughts at four in the morning and the thrashing out of the arguments that would go on in dark moments. He could see the nit-picking stretching ahead of him like a road in the desert, where he would only be able to progress if he examined each grain of sand before moving on. He also knew Anne was right and that what he was doing was wrong. Anne and Victor both knew he didn't have the patience to work with people like Andy, certainly not while there was an ever-increasing stream of similar people. He stared into space weighing up his shrinking life. Moments later he dismissed all feelings of guilt, all thoughts of Anne and of phoning the police.

'OK Andy, I can see you don't want to debate with me and you're humiliated enough. I don't want to belittle you further, I really don't. I would appreciate you listening to me though. I don't want to lecture you so please interrupt me if you feel you have something to contribute.'

'Are you going to let me go after that?'

'Let's explore that option afterwards. I don't want to raise any false hopes.'

'When are you going to fucking well let me go then?'

'As soon as I have a plan. I'm sure it won't be too long after sunrise.'

'Fuck!' shouted Andy thumping the arm of the chair. 'I've got to be somewhere.'

'So have I!' shouted Victor, smashing his fist on the table. 'Fortunately, I have the luxury of phoning to make other arrangements. Now you're starting to see the results of what you do.'

'I don't know what the fuck you're talking about.'

'Of course you don't know. It's not because you're thick, it's because you only think of yourself. The more selfish a person is the less regard they have for others. And that conveniently leads me on to what I hoped we'd talk about.'

'And what if I don't want to listen?'

'Then sit there with your fingers in your ears and look more humiliated than you do now. Come on Andy, join in for goodness sake. Did you know that some criminals have to face their victims as part of their rehabilitation?'

Andy stared menacingly at Victor.

'Anyway, it has proved very successful in reducing reoffending. You Andy, as a thief, have the luxury of having me, the victim, for a face-to-face meeting without being convicted. Because of what you've done, neither of us is able to carry out our plan for the day. You are no richer and I'm no poorer, but hopefully I can give you something and keep it myself.'

'You're talking shit.'

'If I give you knowledge I still retain it, so listen and learn. You came here to take my things with no regard for me or what those things meant to me.'

'You're fucking insured anyway,' Andy spat out.

'You don't know that Andy. You don't know how long it would have taken me to buy a new computer or whether I can afford one or how long it would take to set it up or what valuable files might not have been backed up in my hurry to go out. Those rings belonged to my grandmother. My wife wore one of them until she died. Would you like me to take you upstairs and show you the bed she died in?'

Andy looked at his interlaced hands.

'No, and I don't blame you. I'm glad it was me you tried to rob. Many people never recover from a violation like this one of yours.'

'What violation?'

'You violated me, my space and my house.'

'That means you violated me,' retorted Andy.

'Absolutely correct,' replied Victor.

'And fucking tortured me.'

'That's an exaggeration, but if you want to see what torture is like I'll show you,' said Victor getting up.

Ignoring Andy's recoil into the chair and his uncontrollable coughing caused by his jerking head against the cord, Victor walked out of the room.

'This is torture,' said Victor, showing the first of a file full of A4 colour photographs. 'Don't turn away like that. Take a bloody good look, and yes, he's still alive in this picture in spite of having no eyelids, lips or tongue. His wife was forced to eat them. It's called a double torture. Shall I show you the next one? It gets worse.'

Andy stared unemotionally at Victor, ignoring the photos.

'I'd force you to look but I don't want the bread pudding back, thank you.'

CHAPTER 2

'Hi. Cindy here,' said a crisp business-like voice. A voice that matches the name thought Victor, a voice that anticipates friends, not strangers, or if strangers, a welcoming voice.

'Sorry it's so early. I waited 'til a respectable hour. I have a mobile phone and it has "mom" in its directory and your number rang when I called it.'

'Hang on a jiff.'

Victor heard a phone hit a table and Cindy shouting something inaudible.

'It's probably Lizzy's. She's always leaving it about.'

'And Andy?' asked Victor.

'No, he's very careful.'

Cindy took a deep breath, straightened her back, pulled her dressing gown about her and mouthed 'shit, what now', while holding the phone against her stomach.

'I'm sorry but I listened to some messages before calling. Could we meet?'

'Whereabouts are you?' asked Cindy.

'Within easy cycling distance.'

'I'm just going upstairs to get him and then he can talk to you.'

'He's not there,' said Victor.

'How do you know? Where is he?'

'Please believe me when I say I don't mean to startle you. Andy's quite safe and he's come to no harm.'

'What's this about bloody phones if you know where he is anyway? Are you the police or what? Who the bloody hell are you?'

'Do you want me to call the police?'

'Why?' Cindy rasped, before clearing her throat.

'I caught your son taking things from inside my house last night and I think handing a criminal over to the police is appropriate.'

'Hang on a moment,' said Cindy, pressing the phone against her heart and flicking her long light brown hair over her shoulder. She glanced in the full-length hall mirror, took a deep breath and drew herself to her full five feet-eight inches.

'Listen, my son's not a criminal.'

'In that case I'm sorry to have bothered you. I'll call the police. I'm sure Andy will contact you shortly. You shouldn't have to cope with things like this. Goodbye.'

'Wait!' screamed Cindy.

Victor held his hand over the mouthpiece and breathed a deep sigh of relief. 'I'm waiting,' he said hoping his nervousness couldn't be detected.

'Tell me the whole story.'

'I wish it was a story. Andy broke into my house and stole various valuable items. I apprehended him but I haven't called the police because I don't think it's entirely his fault.'

'You mean he was being pushed into it?'

'No. I'm sure he was alone, but I think he's had an unfortunate childhood.'

'Are you a bloody expert? I've always looked after him. He may be a bit wild but he's no criminal.'

'Then what's he doing in my house stealing things, or is that the wildness in him?'

'Look. I'm really sorry if he's done what you say ------------.'

'Stop there,' shouted Victor. 'I'm being as respectful as I can. There's no "ifs" about it. I didn't go out on a kidnapping expedition in the middle of the night.'

Cindy looked at Homer Simpson's reflected face peeping at her from her nightshirt between the lapels of her dressing gown: inwardly confirming her feeling of being a child. The reflection also showed her sucking the forefinger of her right hand. She nearly cried.

'What do you want me to do?'

'Please listen,' said Victor. 'I'm putting myself out for Andy and possibly you. If you don't recognise that then let's stop playing games, call it a day and I'll call the police. You'll get your thieving son back and I'll probably see you sometime as a witness for the prosecution.'

'I know nothing about you, so who are you? Where's my son? What have you done to him?'

'Fair enough. As I said to your son, I'll answer honestly where I can and I expect honesty in return. I'm a fifty-seven-year-old university professor living alone in a house in Summertown and I found your son in my house late last night. I managed to overpower him without any serious injury to either of us and he's now secure and having food and drink whenever he wants. As a matter of fact, I think he's being treated very well under the circumstances.'

'If his dad were about he'd come over there and kill you,' shouted Cindy.

'Mom. What's going on?' Elly shouted from the top of the stairs.

'It's OK love. Tell you later.'

'I guessed his dad wouldn't be about,' said Victor calmly. 'Where is he? If you have his number, I'll talk to him.'

'You haven't got a bloody clue have you,' shouted Cindy. 'Koos would've been down on you like a shot and you'd be bloody mincemeat.'

'Where's Koos now then?' asked Victor.

'I don't fucking know,' she screamed as a tear ran down her face.

'I'm sincerely trying to help. I've had a shock finding your son in my house. I don't want to spread misery. I understand you're upset. So let's talk.'

'I should call the police now.'

'That's your prerogative.'

'Then what will you do?'

'I'll also call the police and wait.'

'You'll go to jail for kidnapping you will.'

'I'm sure you're correct, and Andy will be punished for burglary, have a criminal record if he hasn't already got one and then I'll be out and who knows what after that.'

'What do you want?'

'I want you to talk to Andy in front of me at my house. I don't want you to talk to anybody else beforehand. Not your family. Nobody. All this is on trust. You, Andy and me.'

'I'm supposed to be at work in an hour.'

'Do you really understand the importance of what I'm talking about?'

'OK. OK. I'll do it. Give me your address.'

'Please confirm your mobile number,' said Victor.

Cindy felt her heart pounding as she read it out.

'Thanks Cindy. When could you be at the Summertown shops?'

'Give me forty-five minutes. What's your address?'

'Please don't rush. It's only just gone seven. Go to the seats near the entrance to the Co-op at eight thirty and wait for me.'

'How will I recognise you?'

'Don't worry. I'll find you.'

'At least give me some clue,' she said into the silent phone.

'What's up mum?' asked Elly, watching her mother run up the stairs towards her.

'Nothing, Elly.'

'Who was on the phone?' she asked while trailing Cindy into her bedroom. 'I heard you talking about Andy. Where is he? He's not here. I've just looked.'

'I don't know and please stop asking questions. I'm trying to think.'

'You do know. You're going to meet somebody. Who is it?'

'Please Elly, just leave me for a bit and get ready for school.'

'If you're meeting somebody why are you dressing in your work clothes?'

'Elly please.'

Elly pulled a long face, slid off the bed and slammed the door on her way out.

I can't bear this thought Cindy, feeling hollow without Elly's normal cheerfulness. She stopped brushing her hair, took off her black slacks and white blouse and threw them on the bed while glancing in the wardrobe mirror.

'I look a bloody wreck,' she said shaking her head from side to side while watching her long hair fall lifelessly, first on one shoulder, then on the other. She tore her bra off after fiddling with the hooks, pushed her tights and pants down in one continuous movement, stepped out with her left leg and kicked the underclothes onto the bed with her right and walked into the bathroom.

'Come on Elly,' called Cindy from the bottom of the stairs. 'It's on the table.'

'Why're you all dressed up?'

'I'm going to a meeting.'

'But you had your office clothes on just now. Please, please tell me what it's about. I know it's about Andy, but what's happened?'

'It'll be OK love. Don't worry. I'll tell you all about it after school.'

'He's not hurt is he?'

'No, he's fine.'

'Is he in trouble?'

'Nothing we can't sort out, but please don't talk about it to anyone,' said Cindy reaching over the table and holding Elly's hand.

'OK,' she replied looking subdued.

'I'll drop you off at school if you like.'

'OK thanks, but you will tell me later won't you?'

'Of course. Sorry I shouted at you but my day isn't working out the way I wanted.'

They went out the back door of the terraced house and across the communal garden to the lockups on the lane that housed Cindy's old Renault five.

CHAPTER 3

I don't feel tired at all thought Victor, stepping into the bright March sunshine and feeling squeaky clean from a vigorous shower. He paused to touch tiny drops of dew hanging from the candy floss of spiders' webs along the garden hedge; inwardly acknowledging that it had been a long time since he'd last felt such an urge. He walked briskly to Banbury Road, stopped opposite the Co-op and glanced at the reflection in an estate agent's window of the seats across the road.

People had come and gone, apart from a slim tallish woman carrying a blue cloth shoulder bag and wearing a long brown sheepskin jacket over black tights. She frequently pushed strands of her long hair from the front of her face to her right shoulder with her right hand.

'Hi, I'm Victor. I spoke to you on the phone earlier.'

'Where are you?' asked Cindy, holding her phone away from her face and glancing about.

'I'm sorry to have kept you waiting. I'll be with you in a minute.'

Victor approached Cindy tangentially, caught her eye and smiled as he normally did with everyone. She smiled briefly and carried on looking into the throng.

'Cindy?' he questioned, turning to face her.

She quickly turned to him and automatically smiled making her face light up before changing her expression to an ill-fitting frown.

'My name is Victor. Victor Elliott,' he said holding out his hand. She took it without thinking.

'There's an empty table over there,' said Victor pointing to a café across the street.

'I didn't come here to have coffee and chat. I want my son back, then I'm going to give him a bloody good talking to and then I'm going to work.'

'I suggest you phone your work to say you'll try and be in this afternoon. This is extremely important and I don't think you'll want added anxiety and, besides, I need your agreement on some ground rules before we get to Andy.'

'What bloody ground rules?'

'I'm sticking my neck out to help your son and in return I need some agreement and recognition from you. I think that's reasonable but if you say no, I'll stop this now because I don't intend to waste my time and energy if you can't recognise I'm doing something positive. I may be arrogant in my assumptions but I don't experience this sort of thing every day and I feel it may be an opportunity for Andy.'

'I've already told the office I won't be there 'till later. Let's skip the café and get on with it. Which way?'

'Come, it's a short walk. How did you get here?'

'My car's in the car-park at the end of the shops,' replied Cindy.

'I suggest you park in my driveway.'

Without a word Cindy walked towards the car park while Victor quickly changed pace to keep up.

'I have to open the passenger door from inside,' she said across the roof of the car as he pulled on the handle.

Victor watched Cindy through the closed window, removing packets of this-that-and-the-other from the passenger foot-well and throwing them willy-nilly onto the back seat. The passenger door sprung open and Victor climbed in and instinctively reached for the lever below the seat to push it back to stop his knees from squashing against the cubbyhole cover.

'It doesn't work. Never did,' she said without any hint of an apology.

Victor pulled the door closed, thought he'd trapped the safety belt but then pushed it open.

'You have to open it wide and listen for a click then slam it.'

Victor opened the door wide, glanced at the hinges and the control mechanism and slammed it shut. 'I think I can fix that.'

'Then you'd be better than the garage,' said Cindy.

'Has this car been in an accident?'

'Which way?' she asked.

Cindy drove into Victor's open driveway and parked behind his old Volvo estate.

'Hooray. They've delivered my car. I've been without it for a couple of days. The house looks empty without it.'

I must be out of my mind coming here thought Cindy while looking up at the three floors of exposed brickwork, the small paned windows with stonework surrounds and the neatly trimmed front garden. She'd wondered who owned houses like these and thought them austere but considered the trees alluring and sometimes drove past on her way to Port Meadow for a walk along the river.

Victor opened the front door while Cindy remained in the car. He waited a few seconds before going back.

'Do you live alone?' she asked through her window.

'Most of the time. My youngest daughter often stays over, but she's not here now.'

'Are you divorced?'

'No. My wife died. Look, I don't blame you for being nervous.'

'I'm not sure I'm doing the right thing.'

'Have you got a smart phone?' queried Victor.

'Why do you want to know?'

'If you have, look me up. It may help you to feel more at ease.'

Cindy dismissed her fears without the phone, opened the car door and stepped out onto the stone-covered drive and crunched her way to the front door with Victor.

'Please forgive me for the untidiness of the place,' said Victor, closing the front door. 'I haven't had the time or inclination for that matter to put things back in their place. I'll leave you in the hall for a moment while I quickly tidy up the front room. Sorry. I'll be quick.'

'I want to see Andy. Don't tidy up. Don't keep me here. Let's get this over with. I can tell you it won't happen again.'

'Please relax,' said Victor 'and please don't think I'm being presumptuous but I've seen and heard the way you assert yourself and I don't think you deserve to be burdened by this sort of thing.'

'You know nothing about me,' said Cindy angrily. 'Nothing.'

'I'm hoping you'll tell me something, especially why you think you should put up with having a burglar in the family,' replied Victor with equal anger. 'I'm ready to learn but first I'll be less than a minute and if I don't do it I'll feel very ashamed of myself. I've not been in there for ages.'

Without waiting for an answer Victor went in closing the double doors behind him. He grabbed a cushion, dusted the piano, the coffee table and two cabinets with it, pulled the heavy dark curtains back lighting up the room, pushed the sash-window up and vigorously beat the cushion sending clouds of dust back into the room. 'Bugger,' he said, leaving the window open.

'Thanks for your patience. I should have thought about that before I went out. This room doesn't get done like the rest of the house. Please sit anywhere you like.'

Cindy walked to a dark red leather chair and sat down, her bag on her lap and its strap still over her shoulder while Victor manoeuvred a matching chair to face her across the coffee table. She looked across the table and felt relieved as she saw people in the street through the open window.

'I'm going to get myself something to drink. What would you like?'

'Water please.'

'I'm making tea or coffee if you would prefer?'

'No. Water will be fine.'

'I'll be back in a few minutes. Please look about. There are plenty of books and magazines.'

Victor closed all four doors en-route to the lounge.

'What did mom say?'

'About as much as any mother would say who's had to face a massive disappointment in her son.'

'Yeah, yeah. Now what?'

'I'm making drinks. Do you want one?'

'If I shout loud enough my mom will be in here like a fucking shot.'

'Not through locked doors she won't,' said Victor, withdrawing a bunch of keys (which he hadn't used) from his pocket and showing Andy.

'You bastard.'

'I'll untie your hands and get you a bit more comfortable. Not long now I hope. Do you want a drink?'

Andy didn't answer.

Victor went into the kitchen and returned to Andy with a coffee and a croissant on a tray and put it on his lap.

The room reminded Cindy of a school visit to a home where she and eight other pupils and two young teachers had giggled nervously after a butler had departed leaving trays of teas and biscuits in what he'd called the south drawing room. She remembered feeling very grown-up sharing similar feelings with the teachers, and for once feeling serious about herself. There had been jostling to be equal to the teachers and she recalled feeling she could achieve things beyond her own experience but didn't know what. Now as she absorbed the atmosphere of the room with its generosity of space and apparent disregard for the passing of time, yet resourced to confront current ignorance, a feeling of loss welled within her as she glimpsed her fifteen-year-old aspirational self, partly replacing her concern for Andy. She let her bag drop to the floor and walked to the bookshelves that were the length of the room and reached the ceiling. She was lost in her thoughts while looking at the blur of book spines and although she heard the door, she didn't look around.

Victor gently pushed the door open with his elbow, saw Cindy and quietly walked to the table.

'I've brought you water and a coffee. You don't have to drink it. Help yourself to sugar and milk,' he said, placing a tray on the low table in front of Cindy's empty chair. 'The croissants may be a bit leathery. I heated them in the microwave. There's honey. The marmalade is home-made; not by me you understand. Haven't got the patience for that sort of thing and there's strawberry jam. You possibly noticed the poor filing on the shelves. It hasn't been good since --- ah well, let's say the last few years. Novels mixed with academic stuff and catalogues have been wedged in where I think I'll find them. You could say it's regulated by the space available, but now that I'm talking to you about it I realise it's been niggling me.'

Cindy returned to the chair and sat down. 'I've come to pick up my son. Please can we get on with it.'

'For goodness sake woman,' said Victor loudly, slapping the table with the flat of his hand. 'At least acknowledge I've done something for your son by not having him arrested.'

'I'm sorry,' she replied suddenly straightening up, 'but this is all too much for me. I'm really sorry for what has happened. I didn't know he would do anything like this. I'm feeling really bad.'

'Please put yourself in my shoes for a moment. I could have tapped into a hornet's nest. I'm aware just as you are of gangs of thugs in this town. Andy could have been in one of those but I'm gathering from what you're saying, we're both in the dark about what he does.'

'I'm sure this is his first time.'

'I don't know if it is and the point is neither do you. I haven't set out to humiliate him or you. I feel for you. I have children of my own who are both doing OK, but I want to assure you I'm not feeling smug. A lot has to do with luck. Peer pressure out-does parental advice almost every time. There's a lot for you to think about I know but please think of this as an opportunity to do something for him. My role is a small interjection but I hope it's significant. Anyway, apart from his pride Andy has not been harmed except for some bruising when I intercepted him and another twenty minutes is neither here nor there. Please try and relax and I'll tell you what happened. Ask me any questions you like and afterwards you may talk to Andy and leave with him and resume your life as though this was simply another experience; or you may go to the police or any other authority for that matter and report me; or you may take any other action including getting your Koos to come here and sort me out as you intimated. It's entirely up to you but I would prefer we agree to be on the same side when Andy gets here and hopefully you can talk to him in front of me. I don't know if I'm putting other people in jeopardy by letting him go so he can burgle some other house. And of course you may want to consider the risks associated with that.'

'What bloody risks?'

'Let's suppose Andy robs somebody after today and that person, or someone else, is hurt and, or, suffers loss. There could be reasonable grounds for litigation against you and me for colluding to protect a known burglar if it becomes known that he burgled this house. You would be less liable than I because you're his mother. Shall we carry on or do you now want to call the police?'

'What will you do if I call the police?'

'Wait here with you until they arrive. You could if you

wish let Andy free, but I can't see him hanging around for the police.'

Cindy put her elbows on her knees and her head in her hands. 'Oh! Shit. Carry on. I'm listening,' she said.

'OK. I came home at about eleven last night and saw someone sneaking about the upper floor of the house with a torch. It was easy to see from the street. I went to the back of the house and nearly tripped over a bicycle next to my shed.'

'Why didn't you call the police straight away?'

'I wasn't prepared to risk having my things or my daughters' things, or my wife's things come to that, stolen while I waited,' replied Victor looking down at the table.

'Where were they while all this was going on?'

'My youngest daughter, Susan, lives with other students and comes home quite frequently and my other daughter, Jenifer, is married and lives a couple of miles away and, as you know, my wife died.'

'Oh my goodness, yes. I'm so sorry.'

'Thanks,' replied Victor without looking at Cindy. 'I didn't have to wait long before Andy walked out of the back door towards my shed. When he put his bag on the ground I hit him on the shoulder with a piece of piping and he fell onto the bike.'

'You could have bloody killed him,' said Cindy vehemently.

'He was so shocked I managed to tie him up with stuff I found in the shed, then I brought him back into the house and tied him to a chair. Please don't look so shocked. His hands have been free. I've given him food and drink, and he's been to the loo a couple of times. His bag contained my credit cards, my computer, some money, lots of other items and my wife's jewellery.'

'Oh no. I can't believe it,' murmured Cindy through the fingers of her hands over her mouth.

'He wasn't forthcoming with any information so I took his phone and I gathered from the messages about dinner being ready, he's used to getting his own way with you, Elly and Lizzie.'

Cindy flinched on hearing her daughters' names. 'I can't see him just handing it over. What did you do? He's had one since he was twelve and I've never touched it, he keeps it so close.'

'Perhaps you should have. Perhaps a lot of parents should have but let's not get side-tracked. I asked for it and he gave it to me rather than have me search through his jacket with a kitchen knife.'

'You mean you bloody threatened him?'

'His jacket was at stake, nothing more. I don't often meet local thieves and I couldn't think of anything else. However, he did say you'd sort me out when you found me. He said you were tough. He said you had contacts but he didn't elaborate.'

'He's not a thief!' shouted Cindy.

'Then what is he?' asked Victor putting his mug down firmly, causing some coffee to bounce out onto the table. 'Don't tell me he's a naughty boy for Christ's sake. You'll end up justifying murder. Think yourself lucky it was me who caught him, because I had no intention of seriously harming him like some people might. Besides the pendulum is swinging towards the victims of crime and it won't be long before judges lose control of juries and they'll return verdicts of conscience instead of the law, and it will be your Andy or somebody else's Andy that'll have his head smashed in by a law-abiding citizen who'll walk free. So, mother of Andy, what do you want to do?'

'I'll talk to him,' she meekly replied.

'What will you say to him?' Victor retorted.

'I'll tell him it's bad,' she said immediately sensing the weakness of her ill-considered reply and reaching for the mug of black unsweetened coffee with no intention of drinking it.

'You'll need a lot more than that if you're going to make a difference. He already knows it's bad but he couldn't care less. What do you want from this? I mean you. Not for that thief of a son of yours. What do you want for you? If you don't know that then you haven't a snowball's hope in hell of changing Andy. That's if you want to. So perhaps you'd better start from there. Do you want Andy to carry on with the things he's doing or do you hope, yes hope only I'm afraid, because it's probably too late to change him; unless something significant happens, and being tied up by some stupid old man may be humiliating but I don't think it's necessarily significant for him.'

'I want things back as they were,' croaked Cindy.

'Were when?' persisted Victor. 'Like yesterday when you were ignorant of Andy's escapade in my house? Or last year when he was probably doing the same thing to some other poor old soul, or years ago when you were pushing him about in a pram? I'm being a bully. I'm sorry, but I got a real fright and I haven't recovered yet. Please let me summarise. First there are many people who consider Andy and youngsters like him to be vermin --- -. No,' said Victor overriding Cindy's attempted protestation, 'let me finish before you start defending the indefensible. Boys and men of his ilk cause misery to thousands of people every year; some never recover from the trauma of even a minor violation and then there's the enormous cost and waste, as well as the damage they cause. There's also the expenses incurred in tracking them down, prosecuting them, imprisoning them and monitoring them, and what I'm beginning to understand, the emotional havoc they cause their families: that's if they're not upholding a family tradition of thieving. Do you have any fault with what I have just said?'

Cindy's 'no' was only just audible.

'Please tell me what you want for yourself,' said Victor.

Cindy drew a deep breath. 'OK. I want my kids to be able to look after themselves. I want them to have OK jobs and be happy.'

Victor picked up his coffee with both hands and looked at the contents without saying anything.

'Isn't that what everybody wants?' she added.

Victor nodded very slightly.

'Well? Isn't it?'

Victor gently nodded again. 'I'm carefully thinking about what you're saying and I don't want to give an off-hand reply. I'm very much aware of your concern for Andy but what do you want for Cindy?'

Victor kept still and silent while Cindy sat across the table from him looking out to the street, seeing nothing and unable to speak for fear of bawling her eyes out in front of this stranger. A minute later she took tissues from her bag, stood up and turned away from Victor, gently dabbing her lower eyelids. She breathed deeply twice and looked down at him before screwing up the tissue and putting it in her coat pocket. 'What do we do now?' she asked.

'I can't tell you what to say to Andy but you've heard me out and given me your time. I'll get Andy. I think he'll be very arrogant once he knows he's free and he may even make a dash for it. Stay here and let's hope he joins us with some civility.'

Cindy stood as Victor closed the door. She glanced at her watch from habit without registering the time and walked to the far end of the room.

'Come and talk to your mother,' said Victor cutting the cord at the back of the chair with a large kitchen knife. 'Go through the kitchen and on through the next room and down the corridor. She's in the last room on the left and please don't try to go through the front door; it's locked. I'll be right behind you.'

After a brief menacing stare, Andy got up and moved quickly through the house and crashed through the pair of doors kicking them open.

'You OK mom?' he shouted.

Cindy swept her hair back over her shoulder and looked along the length of the room to Andy.

'Do ya know what this bastard's been doing? Fucking near strangled me. Come on let's get out of here. He's fucking mad.'

Cindy stood with her left hand on an old leather-topped desk and the other at her side and carried on staring into the distance between Victor and Andy saying nothing.

After a few seconds even Victor was starting to worry.

'Well, don't just stand there mom. Come on, let's get the fuck out.'

Unblinking and as stationary as a manikin, Cindy, feeling ashamed, watched with horror at Andy's behaviour.

'What's going on?' shouted Andy, spittle now visible.

'Sit down,' said Cindy sharply as she approached the chairs. She sat down and picked up the mug of near-cold coffee, but then put it down after a sip and reached for the milk.

'Fresh coffee?' asked Victor.

'Yes please,' she said handing him the mug.

'I'll be back shortly. Would you like some Andy?'

'No I fucking don't,' he said looking menacingly from his mother and then back to Victor as he left the room.

'I bet that old fart is listening at the door. Stop pissing about for Christ's sake mom. Let's get out of here.'

'Are you OK Andy? What's happened to you?'

'That bastard tried to kill me. Look at this,' he said leaning towards her and pulling his jacket and tee shirt to one side.

'That's an enormous bruise. Are you OK?'

'Are you fucking listening? He tried to kill me.'

'I think if he'd wanted to kill you he would have. What were you doing in this house? He told me you were thieving stuff. Is this what it's come to? Is this one of the odd jobs you and your mates do? It doesn't look much like a warehouse job to me.'

Andy reached for his mother's bag next to the chair but she grabbed it, pulling the strap out of his hand.

'Stop!' she shouted. 'You really don't care do you? You don't care about me and you don't care about the man who lives here. And to think I defended you in front of that woman who said you'd been in her car. I told her to get her facts straight before she came around accusing innocent people. I should have bloody well listened to her.'

'I'm going,' said Andy making for the door as Victor pushed it open with his back. 'I'm fucking off,' he sprayed into Victor's face as he smashed the tray from underneath and out of Victor's hands sending up a shower of coffee, milk, sugar, glass and china. The cacophony ended with a single teaspoon bouncing around on top of a Steinway Grand.

'We're fucking prisoners here,' shouted Andy turning to Cindy.

'I've unlocked the front door. You're free to go. I think your mother has seen enough. I'll give her your things.'

'I'm not going without her. What the fuck do you take me for?'

'I've told you what you are. You're a thief. Your mother came of her own free will and she knows she may go any time she likes.'

'For god's sake get out!' screamed Cindy springing to her feet, startling Victor and stopping a bewildered-looking Andy dead in his tracks.

'Fuck you both,' he said striding from the room and slamming all the doors behind him.

Cindy stood on her toes and looked through the window to the path.

'I don't think he'll be there. He's probably gone to the back to get his bike. Shall I get his things for you?'

'I can't leave the room in this state. I feel awful. I'm really sorry.'

'I have all day to do this and besides the morning is just about over and you've to be at work,' said Victor ignoring splashes on his clothes.

'No. It has to be done before it dries. I must do it.'

'Please. No. I started this. It's my responsibility and besides I know where everything is and it won't take me long.'

'We need lots of water. One person will take all day,' said Cindy. 'I'll feel sick if I leave now. I can't go back today. Not today. Please.... let's get it done.'

'If you really feel that way, but I don't want to start feeling anxious on your behalf.'

'Show me where the kitchen is.'

'You're serious, aren't you? In that case I'll get you something suitable to wear. My daughter's not too dissimilar in size. You can't clear up in those.'

'I'm OK, honest. I don't want to trouble you any more.'

Victor waved dismissively leaving Cindy staring at the mess.

'This tee shirt is newly washed. The paint won't come out and it's about your size. It's Susan's. These jeans are also hers but she hasn't worn them for ages. Change anywhere you like, but the downstairs bathroom's a bit cramped,' said Victor gesturing towards a door off the corridor. 'Please feel free to change in either of my daughters' rooms. Theirs are the first two after the stairs and there's a bathroom at the end of the corridor.'

Cindy hesitated for a moment before taking the clothes and heading for the downstairs bathroom.

I'd better get changed myself thought Victor, glancing down at the specks of coffee on his neatly pressed fawn slacks and the expensive tanned shoes he'd not worn for ages. I'm glad I dressed well for this meeting he continued as he took the stairs two at a time. Holding out his light brown leather jacket in the en-suite bathroom, he dabbed at it with a wetted towel where milk had splashed, and assessed the circumstances. I'm obviously bigoted, she's not over-weight or ill-dressed, her command of English is better than I'd expected and she's concerned about her job. If she was on the dole she may have had time to guide Andy better, but I know it doesn't work like that. Is it because children don't respect parents on the dole? What went wrong in her case with Andy? Was he left to his own devices? I'd love to know what makes her tick. She's certainly concerned about the damage. She didn't mention anybody else other than her husband --- no love lost there that's for sure. What was his name? Koos? Not heard that name before. She wouldn't have acted the way she did if she'd known what Andy was up to --- I'm sure she didn't know. What did she think he did for money? What is Andy going to do now? Get his mates and get his own back on me --- I doubt it. He's too arrogant to advertise the humiliation of being overcome by an old man --- that was lucky.

Victor now down to his underpants, soaked the splashes on his slacks with water, pressed a towel on them to take away the excess water, folded them ready for the drycleaners and caught a glimpse of himself in the large bathroom mirror. He dwelled for a few seconds looking at his reflection in the chunky, flecked beige polo neck pullover. Am I younger or older than I look? He moved his face muscles to see the effect of the lines about his eyes and jaw. Not bad, but I wish I'd had the mirror put higher instead of ducking slightly to see the top of my head. Maybe I'll shrink from six-two and won't have to worry. Perhaps my hair stands up too much --- it needs cutting. Jennifer keeps telling me.

He pulled the pullover off satisfied that it hadn't been splashed, folded it and put it in a drawer, then dressed in jeans and an old pullover and went downstairs thinking: I'm glad I've taken my time. I'll go directly to the shed and get the ladder.

By the time Victor returned to the room Cindy had soaked the carpet with fresh water from a bucket and was mopping it up with one of the old towels Victor had left and was squeezing it out into a large bowl she'd found under the sink. 'I'm sorry about all this,' she said feeling and looking contrite. 'We're not going to get the stains off the walls and ceiling but I think the carpet will be OK.'

'I think you've already had more than your fair share of upsets today. If you're happy to carry on, then relax, these things happen and if this is the worst thing that happens today I think we can consider ourselves lucky. I just hope you haven't jeopardised your job.'

'I'm very fortunate - I don't have to worry about that. The admin' team will handle the end-of-day stuff and phone me if there's a problem. I'll sort out the minor issues tomorrow.'

An hour later Victor stopped and surveyed the streaky walls, exaggerating his stance as though viewing a masterpiece. 'It could do with a little touching up here and there but it looks OK to me,' he laughed.

Although Cindy half smiled at his demeanour she felt the pit in her stomach grow as she assessed the damage and the likely cost of repair. 'It will look awful even when it's dry,' she said moving her long hair from the front of her face with her forearm. Victor glanced at her face, saw her smile fade into quivering lips and desperately felt the need to rid her of any feelings of responsibility.

'You've cleared it all up,' he said cheerfully. 'You didn't do any damage. Please don't look so sad.'

'Andy did it and he's my son.'

'He did it. Not you.'

'He can't pay for this,' she said closer to tears.

'There is nothing to pay. This is totally my responsibility and, besides, this is the first attempted redecoration of this room since horses and carts delivered bread to the house,' he said looking at the walls with his hands either side of his chest, palms up in a magnanimous gesture.

Feeling relieved but troubled at not being able to contribute, Cindy half smiled and wiped her eyes with the back of her hand.

'I'll put the things away,' said Victor. 'Thanks for your help. I've put a fresh towel in the bathroom for you.'

'You do the ladder,' said Cindy, 'I'll finish this lot.'

Victor manoeuvred the ladder through the house to the shed and returned to find Cindy rinsing the old towels in the sink.

'Where shall I put these?'

Victor took the towels from her and dumped them in the wash basket.

'My wife wouldn't have approved of the basket in the kitchen but I find it easier and the girls don't seem to worry where it is. I'll leave you to get changed. Leave the shower on for a minute to get the water hot.'

Cindy felt she was trespassing and although eager to leave after tidying and brushing her hair, she was drawn to framed photographs as she made her way along the hall. There were people in turbans, others outside mud huts and one of Victor shaking hands with Bill Clinton. Feeling better but intimidated she went into the kitchen.

'I'll wash these and drop them off tomorrow,' she said, holding the damp clothes in one hand and supporting her shoulder bag with the other.

'If I thought that was the only thing that would cause you to come back I'd insist you wash them,' said Victor taking the bundle from her and adding it to the basket. 'I'm going to have a bite to eat. Why don't you plonk yourself down for a few minutes and join me? Nothing special you understand. Soup, bread and cheese,' he said from the open fridge.

Cindy hesitated.

'I can see that's the closest you're going to get to a yes,' said Victor, gesturing to one of four chairs around an oblong kitchen table.

'I don't want to put you out.'

'You're not. I normally break for lunch at about now and I'd appreciate your company. Fruit juice?' he asked holding a carton of mango in one hand and orange in the other.

'The mango please, but not a large glass.'

Victor loaded the table with things from cupboards, drawers and the fridge, while Cindy arranged two places opposite each other at the table.

'Cheers,' he said holding up his glass of orange to her mango and looking directly at her across the table.

Her smile fits naturally, he thought, as she answered.

'Soup's ready,' he said on hearing the sharp sounding 'ting' from the microwave.

'And thanks for all this,' she said gesturing with her glass.

He tore squares from a roll of paper towelling and placed one on her plate while she manoeuvred her chair into position. He hoped she hadn't noticed him glancing at her knees as she sat. She had.

'I have two daughters – Jenifer, the eldest, lives in North Oxford with her husband Dave. She pops in two or three times a week. Susan was lucky to get a place at Oxford. No, that's unfair. She deserved it. She's twenty. She's keen on law and always has been. She lives in a shared house off the Cowley Road and pops in at least once during the week and almost every Sunday. She often sleeps here. I think they both think I need looking after. Perhaps I do. I hope I'm not boring you.'

'I'm sorry about your wife,' said Cindy watching him pour soup into her bowl.

'She'd been ill for a long time.'

'That's so sad,' replied Cindy concentrating on her soup and ignoring the slight wavering in his voice.

'I've got used to it now. I've not been able to throw myself into my work, but I enjoy my students at the university and I bump along quite nicely. I'm also involved in law - human rights in my case. There's a lot of research required in this fast-expanding world. My students' enthusiasm creates waves that I ride. Wonderful. Help yourself to anything and everything. I'm quite pleased with myself putting this spread together.'

'I've two girls as well as Andy, but I think you know that.'

'Lizzy and Elly, is that correct?'

'Lizzy's nearly nineteen and Elly's twelve. They all live at home. We're near the turn off after Lidl. As for Koos - he's the father of the kids - he's been out of my life for years. He was in South Africa but who knows where he is now? His mother's a sweet old lady and we get Christmas cards from her. No way I'm going back there. Not that he wanted me with him anyway. I went out there soon after leaving school. Supposed to be a trip with my mates before we got jobs back in the UK, but typical me, I got into trouble and stayed. Wow, look at the time! I'd better be off. I have to pick up Elly. Thanks for this,' she said moving her chair back. 'Let's clear up.'

'Leave it all to me. Won't take long. I know where it all goes. I'll get Andy's things.'

Victor returned and found Cindy finishing the washing up.

'Thanks for that. Leave those. I'll put them away.'

'OK,' she replied drying her hands.

'Do you need a hand with any of these?' asked Victor indicating Andy's shoulder bag.

'No. I'll be OK.'

She stood back while Victor opened the front door. She took the bag from him and stepped over the threshold. 'Thank you for everything, not just the lunch. I'm feeling really guilty about the mess though.'

'I'm sorry you had to suffer this and I hope I haven't offended you in any way. The day has been very different from how I imagined it,' he said holding out his hand. She shook it self-consciously and turned to her car as he closed the door.

After driving for perhaps a quarter of a mile, she stopped at the curb, fumbled through her bag for tissues and dabbed away tears. Satisfied with her reflection in the rear-view mirror she drove off.

CHAPTER 4

Incredulity was written across Jenifer's face as she listened to Victor calmly describing the attempted robbery. 'Dad, please say you're making this up,' she said bringing the story to a premature end.

Victor took his feet from the low table and sat upright while his tall, elegant daughter, immaculately dressed in a black business suit as usual, moved around him.

'Why don't you stand in front where I can see you instead of hovering over me like a raptor?'

'You could have been arrested! I could be talking to you through the bars at Wormwood Scrubs,' she said leaning over him, her long dark hair hanging equally divided and presenting her stern face and high cheekbones as a stage set.

'You remind me of Faye Dunaway in Bonnie and Clyde, except you're taller and better looking.'

'Stop it Dad. I'm being serious.'

'Yes I can see that.'

'You still don't know if that's the end of it.'

'There's not much more to tell and I can't see Cindy, and certainly not Andy, bringing charges after a week.'

'You know bloody well what I'm talking about. You of all people should know the possible repercussions and I'm not only talking about the law. You've seen what lengths thugs will go to, to get their own back when they've been humiliated. Street cred to shits like him is paramount.'

'He won't say a word to anybody, and another thing, visitors don't talk through bars.'

'Don't be flippant, Dad. Mum would have been really upset. Don't you care?'

Count to ten before you answer thought Victor.

'Well?'

'I think you should ask yourself what I want.'

'This is ridiculous. A burglar comes here, you kidnap him and get his pathetic no-good mother to come and have lunch with you. I should get Doctor Cunningham to come and see you. You're losing your bloody marbles.'

'I haven't described her as a pathetic no-good.'

'Oh for god's sake Dad, can't you see what sort of people they are?'

'Your mother brought you up to be open-minded and yet here you are making dangerous assumptions and illustrating your bigotry and foolishness.

'You're the fool in this case, Dad.'

'I would prefer you to leave for a while if you're going to be insulting.'

Jenifer stared disbelievingly at Victor and sat down in the chair opposite.

'If anything, I'm getting my marbles back. Your mother passed away nearly three years ago and I can't even describe how much I miss her. I only have to look at you and Susan, leading your own lives, to understand how I'm being carried along with the tide rather than striking out. I know that what happened the other night could have gone completely wrong, but it woke me up to the fact that I had reached a low point. I can't fully explain it to you, but that's my best shot.'

'OK Dad, I was a bit over the top but what you did was so radical and so, so risky. It frightens me to think you could have even considered it. Have you told Sue yet?'

'No. She's probably coming this weekend. She and Mike are going through a rocky patch and I have a feeling she'll be here for a break. I don't think I'm giving away secrets.'

'You and Sue! She's the one who needs you. I've got David but I need to know you're all right. Oh, and by the way, it'll be three years on May the sixteenth.'

'I don't need reminding and I don't want to be reminded. I'm perfectly OK. If anything, I feel better than I've felt for a very long time.'

'Good,' said Jenifer, getting up and putting her coat on. 'I saw Sylvia in town last Saturday. She said she hadn't seen you for a long time.'

'Six weeks to be precise,' retorted Victor more curtly than he'd intended as he put the front door on the latch. 'We went to the cinema and had dinner out.'

Jenifer opened her car door. 'Sorry for the blow up,' she said kissing him.

Reluctant to go back inside the house and face the routine he felt it demanded, Victor pottered about the garden absorbing the last of the sun and thought of Anne when her requirements changed from needing assistance to accepting nursing, and how death had released her from her struggle to be part of the family. It didn't release me he thought, suddenly feeling sorry for himself. Christ almighty, that serene look on her face I hadn't seen for months. 'I'd only been away a few moments,' he said out loud (not for the first time), letting tears run down his face as he imagined for the umpteenth time how she'd spent the last moments of her life with nobody within whispering distance...... and then, he heard himself howling like an animal.

CHAPTER 5

Jenifer's confidence upon leaving the house dwindled as she dwelled on Victor's unenthusiastic hug, but thoughts of off-loading her anxiety onto David buoyed her for the journey home. Oh no, it's his Friday out with the boys she remembered, on seeing his empty parking bay.

This isn't so bad she thought, overlapping the front of her dressing gown, putting her feet up and leaning back into a cushion with a glass of wine, a slab of chocolate and the rest of the bottle nearby. What would mother think of me? What's more, what would she make of Dad? What would *she* do? Jenifer failed to get an answer and ended, as she often did, thinking about her mother.

Jenifer had been twenty when her mother died, but felt she'd experienced her mother's death three years prior when she and Susan had sat around the kitchen table listening to their parents describing what the specialist had said. She remembered Susan saying: 'How can they be so certain? Up to three years? All sorts of things can happen in that time. You're not in pain and we're still going camping in Italy next month.' She remembered glancing at Susan, gathering strength from her own words and then being jolted into action when Susan let out an ear-piercing scream when they both saw a tear run down their father's face. She remembered tingling with fear, jumping from the chair and following her mother as she ran after Susan and how her father had remained frozen.

Jenifer went to the bedroom, grabbed a box of tissues, dabbed wine from the front of her gown, wiped her eyes and returned to the chair to plan the weekend. However, within seconds she fell back to thinking of that day.

'I'm not the one that needs help,' Susan had sobbed, studying her mother's face through bloodshot eyes while she, Jenifer, silently sat on the opposite side of Susan's bed feeling helpless. 'You said yourself,' Anne had said, 'all sorts of things can happen and we're going to Italy. So let's concentrate on the good things to come. OK, Sue my pet?' Susan had reached for her mother and held her tight, ear-to-ear with chins on each other's shoulders while Jenifer watched the back of Susan's head and her mother's face as she freely cried over Susan's shoulder. Although Anne had held her hand across the bed the whole time, Jenifer felt things could never be the same again. She remembered feeling more settled while consoling her father as his tears fell on her neck as he held her. She remembered sighing with relief as Victor cuddled their mother as usual when she turned up for breakfast the following morning and her saying: 'I'm not going to harp on about it, I want life to go on as normal. Talk to me any time about illness or cancer or anything you like. I just don't want anybody pussyfooting around me.' There had been a collective sigh. She even remembered smiling.

Jenifer tipped the remainder of the glass into the sink, put the bottle in the fridge, pulled a tissue from the box and blew her nose.

CHAPTER 6

A day at home for Susan could easily start after midday, but she knew tea in her favourite mug had been placed on the bedside table and she'd felt Victor's kiss on her hair.

'I think my Dad's going to say something,' she whispered without opening her eyes while shuffling over to give him seating room.

Victor shared the story of the break-in with Susan. Rather than explaining himself as he felt he'd done with Jenifer, he remained relaxed until he looked up from his hands to her alert face. She put her arms over his head and pulled him tight against her.

'Don't ever, ever, ever do anything like that again Dad. Not ever.'

Unnerved by Susan's reaction, Victor made no immediate effort to release himself; hence they stayed huddled together for a long time before he gently removed her arms.

'You have to promise me, Dad.'

'I hope we don't have any other burglars.'

'Don't make light of it, Dad. You know what I mean. You could have been injured or even killed. The thought of you alone and exposed like that is making me feel sick.'

'It was reckless but I've been in scrapes when I've been on assignments.'

'You've not been outside international law, but you were in this case and you know it. Don't fob me off by changing the subject.'

'It turned out well in the end. I'll tell you about his mother later.'

'Dad, you're bigger than this. You said your job was to help change things and here you are circumventing the law.'

'I know, I know. Please don't lecture me.'

'I love you Dad. Please look after yourself,' she said holding him again. 'Now tell me about his mother.' Victor proceeded to tell Susan about Andy's mother.

Susan studied Victor's face as he became increasingly animated.

'Can you trust his mother not to take it further?'

'She was a bonus, she was great.'

Susan hugged him again.

'Breakfast in fifteen minutes,' he said.

CHAPTER 7

'What? He didn't tell you?' gasped Jenifer into the phone. 'He's bottling it up. He needs to sort it out. It's been three weeks.'

'I'm sure he's OK,' said Sylvia. 'We saw a film on Friday and he talked about all sorts of things over dinner. If there's something troubling him, I'm sure he would have mentioned it. If you're worried about him you should talk to him yourself.'

'Yes, OK. I'll do that but he's more… I don't know…. distant and less approachable. I'm not explaining myself well. He's become more confrontational with me, I know that.'

He's not obliged to tell me if he doesn't want to thought Sylvia, throwing a cushion onto the back of the chair, causing the cat to scamper.

'You're a dark horse - a burglary and not telling me,' said Sylvia sitting inside her car with her feet outside while Victor helped her with her walking boots.

'Yes. Jenifer said she'd spoken to you. She told me she hadn't given you any details because you stopped her. She also told me you thought I was dealing with it or something like that, whereas she thinks I've gone mad.'

'I've always thought you were mad, so there's nothing new there,' she laughed. 'You want to tell me?'

'I was hoping to have rationalised it by the time we went to the cinema but I'm still thinking it through.'

'Tell me when you're ready, but only if you want to.'

'I'll tell you while we walk because I may never know what came over me. Jenifer was correct though - nobody in their right mind would do what I did. I was lucky it turned out the way it did.'

Victor picked bits from the story and fed them to Sylvia who silently absorbed the facts while sensing his feelings and alert to her own.

'What's this Cindy like?' asked Sylvia after twenty minutes.

'I thought she was going to call my bluff at the start. That was the most nerve-racking bit of the whole thing. She was so aggressive that I found myself shouting at her and that really gave me a shock, but she eventually calmed down when she was in the house. Thankfully she became self-assured when she saw Andy, and unfortunately most contrite after the tray went flying.'

'You're not going to tell me what she's like, are you?' she teased.

'Not a bit like I'd anticipated. She's about forty, long light brown hair that she keeps sweeping over her shoulder. Far more articulate than I'd expected, quite tall, dressed neatly in a blue denim skirt and a sheepskin jacket. Black tights.'

'Hardly noticed her at all then,' laughed Sylvia. 'Jenifer was correct. You could have been arrested and charged with all sorts of things. It could have gone really badly.'

'It didn't and I'm glad I did it.'

'So am I,' said Sylvia.

'I am surprised.'

'Come on, let's walk faster. I'm getting cold,' she said linking her arm into his. 'It's at least a mile to the pub.'

Dressed in padded jackets with hoods pulled down against an unusually cold wind for early April, they walked by the river listening to the continuous squawk of Canada Geese being chased by a barking dog.

'How did the girls take it?'

'Upset, scared, with me feeling chastised.'

Having seen a glimmer of the Victor she'd known before Anne died, Sylvia huddled against him and reflected on the time she'd tried to prise him out of his shell a year after Anne's death. She remembered asking him to join her and her friends for a visit to "Art In The Park". It had been a Wednesday morning when he'd said yes to Sunday's outing. She remembered shooting upstairs to look at herself in the mirror and laughing out loud as she involuntarily smiled at her own reflection in dirty jeans and a blue pullover with holes, thinking how slim and fit she'd felt as she leaned towards her reflection to see the effect on her breasts.

'Penny for your thoughts,' said Victor. 'And don't tell me "nothing". I can feel your hand twitching.'

'Tell you later,' she said smiling.

She slipped back into thinking of that day and remembered skipping to the bathroom, tugging the pullover over her head and while the shower was running, taking the rest of her clothes off and going back to the mirror to look again. First face-on, then sideways and saying to herself, you're more than just OK for fifty-five my girl.

Sylvia and Victor were both thinking of the same event, probably prompted by the slight drizzle, the muddy paths surrounded by new long grass and similarly dressed people anticipating a brighter day.

Victor involuntarily squeezed his arm against his body trapping Sylvia's hand tight as he relived the feeling of seeing Anne for a split second through the glass door before realising it was Sylvia, dressed in similar colours, ready for their trip.

'Now it's a penny for your thoughts.'

'Maybe later,' he replied.

Victor returned to thoughts of that day. He remembered not being able to shake off an instinctive feeling of wanting to passionately embrace Sylvia and only managed to control his feelings by concentrating on the picnic items on the table. She'd kissed him on the cheek and squeezed his hand. He remembered feeling guilty when he looked at her legs through the white lace dress as she crossed the kitchen in front of the brightly lit window. He also remembered then saying, 'where've you hidden your muddy jeans and the pullover with the holes?' And her reply when spinning around on one bare foot in the middle of the room: 'Do you like the dress?' Victor recalled his embarrassment after saying, 'you never remarried after Joe, but I think you've had plenty of opportunities.' She'd replied laughing and brushing the air with her hand, 'I swat them away like flies.'

He remembered feeling he'd gone too far and her saying she'd prefer him to come out with it and her reaching across and touching the back of his hand.

CHAPTER 8

'Hello Cindy. It's lovely to hear from you.'

'How did you know it was me? Oh of course! You put my number on your phone.'

'I didn't look at the phone.'

'Can we meet up? Nothing serious or about the burglary, well not really, but I'd like to talk to you but if it's not OK, I'll understand.'

'Cindy, I'd be delighted to meet up with you. When and where?'

'I've planned a half day on Thursday. Can we meet up in the afternoon? If you can't, I can make any time over this coming weekend or -------.'

'Thursday's fine. Please let me take you to lunch.'

She hesitated a second before saying, 'Thanks. 'Nothing posh though, a café, something light.'

Three months had passed since the burglary and a couple of weeks since he'd thought of Andy, but only a day or two since thinking of Cindy. She'd become a pleasant diversion from his dark feelings. He'd fantasised about her one night and attempted masturbation but had given up, and feeling pathetic, had remained reasonably content in spite of believing his sex life to be possibly over. He was getting out more. Even John, probably his closest male friend, said he appeared more cheerful and even went as far as intimating Sylvia as a possible adventure (he failed to elaborate further). 'I'm released from all of that,' he'd replied, without quite knowing what being released meant.

The day couldn't be better thought Victor. Summer in Oxford, pavement cafés humming, their colourful awnings casting shadows over chatting couples while waiters and waitresses, with a multitude of accents, efficiently glided between tables. Victor, having visited the gym earlier, felt good in a light cream casual suit, blue open-neck shirt and sporting a one-day-old haircut. He approached the restaurant with only seconds to spare, with a modicum of trepidation which conflicted with bountiful excitement when he saw, in the distance, a woman similar to Cindy but slightly taller, wearing a close-fitting yellow and blue summer dress and high heel shoes, sorting through a rotating postcard rack. Thinking Cindy may already be inside instead of waiting as they'd arranged, he quickly glanced about at the many faces in the crowd and increased his step. Out of the corner of his eye, he saw the same woman stop, remove her sunglasses and sweep wisps of hair from her face with her right hand to her right shoulder as a balmy breeze circled the rack. He took a deep breath. She spoke first.

'Hello,' she said smiling.

'You look like a tourist. Wonderful,' said Victor, unable to recollect previously having an eye-level encounter with her. 'Come. Let's find a seat.'

Her mind's-eye picture of Victor differed so much from the one confirming his name for the booking that she suddenly felt completely at sea.

'Thanks for coming,' said Victor.

'I asked you,' she replied looking surprised.

'Oh yes, of course! Sorry,' he said looking at the menu.

'I wanted to tell you what's been going on since I last saw you. I could have told you over the phone but it sounded stupid when I thought about it and it's been nagging me ever since so I thought, bugger it. I'll give you a ring anyway. You could always say no.'

'These last few weeks have been difficult for me. I didn't go back to my kids as the person I was before that horrible day. No, please don't say anything. I've worked at keeping myself different. Almost wanting to preserve myself if that makes any sense. You'll think I'm funny, not funny ha-ha, but funny peculiar.'

'I think we're all funny peculiar, that's what makes life interesting. Unquestioned perceptions lock us up in our own world. You, on the other hand, seem to be searching for something and I have to tell you, I feel privileged that you feel able to talk to me. So don't rush. I have all afternoon if you do.'

'There was one person I thought I could talk to. Someone I thought was a real friend but she went ballistic, telling me what she would have done before I'd finished telling her about the burglary. I refused to go further and we haven't spoken since. And if that wasn't bad enough Charles, my ex-partner, came to the house two months ago to try and make up. When I told him I wasn't interested, he called me a bitch and hit me. Then he cried. I was lucky my neighbour, Jane, came by.'

Victor looked across the table at her and nodded.

'You probably think I deserved it.'

Victor retrieved a small packet of tissues from his jacket and broke the seal. She quickly grabbed it.

'Sorry about that, I didn't come here to tell you any of this.'

'Tell me more,' said Victor looking directly at her.

'No. I hardly know you and, anyway, it's not your problem.'

'That's correct. You hardly know me, so what could be better than to get it off your chest knowing it stops with me. You're upset, and quite rightly so, by the sounds of it. I'm not embarrassed, but your suffering makes me feel sad. So perhaps, Cindy Oosthuizen, you now have some responsibility to stop me from feeling sad.'

'I don't normally cry,' she said dabbing her lower eyelids, 'and certainly not in public.'

Victor stayed silent.

'Liz's pissed off with me because I'm being calm and rational through her emotional ups and downs, and Andy's pissed off with me because I challenge everything he says. I think Elly appreciates what I'm doing but gets seriously pissed off when she can't have her own way. I bet you're thinking you've been invited to lunch by some silly bitch who's completely lost it.'

'You can't have lost it. The pathway to failure is paved with good intentions. You, however, have gone beyond intention. You've arranged to be here. You may not necessarily need help but you've confirmed losing a close friend and I may be mistaken, but I sense you calling out for help, and that's a sign of intelligent behaviour.'

Rather than tough it out, Cindy let tears run down her cheeks before using a further tissue. 'Sorry about the swearing,' she sniffed. 'It's a bad habit and I don't need telling it's a lack of expression. I know it.'

Victor resisted (with difficulty) the temptation to touch Cindy's hand. 'Take all the time you need,' he said. 'Don't rush.'

Cindy started talking logically about her plans for moving, becoming more and more animated after ten minutes and a few sips of rosé.

'Do you think moving will solve most of your problems?' asked Victor.

'It's already created problems, but they're the ones I should have been dealing with. Elly's school for a start. She'll be moving, but because I've thrown myself into sorting her out, it's made me much more concerned about her and she's lapping it up. I can see that. I know deep down I've stopped running away from responsibility. I feel guilty about Liz and Andy but I can't choose to start from somewhere else. I'll be stretched financially but I know it's right.'

'And how do the others feel about the move?'

'Liz's half living with her boyfriend and treating the house like a hotel whenever she likes. He's a nice guy and would love her to move in with him permanently so it's make-up-her-mind time. She earns enough at the Science Park to get her own place if she wants that. I've told her she can move with me and carry on sharing a room with Elly. I've asked Andy to move in with me on my terms. Elly's the only one excited about it. I should have done it years ago, but what with Charles and so-called friends, it felt impossible. Then you mentioned peer group pressure that day and how it beats family influence and I saw my own peers and my kids' friends and I asked myself: have they got my interests at heart? The answer hit me like a brick and I suddenly realised I was living inside a fucking soap opera. Oops, sorry.'

Cindy paused, removed another tissue, dabbed her face, leant back in the chair and stared into space above Victor's head before bringing her eyes down to focus on him.

'Your parents?' asked Victor.

'I went with them to South Africa when I was six and they split up a few years later. They argued a lot and my Mum thought a new country would change things but it didn't and he was soon up to his old tricks and eventually one of his girlfriends became pregnant and he drifted away. I came back here with my mum and stepfather. He was better than any father, but he died when I was thirteen. He called me Cindy Loo. I loved him. The last I heard of my real dad was from one of his old drinking mates at Mum's funeral in the UK. He thought he'd gone mining in Western Australia and didn't think he'd taken anyone with him.'

'And the father of your children?'

'Koos. He was just like my Dad, had affairs, begged forgiveness, had affairs and begged forgiveness. How many would you like to hear? And on top of that, drank brandy and coke until he fell over. That was at least once a week. He wasn't like that when I first knew him. I used to think it was my fault. Maybe it was, but it's too late now. I saved up and went back to South Africa with a schoolmate for a long holiday before we needed to start work proper. Some bloody gap-year that turned out to be. I got pregnant and stayed. Eight years ago I came back here. I think Koos's parting words were 'fuck off then.'

'So, you've heard my story in a nutshell. More than I've told anyone. Hope you weren't bored. I really needed to see you and say thanks, face to face.'

'Thanks for what?'

'You listened to me at your house,' she said vehemently, 'and you're listening to me now.'

'I could sit and listen to you for ages,' said Victor.

Cindy laughed nervously while looking into Victor's face. 'Andy got a big shock, in spite of what you might think, and it's done him the world of good, not that he'd admit it. He could've been locked up. My life would've been a bloody misery. And you took an enormous chance. So thanks.'

'I was going to say it was a pleasure but that sounds crass; but since we are being honest I can tell you it was a pleasure. It was probably what I needed.'

Cindy put her head on one side, looking quizzical, then changed her mind about questioning him and instead raised her near empty glass towards him.

'Thanks to you and of course my new flat.'

Victor raised his glass, clinked it against hers and held it suspended while he thought for ten seconds or so, causing her increasing anticipation. 'I want to acknowledge what you've set out to do without seeming patronising. Perhaps I'll leave it and say….. to Cindy's future.'

'Oh, thank you, Victor. I'm really touched.'

'Now tell me more. I thought Elly would have been short for Elizabeth but you have a Lizzy as well.'

'Her real name is Emma. I called her Elly when she was five to encourage her to part with her stuffed elephant which she wouldn't let out of her sight. It didn't work but then suddenly at the age of six, and I was there when it happened, she looked at the floral rags with three legs and no trunk and said it looked nothing like an Elly and within minutes it went from the best loved thing in the world to a piece of rubbish. I'm sure there is a message in there somewhere. I then called her Emma but she gave me a frown with half-closed eyes, which means cross-beyond-words in her case, and so it's been Elly ever since. I'm sure she will tell me one day she looks nothing like an Elly and it will be Emma again. It will happen when boys ask about her being called Elly and she will make up some story to hide the truth and I will be sworn to secrecy, never to tell and cross my heart and hope to die.'

Cindy stopped talking and Victor smiled.

'I'm wittering on.'

'I could sit here and watch you talking for hours. I find it delightful.'

'Some other time,' said Cindy.

'Well, if you need help with your move give me a shout. I have a large estate car you could use.'

'I may very well do that. Do you really mean it?'

*

She's probably well ensconced by now thought Victor, looking at his diary and realising only three weeks had passed since their lunch. He put a note two weeks ahead for a possible call, which he, when the time arrived, felt foolish and didn't make. Two weeks later and feeling strangely bereft, he answered the phone.

'Hello, Victor. I hope you got my little card thanking you for the lunch.'

'I did. Thanks for your lovely words.' (He didn't mention its status near his computer in his small study on the first floor).

'If you were serious about helping me move, it's the weekend after next.'

'I'd be delighted. Give me some idea of times.'

'I have both places all day Saturday and the van is scheduled to be here at seven. I'll have my personal stuff ready. So how about eight to start loading both cars? Is that OK?'

'Saturday morning at eight, get everything moved by late afternoon and then have supper. How does that sound?' said Victor.

'Bloody wonderful,' she replied, punching the air. 'You're a star!'

CHAPTER 9

'I was hoping to have a lazy breakfast with you tomorrow. Where are you going?'

'I'm helping a friend move house and it looks like it'll take all day.'

'A friend, my father has a friend,' mocked Susan.

'It's nothing like that,' he replied, feeling guilty before realising he wasn't.

'Oh! Nothing like *what*?' she asked playfully.

'No. Really, it's nothing.'

'Oh! No, of course not, not my innocent darling Dad. I'm waiting. What's her name?'

'You don't know her.'

'How do you know?' she replied in her "don't-make-assumptions-with-me" voice. 'I bet I know her name.'

'No you don't,' he said trying to sound casual. 'OK. Now I'm going to stop.'

'Oh no you don't. I'm not letting you off the hook,' she said looking down at him in mock strictness.

'How come you and your sister hover like raptors when you're having a go at me? And if you're so clever, tell me her name.'

'Let me see,' she said, drawing herself to her full five feet ten inches in studded high heels, putting a finger to her lips and looking towards the heavens. 'It begins with a 'C'.'

'Now I know you're guessing.'

'OK.' she replied, with exaggerated deliberation, 'the second letter is an 'I' and the last is a 'Y'.'

'What's her full name then?'

'Oh no, I want to hear you say it first.'

'Cindy,' he said.

'Wow. I was so close.'

'You really enjoyed that, didn't you?'

Susan laughed, bent down and kissed him on the forehead. 'Now that wasn't so bad was it?'

'OK. How did you know?' he said, getting to his feet to help her clear the table.

'I've heard her name many times since you turned into a wild law breaker and besides, if it had been anybody else --- no I'm not going to say. I'm not showing you my toolkit for reading you like a book.'

'I knew I'd reared a wicked witch,' he said holding her head and planting a kiss on her cheek.

She turned and half danced to the kitchen.

'I didn't phone her. She phoned me,' he shouted after her.

'How much not to tell she-who-will-be-obeyed?' she asked from the doorway.

'You shouldn't refer to your sister like that. She's really very sweet.'

'Only since you stood your ground. Yes, you didn't think she'd tell me, did you?'

'I am surprised.'

'She didn't go into details but whatever you said gave her a scare.'

'I hope it didn't come across as brutal as you're describing.'

'Probably not. She needed to get it off her chest though. We chatted for a long time about our wayward parent.'

'If it brought you closer together, it was worth it.'

CHAPTER 10

Wearing blue jeans, trainers and a blue and white Florida Keys tee shirt, Cindy was biting her bottom lip and too occupied with two men wobbling a glass-fronted cabinet up a steep ramp into a large van to notice Victor backing his old Volvo into a nearby space.

'Hello Victor,' she said a moment later, 'where are you?'

'Admiring the buzz of activity near your front gate.'

'Wonderful,' she said pocketing her phone and walking to his car. Walking close behind was a slim five-foot nothing girl who, apart from her dark complexion and hair that hung in ringlets, had Cindy's sharp features and natural smile.

'Welcome to my abode on this beautiful sunny morning. This is my youngest, Elly. Elly, this is Mister Elliott I told you about.'

'Hello Elly,' said Victor, 'my name is Victor.'

Elly looked from Victor's face to his outstretched hand into which, she placed her own, leaving Victor to shake it while she looked down at her white trainers.

'Can I go in the van, mom?'

'Afraid not, love. Have you finished sorting out the things you want? If you haven't finished in the next half hour we're taking the lot.'

Elly's crystal clear dark eyes opened wide and her mouth formed a perfect 'O' in surprise. She spun around spreading her ringlets out from her small face like a miniature merry-go-round, and ran back through the gate.

'Morning,' said Victor pecking Cindy on the cheek.

'I'm so pleased you're here,' she said turning her head for a second peck.

'This box's not marked, love,' said one of the removal men as he passed.

'Oh!' said Cindy taking a marker pen from her pocket and following him into the van.

'I'll get the guys to bring my personal stuff to the car. It's boxed up. You stay here and look after things.'

Victor stopped adjusting the car's seats when he heard a familiar voice.

'Hello Andy,' said Victor holding out his hand.

Andy hesitated, quickly glanced at a nearby nineteen-year-old girl, who'd stopped walking, and allowed his hand to be shaken.

'It's your fault she's fucking moving,' said Andy.

'Bloody good job she is,' said the girl.

'This has fuck all to do with you,' replied Andy, still looking at Victor.

'So you're Victor,' she said watching Andy walk on without her, before focussing on Victor.

'I am. And you are?'

'Kirstin. I'm Andy's girlfriend, but you wouldn't think it the way he speaks,' she said turning to follow Andy.

'All of us accept abuse now and then in order to get by. Unfortunately, the younger we accept it, the more of it we're willing to take.'

Kirstin turned back, went to a low wall a pavement-width from the car and sat down with her silver, mock leather handbag in both hands on her lap.

'Andy's pissed off with you. He thinks you're the cause of all this,' she said, nodding in the direction of the van.

'Let's hope it's for the good,' he replied.

'Was it your idea?'

'If you mean did I suggest moving, no. I don't know Cindy well enough to suggest anything. She knew I had an old car to help her with the move though.'

'She likes you, you know.'

'Good. I like to be liked.'

'Hi, Kirstin love,' said Cindy.

Kirstin smiled widely at Cindy without getting up.

'Is everybody inside?'

'Liz is working this morning, but she'll pop over to the new place this afternoon, otherwise it's us,' said Cindy, making a circle with her index finger. 'And Elly of course. She's moving her things from box to box and back again. You'd love to help her, wouldn't you?'

'Sure, see you.'

'Elly's things will go in my car,' said Cindy, adding a box to the pile she and Martin, one of the men he'd been introduced to, were building next to the tailgate of the Volvo. 'She's making grown-up decisions at the moment. She's going through what I'm going through. Is it OK if you go to the house before I do?'

'Just tell me what to do and I'll do it.'

'The address is on the front, you can't miss it,' said Cindy giving Victor a transparent bag containing keys and papers. 'It's off Divinity Road. The car spaces are marked. Mine is number two. They've coned off the front for the van but you'll need to open up for them. Each item is labelled and it's obvious which room is which but if things end up in the wrong rooms. Too bad.'

Victor arrived at the block of four apartments on two floors and drove through an archway to the back, parked and stepped into a walled garden of well-spaced birch trees, various acers and a trimmed lawn. He opened a large glass door leading to a wide, well-kept corridor linking the front and back of the block, then opened the apartment and went into the street.

'So, this is Cindy's new place,' said the driver, letting himself down from the cab. 'Nice. I bet she's pleased she's moving.'

'You know her?' asked Victor.

'Should do. Worked with her for the last six years. She's got special arrangements to use company trucks providing the sides are covered with tarp. Head of office she is,' he said deferentially. 'Isn't that right Martin?' he shouted while Martin released the van's doors.

'Do you two want a hand?' asked Victor.

'No mate, show us where to go. Three'll only get in the way. Thanks all the same.'

Victor was still unloading his car when Cindy's fully laden Renault pulled in with her and Elly squashed forward.

'Can't have you slacking. I've arrived in time for you to help me with this one,' she laughed.

'Take the things into the kitchen Elly. Don't get in the way of Ed and Martin.'

'I saw one room's already full of things,' said Victor.

'Andy moved his stuff very early this morning. I say Andy, but when I saw what his mates carried, I did wonder what was left for him. Then he sauntered back at the same time you arrived with no intention of helping.'

'And where do you want these to go?' asked Victor, pulling a large cardboard box of open shoeboxes filled with papers from the back seat of Cindy's car.

'That's my professional filing system. On the bed in the large bedroom for now.'

By five o'clock the apartment had been swept and made liveable and cardboard boxes had been reduced to flat sheets ready for removal.

'Kirstin won't come without Andy,' said Cindy, putting her phone in her bag. 'I could hear her pleading with him to come. Oh well, it's his loss. That leaves you, me,' referring to Victor, 'and Elly. Liz and her boyfriend, Paul, will meet us at the restaurant. It's a real adventure, walking to Cowley Road for the first time from my new apartment. I feel like a kid.'

*

'Thanks,' said Paul sipping a beer and looking at Cindy.

'What for?'

'Liz would have carried on living between Abingdon and Oxford for ever if you hadn't moved.'

'You'll have to work hard to keep her. She knows she can come and live with me if she wants.'

'No she can't,' said Elly momentarily halting her conversation with Victor, 'I've got my own room now.'

'Don't worry, little Elly, I won't sneak back and throw you out.'

Elly feigned indifference to Liz's cajoling and eagerly questioned Victor further about his daughters.

'Are you going out with my mum?' she asked, looking directly at Victor.

'Victor helped today because I asked him and he said he would take us out for a meal to save cooking after all the moving.'

'How do you know each other?' Elly persisted, her head twisting from one to the other.

'Victor kindly sorted some things out for me a few months ago and now we're friends.'

'To friends,' said Victor holding his glass of wine towards Elly's Coca Cola.

'Can I meet your daughters?' she asked, clinking her glass against his and smiling.

'Drink up, we're off,' said Cindy, 'it's late'.

They said goodbye to Liz and Paul who'd arrived by car.

'Look after my room for me,' said Liz, hugging Elly.

Paul revved the second love of his life for a brief wheel spin and his Subaru Impreza joined the buzz of the late night traffic on the Cowley Road.

'I don't know what went on but something happened. Andy won't talk but I know he had something to do with it and now look at Mum, falling over herself for him,' said Liz the moment the car pulled away. 'How old do you think he is?'

'Happiest I've ever seen her,' replied Paul, feeling happy himself, especially with Liz's things in the boot.

'At least come in for a coffee,' said Cindy, betraying the tiniest amount of desperation.

'I'd love to but I think I'll be on my way,' said Victor. 'Good night Elly.'

'Night,' she replied turning to the apartment.

'Please come and have a snack with me in the near future,' said Victor quietly. 'How about some time next week? Bring Elly if you want.'

CHAPTER 11

Feeling out of his depth, Victor watched Cindy. She was half running for the first few steps and then approached him as he stepped from his car into the August heat at the DIY centre.

'You're staring at me.'

'You look wonderful.'

'Thank you kind sir,' she replied curtsying to the limits of her tight black skirt and high heels. 'I must have done something right. You're the second person who's said that this afternoon. Leave your car here. I'm taking you for drinks and a snack,' she said pulling his arm and walking towards her car.

Thud went the passenger door before springing back open.

'Arm out the way,' she said leaning across him and slamming it harder. 'I want to hear about you. I know once I get started I won't stop. I feel like I'm buzzing.'

'Tell me more.'

'You're not tricking me like that.'

'I feel good,' he replied.

'Good. That makes two of us. I've nobody to talk to about the day we met. Have you?'

'My girls and a friend of ours, Sylvia, who's like an aunt to them.'

'Not a real aunt then?'

'No. A long-time friend.'

'I bet none of them approved of your actions.'

'You're correct there.'

'Sorry about the questions, but that day changed my life. It was the best present I've ever been given,' she said, leaning across and giving him a kiss on the cheek and switching the engine on.

Victor felt the hairs on the back of his neck move. He gripped his hands together for fear of touching her and felt his eyes water as he stared ahead. He turned to the window, coughed and pulled a packet of tissues from his jacket.

'Frog in my throat. Sorry.'

'You know more about me from a few hours, than people I've spent years with. I've cried and laughed, and I think you have too.'

'Perhaps we're bonded by a common secret which allows us to plumb depths we wouldn't necessarily share with others.'

'Stop intellectualising it, Victor. I like you and you like me.'

Feeling as though he was recovering from a minor trauma, Victor followed Cindy through the pub to the back garden, picking up a menu on the way.

'I'm getting the drinks and ordering the food. What would you like?' asked Cindy. 'You're getting the blame for a strained relationship,' she added.

'Oh yes, tell me more.'

'Apparently you made an impression on our Kirstin and she told Andy he's abusive and she's not taking any more of it.'

'I'm surprised she gave my brief comment any thought.'

'Yep. It's good for Kirstin. Wish I'd picked up on something like that at her age. The trouble is he'll find it difficult to find someone as good.'

'You two must have been close.'

'We still are. She's lovely. I can see her getting a really nice guy, and Andy getting some airhead while I just sit on the side-lines. What would you do?'

'Ask him about his next girlfriend,' said Victor.

'He hasn't got one. Kirstin's still on the edge of his life but I know she's holding back. It's only a matter of time.'

'No. I mean ask him what he thinks his next girlfriend will be like. It might make him think.'

'We don't have those sort of chats.'

'Ask him to meet you for a bite to eat.'

They sat silently sipping drinks in the evening sunshine watching people who were watching people.

'I think I will,' she said after a few moments, 'he might treat me differently being away from the house.'

'If it works I'll take the credit. If it doesn't, we never had this conversation.'

Cindy laughed.

'Come on, Victor, tell me about your girls.'

It wasn't 'till he felt chilly and saw the deep red of a sunlit wall that he realised he'd been talking non-stop for over an hour about Susan, Jenifer and Anne. He looked across the table at Cindy and couldn't recall her carrying a jacket, let alone putting it over her shoulders.

'You said we had until eight and now it's a quarter past.'

'Don't worry Victor,' she said, putting her hand on his.

Smiling at her, he rose from the wooden bench. 'Come, I know you have to pick up Elly.'

'Oh yes! She thinks you're great and said I must say hello.'

*

Everybody should have a cat to come home to thought Victor, upon hearing Pib (puss in boots – black legs under a white and black body) flow down the stairs to greet him. He'd driven home from seeing Cindy, unable to reconcile his thoughts, and now seeking sanctuary in routine. Half an hour later, with a mug of tea, Victor sat propped up in bed with an unopened newspaper and a purring Pib, unravelling the evening to rid himself of a residual malady from thoughts of Anne. He'd started to tell Cindy about Anne when he inadvertently unearthed intimate details causing him to feel emotionally fragile and forcing him to stop. Now, in the security of his bed, he felt he had to revisit the scene and the feelings in the hope of some sort of closure or burst.

He'd ached with unfulfilled feelings before Anne died. They'd cried together when their mutual loss became articulated from what had been an explorative conversation. She'd wanted him to have sex with her in spite of her illness, but he couldn't disinter desire from beneath layers of his concern, regardless of what they attempted to do for each other. Each had been left with their own interpretation of the event, knowing it wouldn't be repeated. A month later she was dead.

CHAPTER 12

Each of the three bangs on the front door seemed louder than the one previous. Susan stopped what she was doing and opened it to a medium-sized man.

'May I help you?'

'No, it's OK,' he grunted as he turned away.

'My Dad will be back shortly,' she called across the widening gap. She called again when he reached the gate, 'Shall I tell him Andy called?'

Andy turned and faced Susan who was smiling while gathering her hair and stretching a band over it. He faltered for a moment before walking back.

'You're back, so I guess you're Andy,' she said light-heartedly.

'And if I am?'

'I'm Susan, the youngest daughter. You may come in if you are.'

'How did you know?'

'Your name? Easy peasy. You fit my Dad's description, except for the sunglasses.'

Andy took his sunglasses off with one hand and stood looking up at Susan on the step above.

'You look as athletic as your description,' said Susan mimicking his tough stance. 'Come in, Dad won't be long.' She invitingly stepped aside. 'Would you like a drink? I'm having a white wine, but we've got more or less everything.'

Papers on the hall table moved. 'Quick, the back doors open,' she said, pulling his elbow to hurry him through against an increasing draught. A loud thud reverberated through the house. 'Too late.'

'When's he back?'

'Did you arrange a time?'

'No. I want to see him,' Andy curtly replied.

'Oh sorry, I thought you were early. He doesn't know I'm here either. I've only just read a note to say he'll be back at about five-thirty. He always leaves a note for me even if I've not seen him for a week. It's his way of maintaining feely contact. Sweet, isn't it? I'll wean him off it when I'm ready. Oh! And you don't have to worry, I'll make myself scarce when he gets here.'

'I'll have a beer,' said Andy.

'Hooray! Plonk yourself down in there,' said Susan, pushing open one of the double doors of the front room. 'I'll be back in a moment.'

Andy walked into the room and in a flash remembered not only his mother acting strangely, but also the smell of the coffee, the pain of his shoulder and the abrupt loss of his mother's support and her uncharacteristic coldness towards him. He re-experienced the feeling of being humiliated by her in front of Victor but consoled himself with the belief that he'd fully asserted himself by his dramatic exit. But even that now felt fragile.

'Aren't you scared, having a thief in your house?' asked Andy taking the glass.

'My Dad said he thought deep down you were a good guy, apart from being a thief that is. He didn't say the last bit,' she laughed, raising her glass to Andy without taking her eyes from his face. 'Cheers.'

'Ta,' said Andy.

'I'm intrigued,' said Susan, tucking her feet beneath her and pulling her maroon skirt over her black tights. 'What are you meeting my Dad about? I'm dying to know, or shouldn't I ask?'

'He's seeing my Mum.'

'I know. She sounds great. I'm dying to meet her.'

'I don't like it. He's fucking up my life with his fancy advice.'

'What should we do about him?' she mocked.

'I'm fucking off,' said Andy getting to his feet.

'No. Please don't go. I'm sorry. I'm being flippant. Please let's start again.'

Re-seating himself, Andy looked directly at Susan for the first time.

'Please tell me about yourself. It's not idle curiosity, really. You and your Mum have been good for my Dad. I feel I'm getting the Dad I used to have before Mum died.'

'I don't like what he's doing. They see each other all the time and she's getting fancy fucking ideas. She's even moved out.'

'What? You mean my Dad and your Mum have shacked up together and this house is just a pit-stop?' she said, straightening her back.

'No. I'd fuck him up if he did that.'

'What are you talking about then?'

'He's fucking with her brain. That's what he's doing.'

'You mean he's carrying out psychological experiments on her? I can't believe that. I'm sorry, that's not my Dad.'

'No,' said Andy, crashing his glass to the table.

'Then what are you telling me?'

'I'm telling you that every time he sees her she comes back with fancy fucking ideas.'

'What sort of ideas?'

'Moving fucking house for a start.'

'I'm sure he didn't tell her to move. That's not the sort of thing he'd do.'

'He put fancy ideas in her head that's for sure.'

'So, she moved out and left you with nowhere to live?'

'Not exactly,' faltered Andy.

'Then what?'

'She's got a new place.'

'And it's not big enough for you. Is that correct?'

'I've got a room in a shared house with some mates, but they get on my tits.'

'I still don't know what my Dad has to do with it. You're about my age. Isn't it time to be independent anyway? You've got a room with your mates and your Mum's got her new place.'

'It's crap living with my mates.'

'Well I guess you'll be moving out in that case. Couldn't you move in with your Mum while you get sorted? I'm sure she'd let you doss down in her lounge or something. She wouldn't just throw you out, surely?'

'I've got a room at her place.'

'What? Now it's my turn to say fuck. You mean you're spoilt for fucking choice?'

'I've had enough of this. I'm off,' said Andy getting up.

'Have a good evening,' she said following him to the front door.

He strode to the bus stop. 'Fuck'm all,' he said to himself.

CHAPTER 13

'Oh, no! I can't believe it,' said Cindy putting her hand to her mouth. 'Andy went to your house! What did he want?'

'Susan said he was concerned about my influence over you and wanted to see me.'

'Why didn't he wait?'

'She said he wanted to warn me off but changed his mind and left in a huff without finishing his beer.'

'What do you think?'

'I think she gave him the third degree and he couldn't take it. I personally think he was brave going to the house like that.'

'Anything else?' she asked staring at her half-finished lasagne and putting the knife and fork together across the plate.

'You look sad.'

'I've let him down and now he's dragging me backwards. I've made all sorts of suggestions: work, further education, outside advice. I even set up an interview for him when he said he could do warehouse packing. And do you know what? He didn't turn up or apologise. Made me look bloody stupid.'

'It's one of the problems we'll handle. There'll be more, but that's also OK.'

'I love the fact you say "we", but it's not "we" is it? It's me that has to handle it and that's on top of the dreadful meeting at the coffee shop I told you about. He's upset me time and time again and now he's trying to control my life.'

'He hasn't changed my intentions. Has he changed yours?' asked Victor.

'No, I guess not,' she replied, then paused for a second and smiled. 'So, you have intentions and what might they be?' she asked, raising her eyebrows, sitting upright and putting a hand to her heart in mock surprise.

Victor laughed. 'I like meeting up with you.'

'I love it,' she replied. 'What else did Susan say? She must've known why he left in a huff.'

'It was about his choice of accommodation, but she didn't go into detail. She's a natural lawyer and would have led him into an intolerable trap.'

'That might be why he's spending most of his time at the apartment. The trouble is, although he hardly communicates, the fact that he's in the house prevents me from feeling free to work,' sighed Cindy.

'What work is that then?'

'I decided to get some formal qualifications. Chatted with head-office about my options and hay-presto, HR said they'd pay for my accountancy course and they've given me half a day a week to study. I've still got my salary but my contract's been revised to a year's notice on my part and one month of theirs, which suits me anyway.'

'Congratulations.'

'Hold those 'till I've passed, but thanks.'

'I know what it's like working with interruptions. You're welcome to use my old study. I had it redecorated with coffee about six months ago,' Victor laughed. 'It's a bit dark but it has a desk. I'd feel good to know it was used. I'm out most of the time or in Anne's study on the floor above. The Wi-Fi's good throughout the house and the kitchen's down the corridor. I used to have students going in and out in the old days, but now I use the college.'

She searched his well-shaven rugged face, his greying thick hair, his mouth with a small vertical scar above the top lip, his nose (she thought Greek) and settled on his clear blue-grey eyes smiling back at her. She reached for his hand and squeezed it.

'Come, I've got shopping to do and it's my turn to pay,' she said.

CHAPTER 14

'So,' said Susan bouncing bare-footed. 'If I sneak home on Wednesday, I'll meet the wonderful begins-with-a-'C' and ends-with-a-'Y'. Can't wait. What about, she-who-will-be-obeyed?'

'Cindy knows you may arrive at any time and wants to meet you. Who's she-who-will-be-obeyed?'

'OK I'll stop that. Jen seems a tiny bit more accepting but I don't think she'll be happy.'

'I don't need her permission, but I had a long chat with her, just like I'm having with you. She expressed her reservations but in the end saw it as charitable. Cindy said she'd only use this room on the understanding there was total agreement from the family.'

'You have my total blessing,' she said hugging him. 'Did you tell her about Jen's reservations?'

'Not entirely.'

*

'The desk has been refurbished.'

'This is wonderful,' said Cindy looking about. 'Thank you so much, Victor.'

'I've cleared the drawers for you.'

'I can smell new paint. Did you do it yourself?'

'Some of it. I'd grown to accept the grey ceiling and the fading red walls, not knowing it could be different. It looks light and airy, don't you think?'

'It certainly looks that. It looks wonderful. I don't remember it being so open.'

'The piano's back in the lounge.'

Cindy stroked the green and red desk inlay. 'You've done a lot to this room and bought a new fancy swivel chair and an angle poise lamp, I see.'

'You noticed that then.'

'One day I'll tell you the memories this room brought back.'

'I enjoyed doing up this room,' said Victor glancing at his watch. 'Susan will be here any moment. I said one-forty-five but punctuality's not her strongest point but once she's here, she'll not let you get much work done.'

'I can't thank you enough.'

'Enjoy working here - that's good enough for me.'

'Hi. I'm home!' shouted Susan from the front door.

'We're in here,' replied Victor.

Susan's broad smile, happy eyes and long dark hair seemed to pull the rest of her near-six-foot figure into the room. Without dropping her overloaded linen shoulder bag, and before Victor could get the first syllable of an introduction out, she'd reached Cindy.

'Hi. I'm Susan and you're Cindy,' she said taking Cindy's forearms. Cindy did the same and they remained looking into each other's faces until their smiles grew into laughs, then Susan kissed her on both cheeks.

Victor prepared himself for some put-dad-on-the-spot banter while watching his daughter's naughty smile coming towards him, but to his relief, she kissed him and gave his arm an extra squeeze.

'I'm making coffee or tea or both. Who would like what?' asked Susan, as she dropped her bag onto a chair.

'Tea please,' said Victor looking at Cindy.

'Um--- tea, thanks,' said Cindy.

'That was a whirlwind,' said Cindy, sensing the vacuum where seconds earlier Susan had been.

'She hasn't started yet. Moves like a gazelle, but when she stops she sleeps like a bear in winter.'

Cindy laughed and turned to the desk. 'I hope you didn't do all this for me. You know it's only for an afternoon a week. I really feel spoilt just being here.'

'Come on, let's get your computer set up. There's a power socket under the desk and I'll get the code for the Wi-Fi,' said Victor scrolling through his phone.

Susan returned with a loaded tray and spread the items over the large low table.

'You've met my son. Sorry he was such a nuisance.'

'He wasn't. How's he getting on?'

'Been very quiet of late. But I have to admit something's changed. He's less aggressive. He told Kirsten, that's his ex-girlfriend, he's looking for a job but I can't see him getting one that easily knowing how he's been behaving 'til now. He said he'd answered an advert for a delivery driver, but he's only had his licence a few months and they couldn't take him on because of the insurance. It's sad but I can't talk to him about these things without him getting angry.'

Each time it looked as if the talk about Andy would change, one of them flicked it back into play until Susan got up from the couch.

'I think we should drink a toast to him. I'll get some wine,' said Susan, not waiting for an answer.

'Red or white?' she asked stooping over the table.

'Whatever is being opened,' said Cindy.

'That will definitely depend on you. Neither will last long in this house,' she lied, while mischievously glancing at her father.

'White please,' said Cindy.

Susan poured three glasses without asking Victor.

'To Andy, who's pulled us together,' proposed Susan.

'To Andy,' said Victor.

'I'm going to have a quick zizz before I go out. Lovely to meet you, Cindy. Don't let my Dad organise you too much,' she laughed, gently hugging Cindy before gliding from the room with her bag in one hand and her glass balanced in the other.

'She's wonderful,' said Cindy.

'Yes. She was less turbulent than normal, thank goodness. I'll leave you to get on. Help yourself to anything and give me a shout if you need help. Susan won't hear a thing 'til her alarm goes off.'

It had gone five by the time Victor came downstairs in answer to Cindy's call. She'd opened the front door ready to leave. 'Thanks for everything. I'm off to pick up Elly from her friend's house. Saturday at ten, normal place in Cowley Road?'

'Sound's good. Oh yes, here's a set of keys. I have another set inside. Use them any time you feel like escaping.'

'Is that wise?' Cindy replied, 'what about your daughters?'

'They both know you may be here at any time. Not just Wednesdays.'

'This means a lot to me. I hope you don't get a bad name or anything like that.'

'Like what?' laughed Victor.

'Oh, I don't know. Your friends mightn't like it. Have you thought about Sylvia?'

'Why should it upset Sylvia?'

'Victor, you may think you know everything, but you don't,' she said, pecking his cheek.

CHAPTER 15

By November, Wednesday's routine started with a quick lunch. Victor would wash up and go to his study and Cindy to hers, then a quick tea and biscuits at about three-fifteen after a shout from one of them. At five-thirty the alarm would sound on their phones and it was a toss-up as to who would pick up Elly (along with the evening's meal).

Cindy never ceased to be surprised at Victor's interest and patience while he listened to her talking about her concerns. She felt uplifted by him and automatically, and subconsciously, prepared herself for the evenings. Elly delighted in similar treatment and if time allowed would reserve difficult schoolwork for Victor's help. They both loved listening to him talking about his university work, Elly especially eager to hear about his students. Occasionally Victor would think Cindy had drifted off into her own world and he'd start to wind down, but then she'd throw in a question his students had not conjured up and a debate would generate with Elly throwing in her penny's worth without fear of criticism.

At about nine they'd part with kisses on cheeks, leaving Victor with a strange sense of loss, Cindy feeling unfulfilled and Elly looking quizzical.

'I've got to come clean, Victor. I've become a scheming little bitch,' said Cindy after an unusually late dinner on a Friday. 'You know Elly's sleeping over at her friend's. Well, it's not by accident. I know Susan's away and I don't want to go home tonight and it's Saturday tomorrow.'

'This is fighting talk,' said Victor with mock conviction.

'I've thought about you so much in the last few weeks. You remember how harsh you were the morning we met? I fought really hard to keep myself together. Now I realise we were both so alive that day. That day changed the way I look at things. What did that day do for you, Victor?'

'It's difficult to describe but I think I can define myself more clearly now. I've always enjoyed my work, but I'm pushing boundaries again and getting good feedback from students and colleagues for that matter. I love you being here. Elly's added another dimension to my life and I think my relationship with my girls has clearer boundaries.'

'Would you say you were more comfortable?'

'What's that supposed to mean?'

'Do you feel more comfortable because I'm here with you?'

'What do you think?'

'I see how you look at me and I see how you occasionally look at other women. You are comfortable but you're not confident. You were confident that morning. You had a mission.'

'Do you think I'm a silly old man with a young woman?'

'Is that how you see yourself?'

'I must confess, sometimes.'

'How do you think I see you?'

'This is getting too deep for me, Cindy.'

'No, come on; how do you think I see you?'

'I think you like me and I know you appreciate the things I do for you, and I know you enjoy the things we do together.'

'You *think* I like you?' questioned Cindy.

Victor sipped his Merlot without making eye contact while she waited.

'I don't want to stay over for convenience's sake, Victor.'

Victor stared at his empty glass.

'You could ask me to go home now that you know I want to sleep with you tonight, but you won't because you know I'd be hurt. You don't have a mission, do you? In fact you're scared. I want you to know I know. I'm right, aren't I? Or, as per your correction of my English, I'm correct am I not?'

'I'm sure there's some truth in there somewhere,' said Victor looking directly at her.

'I've fallen asleep feeling sorry for myself, Victor. I have a wantingness I can't fulfil. I'm greedy for knowledge about things I don't know or even understand. You woke me up. You said to me that first morning: "what do you want for yourself?" I think you said it twice.'

'That's good, isn't it?'

'You said it to me because you wanted to open my eyes. I know now you were also shouting at yourself. And I'm not guessing.'

Victor picked up his wine glass, went to take a sip, realised it was empty and put it back without looking at Cindy.

'I thought I'd fallen for you because you made me feel good about myself but even I'm able to rationalise that. Then I asked myself if it was because I recognised your need for love, but then -------.'

'Like loving a Labrador?' questioned Victor.

'Why not? Do you feel like a Labrador?'

'You might have something in your reasoning.'

'Listen to yourself. Do you sound like you did that morning?'

'What are you trying to say, Cindy? Give me something I can get my teeth into, for god's sake.'

'I know you Victor. I've seen your anger and I've seen your passion. May I stay or am I out?'

'Of course you may stay.'

Cindy sighed, poured a little wine for Victor and studied the back of his hand while she kneaded it thoughtfully.

'I don't expect miracles and I don't want to think about expectations. I just want all of you. Now I'm drained. Please kiss me properly and let's go to bed.'

Victor reached across the kitchen table, held Cindy's head and kissed her.

'Let's clear up.'

'No. I'll clear away,' he said.

'I'm not going to argue. I'm going to have a shower.'

'Towels are in the large cupboard at the end of the landing.'

'I told you, Victor. I'm a scheming little bitch. I've brought everything with me.'

Victor loaded the dishwasher, closed it, pondered, opened it, put a tablet in the tray, closed it and forgot to switch it on. He tidied the room, cleaned the stove surface, wiped down the table, swept the floor and jumped when Cindy spoke.

'I've just come from your bedroom and the bed looks like a slice of luxury. Pib looks a bit worried though. Hurry up,' she said, pulling her dressing gown around her 'and pleeeeez don't be long.'

He stood with a shower towel wrapped about him and looked at the back of her head as she lay on the far side of the bed facing the window.

'You took a long time,' she said quietly as she turned her head. 'And please take that towel off.'

'I was enjoying looking at you before I get my things.'

'Please don't put anything on, but you must take the towel off. It'll be damp.'

'I'm being ordered around in my own bedroom by a bully.'

Victor switched the light off and joined her under the duvet as she turned to face him. They lay looking into each other's faces for a few minutes, imagining shapes in the near darkness until Victor kissed her eyelids closed and held her against him.

'I needed this so much,' she whispered.

He whispered something she couldn't hear, she kissed him, turned to the window, moved her body up against his, felt for his hand resting on her hip and moved it to her breast.

Cindy tried to imagine Anne's daily life at her age, but after a short while she failed to focus and her thoughts turned to nonsense and instead of fighting it, she let go. Victor on the other hand, almost afraid to move, struggled to differentiate the nurturing feelings he had towards his daughters and Cindy. An hour later he fell into a fitful sleep.

Before first light Victor gently pulled the duvet from his side and placed it behind Cindy and got out of bed. He unhooked his dressing gown from the door and crept downstairs to the kitchen, glancing at the green glow of 06:45 on the microwave's clock and then at the blue glow of 07:46 on the oven clock. A few minutes later and after some fiddling, both clocks and his phone read 07:59. He made a mug of tea, leaned against the kitchen counter-top feeling pleased with himself and dropped a tea bag into Susan's mug, took another mug from the cupboard, emptied Susan's mug into it and put Susan's mug back in the cupboard.

Cindy leant against the doorjamb watching Victor padding bare-footed to and fro and listened to his mumblings.

'It's only a mug you silly old sod.'

'Muttering to yourself about mugs. You should be careful, someone may be listening and have you carted off to the funny farm,' said Cindy.

'You made me jump.'

'Good,' she replied with a smile.

'I want to know about the mug. Why can't I have my tea out of it?'

Victor pictured the Red Squirrel on the mug with Susan's face half hidden but couldn't quite recall her age.

'Come on. Tell me. You've had time enough to fabricate War & Peace.'

'It's of no significance. It seems to be Susan's favourite, but today I think you should have it,' he said, retrieving it from the cupboard and tipping the bag back in.

Cindy pulled her blue and red silk dressing gown about her, wrapped one arm about Victor, reached for another mug from the cupboard behind him and placed it next to Susan's. She tipped the teabag from the one to the other and kissed Victor's cheek.

'I also think you should keep thoughts about daughters separate from those about me,' she said, wrapping both arms around him.

CHAPTER 16

'When did you last see Dad?' asked Jenifer after a few minutes of banalities with Sylvia over the phone.

'Five weeks ago for lunch here, but I saw him in town the other day.'

'Was he with anybody?'

'Why are you asking, Jen?'

'Just asking.'

'He's OK isn't he?'

'You could say that.'

'That sounds ominous.'

'I think he's going mad.'

'He's not mad. He's in love.'

'So you know about Cindy then?'

'Come on Jen, you're phoning me on a workday afternoon. What's the matter?'

'Sorry Sylvia, I feel I've got nobody to talk to and ------.'

Sylvia, sensing Jenifer was close to tears interjected, 'Take your time Jen, I won't go away.'

'I didn't mean this call to go like this. Sorry.'

'Would you like to meet, love?'

'Please,' sobbed Jenifer, 'may I come now?'

'Make it forty minutes, love.'

Sylvia had been up since seven, she'd put on warm gardening clothes over faded pink woollen pyjamas in her eagerness to grab what looked to be a clear early March day and had sat on an east facing wall in her large garden eating cereal. She'd meant to change before breakfast and then again before lunch, but after a mid-day snack, she saw no reason to dress. She glanced at her iPhone. It was four-ten.

'Can't come tonight,' said Sylvia, 'the meeting will have to go on without me. Sorry about that. I was looking forward to it but something's cropped up and I don't want to be anxious if it takes long,' ------------- 'no, nothing serious. Yes, I'll come if there's time. Bye Emma.'

Sylvia showered, changed into jeans and a white shirt but stopped brushing her hair when she heard tyres crunching on the gravel in the drive and ran downstairs.

'I'm pleased you wanted to come,' said Sylvia taking a tissue from her pocket. 'Come my lovely Jenifer,' she continued supporting Jenifer's chin in her cupped hand and wetting a tissue with spit as she began to dab at streaked mascara on Jenifer's face.

'I thought I'd tidied myself up. Must've had watery eyes in the car. Should've checked before I got out.'

'You'll do, my girl,' said Sylvia kissing her on the nose, 'Let's go in the garden. It's rare to get such a warm afternoon - seems a shame to waste it.'

'I'm sorry to burden you with my woes. I was feeling sorry for myself. You caught me in a moment of weakness and now I'm feeling silly. I'll be OK.'

'I'd like to hear about your woes and moments of weakness. Moments of weakness; sounds like something will tumble down if you stop holding it up. Feels like hard work to me. So what's it all about?' asked Sylvia while searching the fridge for Jenifer's favourite fruit juice.

'I'm waffling. Take no notice of me, Aunt Sylve.'

'I haven't heard you call me that for years.'

'Call you what?'

'Aunt Sylve.'

'I didn't, did I?'

'Yes. You really took me back.'

'Oh, I'd no idea.'

'Come on, love, let's go into the garden. Bring those old cushions with you.'

Jenifer stretched out her black stockinged legs, rested her heels on the warm paving slabs and cradled a glass of pineapple juice on her lap. Sylvia tucked her bare feet under the bench, with the flat of her toes touching the ground.

'I know I'm uptight. I can't help it. It's the way I am. I can't just let things happen like Susan does. I'm driving David away, I can feel it. He's always out with his mates after work. Dad holds me at arm's length, not literally of course, but we don't engage. He's with that woman and he knows I don't like her. Everything's changed since that bloody burglary. Susan even thinks she's fun. Can you believe it? Fun? And as for her son, I don't even want to mention his name. He went to the house to confront Dad and he wasn't there but Susan was, and they had a tête-à-tête. Well, ever since then, whenever I try to bring the subject up with Susan she completely blocks me with something frivolous and then she says I know nothing about him. I can tell you I don't want to know anything about him. He came into our house in the middle of the night to steal things and nearly got away with it. Can you imagine it? Mum's things just disappearing like that?'

Jenifer made no attempt to stop tears from dripping onto her black skirt.

'I'll be back in a moment,' said Sylvia.

'Here Jen, my love,' said Sylvia, placing a box of tissues on her lap.

'I'm sorry,' said Jenifer pulling a chain of un-separating tissues from it. 'I'm sure they make these stick together to sell more,' she said half laughing through a sob. 'I'm sorry. I'm only thinking of me. I know you like Dad more than you let on. Oh God! I didn't mean to say that.'

'Of course I love your Dad and he'll always be a dear, dear friend, but he has his life to lead and I have mine. Come my love, let's make some supper.'

'I'd love to but I need to be home for David. He may, just for once,' she said, sarcastically, 'go directly home from work and I must be there.'

'I don't want to pry Jen my love, but if he goes out with his mates after work and you wait for him, aren't you setting yourself up for disappointment? Can't you just phone him and find out?'

'No I can't. He'll think I'm checking up on him.'

'If he goes out with his mates and you've waited for him, what do you both feel when he gets home?'

Sylvia broke the long silence. 'Jenny my darling, you know the answer. You'll feel let down and frustrated and he'll probably feel guilty. Where's this going to end up? Is it a battle for control? Are you feeling insecure? What's going on?'

'You're right as usual. I'll phone him. Thanks.'

'Everything OK?' asked Sylvia upon returning from the kitchen.

'I think he was relieved.'

'Open some wine and help me with supper. I want to hear everything.'

CHAPTER 17

'I'm taking advantage of you Victor,' said Cindy looking down at her bare feet swinging back and forth while sitting on the kitchen counter top with her hands spread out on either side and her black-rimmed reading glasses lying nearby.

A tingling sensation passed through Victor as he anticipated her next words. He looked at her without smiling, knowing something had been brewing since her arrival.

'It's been two weeks since I slept with you, Victor, and I'm feeling like a conniving little bitch. I'm spending a lot of time working out ways of sending Elly off for the night so I can spend another night with you. I know you're nervous about sleeping with me and would possibly rather not repeat it. No, please don't say anything; I might have got it wrong but I still want to say it. I think it's because you value your past and sleeping with me will somehow taint it. It probably stops you from getting an erection. Sorry, I didn't mean to go that far. No, no, please let me carry on, this is so difficult for me. If I stop now I won't be able to get it out and it's been going round and round in my head until it hurts. I'm not in your class. Sylvia is, and if you'd wanted someone to sleep with she'd have jumped at it and I wouldn't be here. I've got tons of baggage and if you sleep with me - oh fuck it, Victor, I mean if you have sex with me you'd probably feel you'd cheapened yourself and taken Anne, Susan and Jenifer, especially Jenifer, with you.'

Victor moved towards her but she held the palm of her hand towards him.

'Please listen, Victor. I really do understand what it means to you to have somebody else in your bed. I know it's difficult and probably brings up painful feelings but I don't want to do any more conniving. It was bad enough last time.'

She looked at Victor, head height, barely eighteen inches away, feeling forlorn and unkempt from a sleepless night but determined to see it through.

'Take a good look. You have to accept me as I am now or ----.'

Victor moved closer, gently pushed her legs apart and stood in-between her knees, his forehead against hers. They remained silent for a long time before Victor parted her hair and kissed her forehead. She hardly responded.

'Since we are talking with the veneer pulled back,' said Victor standing back, 'I have to confess, I sometimes find it easier to be an observer rather than a participant. Does that make sense?'

'When did you last have an erection?'

Victor hesitated, studied her deadpan expression and lifted her chin until their eyes met.

'I still want an answer,' she said without smiling, 'because I feel you're making it out to be a problem while I'm not.'

'A long time ago.'

Cindy put her arms around Victor's head, held him to her cheek and kissed his neck.

'I'd like you to sleep here when you can arrange it,' whispered Victor. 'I'm terrified, but the thought of having you in my bed is joyfully overwhelming. I know it will bring up big issues for me, so perhaps I should look at it as -------. No. I look at it as a journey.'

'Joyfully overwhelming, what a pompous speech! I love it,' she said, half grinning, half crying. 'Joyfully overwhelming--- I must hold onto that. Joyfully overwhelming,' she slowly repeated while looking into the space above Victor's head. She pulled herself towards him and closed her eyes tight. He lifted her from the counter top and lowered her to the floor. She carried on holding him whilst on her tiptoes and hugged him so hard it caught his windpipe, causing him to cough.

'Don't die on me now, not now,' she laughed, tearing a square from a kitchen towel and wiping her face, 'and where's the tea and biscuits you were bragging about?'

CHAPTER 18

'Next Wednesday for the night,' whispered Cindy into her office phone. 'Are you OK with that? And if you can spend time with me on the Thursday, I'll take the day off. I'll get to you at about seven thirty. If you hesitate for more than two seconds you'll really hear me cry. No. That was mean. Please be honest. If it's no, then it's no and I'll do my best to understand.'

'And Elly?'

'She'll be sleeping over at Carol's and her mother will take them to school. Elly's delighted.'

'I'm not even going to look in my diary. Wednesday it is.'

Cindy felt apprehensive when she saw Victor's name on her office telephone the following Monday.

'Be in your glad rags. We're going out to dinner on Wednesday first.'

'Before our joyful overwhelming?' she laughed.

'Consider it an integral part. I've booked a restaurant for eight.'

'That's really lovely Victor, so long as you don't intend to eat there all night?'

At seven-fifteen Cindy rang the doorbell rather than use her key and Victor, dressed in a light cream linen suit and a blue open-neck shirt, opened the door.

'Great haircut as well,' she said pecking him on the cheek and moving into the house.

'Wow! You look fantastic and taller,' replied Victor helping her with her long black coat.

'Thank you, kind sir. You look pretty dishy yourself.'

'Ice cold Prosecco in a champagne flute or lukewarm tap-water in a chipped tumbler?'

'I've never been so spoilt for choice. Should we be drinking before we go though?'

'A taxi will be here in fifteen minutes.'

'This evening's getting better and better,' she replied, while following Victor to the kitchen where two glasses were sitting on a small tray.

'Here's to a lovely evening with a lovely woman.'

'Victor, I feel lovely tonight. I'm not going to deny it. Here's to you.'

'There's no hiding in there,' said Cindy taking Victor's hand to duck out of the cab. 'This restaurant looks wonderful.'

'I hope you weren't banking on a secluded table with dim lighting, besides, glad rags are not for cosy chats in corners. Did you want to hide?'

Cindy pulled on Victor's hand stopping him at the entrance and looked into his face. 'This is so much more than dinner and you know it and I love you for it.'

Victor pecked her cheek and pushed the door as the maître d opened it.

'Hello Victor, good to see you,' came a voice from a table while he and Cindy were being escorted.

A small stocky man of about sixty, wearing a colourful bow-tie that blended with his cheeks, rose from a chair at a nearby table and reached out his hand with the expectancy of a long lost friend.

'Hello Ed. Good to see you, and you too Mary,' said Victor shaking Ed's hand and nodding towards a smartly dressed woman in her late fifties sitting at the far corner of a table of four.

'Allow me to introduce Cindy Oosthuizen. Cindy, this is Edward and Mary Johnson.'

'And Lucinda and Patrick Fairweather,' said Ed. 'Victor Elliott,' he continued with an introductory gesture.

Lucinda and Patrick smiled and nodded while Ed continued standing.

'At last, I get to meet the mystery woman,' said Ed laughingly as he held out his hand to Cindy.

Cindy shook it more firmly than she'd intended.

'Please join us,' said Mary. 'They can easily add two places to this table and we've only just got here ourselves.'

'Lovely thought,' said Cindy quickly, while smiling broadly and taking Victor's hand, 'but we've a lot to talk about.'

'Thanks Mary, it's a lovely thought but Cindy's correct. We need to take the opportunity while we can, but I hope we can make it another time. It's good to see you, and you're both looking so well.' Victor smiled and nodded towards the other couple and led Cindy to their table, where the waiter was standing behind a chair.

'I didn't mean to grab your hand like that,' said Cindy.

'Was it you that grabbed my hand? I thought it was the other way around.'

'I'm sorry I spoke out so quickly.'

'You knew Ed was itching to have you seated next to him.'

'Oh! Come off it Victor. What did he mean, mystery woman? Should I take it as a compliment or what?'

'That is typical of Ed. Think no more about it.'

'OK, but where did he get information about me? I find it amusing, but a bit unsettling. Are there lots of people talking about me, -- us?'

Victor leant over the table and whispered into Cindy's ear as she took a sip of sparkling wine.

'Shall I tell them to go and get fucked or shall I shout about the cost of this wine being ten times that at Tesco's? Your choice.'

Cindy sprayed wine over the table as she failed to contain a laugh, and although she quickly restored herself, she'd attracted not only the attention of Ed's table but most of the surrounding ones.

'That's much better,' he said as she dabbed her face with the napkin, 'I've got my Cindy back.'

'Oh, it's my Cindy, is it? I like the sound of that. Now tell me. Are your friends talking about me?'

'I think I've become a thing of interest to people like Ed. Most people take an interest in others when there's been a change. We all do it, it's part of socialisation and it's mostly harmless speculation. My little academic world will know all about it by Monday now he's met the tall, elegant, assertive, beautiful, not to mention young, Cindy Oosthuizen.'

'And how do you feel about that?'

'I'm delighted and I'm glad you met Ed. Most people think he's brash, but I think he's an open sort of guy. How do you feel?'

'I'm over the moon Victor.'

'Tell me what you've been up to. We've not been in the house at the same time for ages. I've missed you.'

'I've been prioritising my life and concentrating on things I can influence like Elly's education, my studies, my work and my apartment. I'm feeling guilty about Andy but at last he seems to be doing something with his life, so perhaps I should relax a bit. He's been using a van for a few weeks but he won't tell me anything, just says its work. I've been tempted to investigate but quite honestly I don't want to get involved unless he volunteers it. But the other evening a well-spoken man phoned and asked me if I was Mrs Oosthuizen. I thought he was a rep selling electricity or gas or something and nearly put the phone down but he was so apologetic. He said he was Mark somebody or other and wanted to get hold of Andy to make an emergency delivery. He asked me if the van and the keys were there. He said the other vans were out of Oxford. I wondered what I was letting myself in for. Anyway, I went into the street and saw the van near the corner and the keys were in the dish near the door. I was so nervous of Andy's reaction that I told this Mark fellow that I couldn't just hand over the van without Andy knowing. He then said he would leave his BMW for Andy and they could swap back in the morning. I then told him to come and get it. Ten minutes later this dishy, thirty-something in jeans and leather jacket arrived, shook my hand and tried to phone Andy again but could only leave a message. Then he scribbled a note and left the keys to a BMW in the dish and was gone in a flash. I felt so guilty not knowing what Andy does that I couldn't ask. I feel so left out. It's horrible.'

'Slow down, we've got all night,' said Victor.

'I'm afraid Andy will get really nasty and I'll lose what I'm trying to preserve.'

'As far as I'm concerned I could sit looking and listening to you all evening,' said Victor.

'That's because you're mad,' she laughed. 'Please let me be selfish tonight and let's talk about something else before I start worrying. I want to be taken home later for a joyful overwhelming or should that be overwhelmingly joyed? Whatever it is, I've brought lovely underwear and a matching top for the occasion and you have to say you like them whether you do or not. No pressure. Just love me for now.'

'I do,' he said casually, raising his eyebrows and looking directly at her.

'I said you were mad,' she said smiling back and putting her hand on his.

They'd entered the house through the front door many times together but now Victor hesitated and turned to Cindy. He pushed her hair to one side and gently kissed her closed eyes and the tip of her nose while she held him.

'You can carry on doing that.'

He kissed her nose again, turned and pushed the door open.

'OK young lady, what would you like?'

'I want to be taken to bed. I want you to hug me and love me. And Victor, please relax completely. I really mean it. There's no pressure. Just hug me and love me.'

Dressed for bed, Cindy sat at the dressing table brushing her hair and surveyed the room sensing minor changes without the benefit of familiarity to establish exactly what. The picture of Anne she'd studied on her previous visit no longer sat high on the chest of drawers overlooking the bed, and yes she thought, all the bedclothes are new and he's put a rose on the pillow with a chocolate wrapped in gold foil.

As soon as she heard him switch the bathroom light off she stood up.

'You look wonderful. No need to ask,' he said, looking across the room at her. 'Did you like my bowerbird impression?'

'Touched is all I can say.'

Neither could remember getting into bed but once there, they stroked and explored each other like a pair of teenagers and although only Cindy reached orgasm, they fell asleep after an hour in a tangle of arms and legs.

The morning however, in spite of being strangely painful and wonderful for Victor, produced unexpected results to the delight of both. He then drifted into a deep sleep.

The note propped against the bedside lamp adjacent to the now cold mug of tea read: 'You didn't even wake when I kissed your stubbly face and I hadn't the heart to wake you, you looked so peaceful. I'm coming back at about one for lunch and then we'll go for a walk. Love you so much, Victor. XXX - C.'

CHAPTER 19

'Oh, yes! And when were you banned from the house?' asked Victor.

'I know when to take a hint,' said Susan from her superior position perched on the kitchen counter. 'Oh! I just wondered. You replied after you'd asked what I was doing on Wednesday. Your face lit up when I told you I'd be at my place. So I stayed clear of here, knowing my very own father was up to mischief,' she mocked.

'I've made coffee for you for a change and because I'm being severely neglected, I bought myself some Danish pastries. If you're good, you may have one,' she said, bouncing onto the floor and removing a plate from the oven. 'I heard you stirring. Another two minutes and I would have called you down anyway. Did you lock yourself in your study all morning? It's gone midday?'

'This is a very pleasant surprise without the interrogation. How did you know I was here?'

'A little bird told me. Actually, it wasn't what the little bird said it was more like what it didn't say.'

'So you've seen Cindy?'

'Got it in one. Saw her in the supermarket. I could have

spotted her with the lights out. She positively glowed. I can tell you one thing though.'

'Oh yes. What's that then?'

'My Dad definitely looks happier.'

'Glad to hear it, and so that there's no guessing, Cindy was here last night but that doesn't mean that you should stay away.'

'I won't. I hope you don't get hurt though.'

'I'm old and ugly enough to know the pit-falls.'

'It's one thing knowing them, it's something else if they happen.'

'OK wise one, what have you been up to?'

'No, tell me more. How's Cindy, really?'

'Well, we went to dinner at Raymond's and chatted until we were just about the last to leave and today she'll be here for lunch and then we're going for a walk.'

'I'm so much more interested in the bit in between but I think I'll leave that alone. How is the wayward son now that he has a job?'

'Who told you he had a job?'

'Good old Mark ended up giving him a driver's job at the workshop. It's not full-time yet but looks like it will be as Mark sees it.'

'Who's Mark and how come you know more than Cindy or me?'

'Mark, you know Mark, Jen's ex-boyfriend. I bump into him every now and then. He's always running around like a mad thing and I thought he might have a job for Andy. Andy doesn't know any of this. I think he's so arrogant he would go it alone and fail rather than get help. I got his number from Cindy a long time ago and said I would look out for him.'

'You never cease to amaze me,' said Victor, 'but how did Mark contact him without Andy answering an advert?'

'Dad you ask too many questions. I simply told Mark about Andy and to make up any story he liked and to avoid going through his mother, and if he was happy with him, to make sure he gave him as much responsibility as he could take.'

'He obviously liked him then,' said Victor.

'Please don't tell Jen. She really doesn't like him. She thinks he and Cindy are responsible for upsetting her world. Sorry Dad, I hate collusion.'

'Haven't heard a thing,' said Victor.

'What thing?' laughed Susan. 'And I'm glad you're with Cindy. Beware of broken hearts, won't you?'

'More wisdom from a wicked woman.'

'We're more wicked than you could ever imagine in your wildest dreams.'

'OK, I've got the message.'

Victor cleared the table while they chatted.

'What time is it?' asked Susan with some alarm.

'Twenty-five minutes past twelve,' said Victor feeling slightly alarmed on her behalf.

'Oh Jesus, I'm supposed to be meeting Jen in town in twenty minutes,' she said racing up the stairs.

*

'I rarely see my elegant sister nowadays and I end up late. I'm really sorry, Jen.'

Jenifer, pale-faced, heaved herself out of a settee and without speaking, uncharacteristically hugged Susan, who jettisoned her excuses and defences against anticipated censuring and held Jenifer equally tight, and long enough for Susan to understand things weren't as they should be.

'David's having an affair,' she blurted out between involuntary sobs.

Susan took Jenifer's bag from the settee and gently ushered her towards the exit. Outside amongst the throng, Jenifer retrieved her bag, and with Susan's assistance, most of her composure, then nodded when Susan suggested walking along the river.

'I thought you'd tell me it was expected. I know everybody else has twenty-twenty vision when it comes to looking at Dave and me, and then Sylvia, warning me about being a control freak. She didn't exactly say it but that's how it felt.'

'You've told her?'

'No. That was weeks ago. I was being silly and she caught me unawares. You know what she's like. Just like Dad; her silences extract everything when you least expect it. I went there from work. I phoned Dave to say I wouldn't be home 'til late. I could hear lots of laughing in the background so I knew he was with his mates. I left my car at Aunt Sylve's and collected it the next day. It was a lovely and --------.'

Susan listened to Jenifer's diversion from David and his affair, feeling slightly redundant as Jenifer gradually regained confidence. However, she abruptly interjected without choosing the moment.

'We both called her Aunt Sylve when we were in trouble.'

Ignoring other walkers, Jenifer turned to Susan, threw her arms about her and cried, causing Susan to do the same.

'Ask me then,' said Jenifer, wiping her eyes.

'I'm not going to bombard you with questions. I know my big sister well enough and you'll tell me when you're ready.'

Linked together, they walked in silence for a few minutes.

'It's more than an affair Sue. He's moved out and he'll be collecting the rest of his things today. He met some bitch months ago and he's been screwing her ever since. No investigation on my part. I simply asked him her name because I told him I felt I wasn't part of his life any more. I'd have felt better if he'd begged forgiveness or at least argued, but he said he would have told me soon enough. That's when I screamed "soon enough for what you bastard?" I'd completely lost it by then and told him to get out. And to think I'd been humiliating myself by trying to be attractive for him, even dressing in flimsy, expensive and uncomfortable underwear. I feel like a prostitute when I think I was competing with that bitch. I didn't go to work yesterday and I'm glad. I got my mind together, and believe it or not, had a good night's sleep without turning over in the middle of the night and feeling as though I'd cut myself in half with a piece of string between my legs: and they call it sexy underwear. I know I can face Monday with a good start.'

'You don't want to be there while he's taking his stuff?'

'No. He won't take anything of mine and he won't be interested in household things. In some ways, it's a relief. Please don't say anything until I've spoken to Dad this evening, that's if he isn't totally preoccupied with his tart.'

'Now now,' said Susan.

'Well what do I call her then, his bit of fluff, his floozy, his bit of rough? Or does that only apply to men?'

'You could go to the house and see Dad now if you wanted,' said Susan.

'No, I couldn't bear bumping into whatever you want to call her. I'll ring him when I get back.'

'Please let Dad know today. I'm staying there for a couple of days and I can't act like I know nothing.'

*

Susan helped Jenifer move furniture within her apartment, and by the time the spare bedroom had become a study and a bottle of Merlot was just about empty, both were laughing at Jenifer's comments about burning the bed linen instead of washing them and "Dave and his bitch".

'It's seven-thirty, Dad's probably home and what's-her-name's probably attending to her brats. I'll talk to Dad,' said Jenifer, sharing out the remainder of the bottle before disappearing into the bedroom.

Susan had almost finished preparing something to eat when Jenifer, less hysterical, joined her in the kitchen.

'It would have been better if he'd said "I told you so" but no, I could hear it in his voice. He was really upset for me. Bloody well started me off again.'

CHAPTER 20

'Hello,' shouted Jenifer from the front door.

'In the kitchen,' Victor called back.

'It's such a wonderful day I thought I'd walk,' she said kissing him.

'You walked?'

'I do have legs,' she said, looking down at her shoes in mock surprise.

'I have to say, you look wonderful,' said Victor.

'You expected to find me in a complete mess after last night's phone call.'

'A mess is an exaggeration, but I expected to be picking up a few pieces. Glad to see you looking so good. Are you OK?'

'Dad, I'm fine. Yesterday was bad. But you probably got all that from Susan. I didn't expect to pour it all out to her but her seriousness disarmed me completely. She spent all day with me and I ignored any plans she may have had. And it was Saturday. I apologised this morning when I woke her for lunch. She laughed it off. I probably need to be more like her.'

'You haven't changed your mind since last night?'

'About getting a quick divorce? No, the quicker the better. I've brought a list of things I must do, but I'd like you to go through it.'

'Use the desk in the front room - there's a printer there. I'll join you in a minute or two.'

Assumptions gave way to shock as Jenifer entered the room for the first time in well over a year. It was light and airy. She detected a delicate and unobtrusive scent, and caught herself sniffing the air before feeling disturbed, verging on distraught. Her medium height heels clicked on wood where carpet had been as she approached the desk. In place of old floppy wooden swivel chairs with green cracked leather seats, were three modern five wheelers of cream and chrome. The familiar stains and dents had been sanded out of the leather-topped desk revealing light oak that hadn't seen the light of day for over a hundred years. She looked in awe at the categorised books before taking 'How to Talk Finance by Ted Wainman' from an array of new books on new matching shelves immediately behind the desk, and leafed to pages marked with Post-it notes where Cindy had written references.

'What do you think?' asked Victor, making her jump.

'It's changed.'

'When the carpet people arrived to quote for a new one they pulled up a section and I had a good look at the wood underneath. It's the original floor sanded, filled and sealed. The rugs come from Ikea and I had the curtains made locally. It's a wonder the old ones didn't fall down with the weight of dust. There were some unhappy spiders that went out with them.'

'Does Joan still come and clean?'

'She does every room except this one. Cindy does it. Let's have a look at your list.'

Actions required and names to be contacted precipitated from Jenifer's evolving list which culminated in a final print-out at five-thirty.

'Come. I'm taking you for an early supper. That's if you're not expecting you-know-who to be here later.'

'Her name is Cindy Jenifer, and I've cancelled everything to be with you today.'

'I'm sorry Dad, but you know how I feel; and as for her no-good son, I hope I never meet the bastard. Just thinking about him gets me worked up. Come on, we'll walk to Banbury Road and see what restaurant looks appealing.'

'Let's go by car. It's chilly and you came without a coat.'

'Don't worry about that,' she said, rummaging through the rail in the hall cupboard. Victor watched Jenifer pull out Anne's long, dark mauve coat, shake it, inspect it and put it on. She pulled it about herself with her hands in the pockets without fastening the buttons, looked at her reflection in the mirror and with a sideways glance smiled, removed a couple of tissues from the pockets, walked to the small bathroom and flushed them away.

'Ready, Dad?' she shouted while washing her hands. 'Please bring mum's clothes brush down.'

Although Jenifer was taller, Victor felt unnerved by the similarity as Jenifer turned around with the same expectancy of having the back of her coat brushed.

'Was she coming today?' asked Jenifer, as she walked with her arm in his.

'Yes. I didn't tell her about your problems, but I did say I needed to talk to you. She doesn't probe. She's sensitive to family issues.'

'I'm sorry Dad, I just can't even think about her and I don't want to hurt you. And let's not call them problems. There are things we, I mean I, need to do. Problems would be like being pregnant.'

'You're not, are you?' asked Victor, stopping to look at her.

'Not that I'm aware, but we did have sex in the last few weeks, but I'd rather not go there either.'

They walked on in silence with Victor feeling warm from a flash of fantasy of a baby about the place. He then involuntarily drew a deep breath thinking of Cindy, realising he'd abdicated from responsibility of even talking about contraception to her. His mind settled while he continued his flight of fantasy by imagining Cindy pushing a double buggy and almost laughed.

'Penny for your thoughts Dad.'

'It's nothing Jen.'

'What if I was pregnant is what you were thinking.'

'Something like that,' replied Victor.

CHAPTER 21

After hellos and niceties on the phone, Mark asked Susan if she had time to talk about Andy.

'He's doing OK isn't he?'

'Yes, he's been on a couple of courses and did really well. He's installing equipment and he's good with data networks and can do most of it without phoning back to the office.'

'There's something serious. I know it. You don't do small talk and we've been on the phone for five minutes already. What is it?'

'I need advice. May we meet? This evening if possible?'

'Carpenter's Arms at six-thirty?'

'See you there.'

'This is delicate,' said Mark. 'It's happened three times and is beyond coincidence. Andy's worked with a lot of client companies where we have support contracts and he's organised replacement computers for a few of them. That's not unusual. We bring the old ones to the scrap store and rob them of parts for spares and send the rest for recycling. We charge the client where we can for the new equipment unless they have a comprehensive maintenance agreement. I think – actually - I know some of the equipment is being removed from the client with no recording and I found that somebody had been buying hard drives for some of this equipment and selling the whole computer to another company. We've won a few new clients recently and our unique numbers have been discovered inside their equipment. All can be traced back to support work carried out by Andy.'

'I'm so sorry to have got you into this, Mark. I really am.'

'That's not why I'm here. This sort of thing goes on all the time. I'm more concerned about your Dad and Andy's mother. In spite of what Jen says, I know they're happy together. I saw them in town the other day. They were like a couple of kids.'

'Cindy will be upset. She used to anticipate this sort of thing, but she's been more confident about him now he's got a real job.'

'Thought as much,' said Mark.

'This is such a shame. Dad's more relaxed about Andy and he loves Cindy to bits. What's the next step?'

'We're getting our systems in order so we'll be able to track things more accurately. I'll think of a way of talking to him without a showdown. I thought we should talk first because you normally come up with some bright idea.'

'Wow, what a compliment and there I was thinking I was a pest when you were with Jen and I was the baby sister getting in the way.'

'You were a little pest. You probably saved your sister's good name on a number of occasions.'

'Pity I got in the way. Things might have been very different. I hope you haven't lost a lot of business through this. You were the only real person I could think of to help Andy.'

'If it helps at all he's more than earned any loss we've incurred so there's no need to be down-hearted. Now tell me about your beautiful sister. I've heard things on the grape vine.'

Susan perked up at the thought of Jen being with Mark, and had never known the reason for the breakup of their one-year relationship.

'No Susan, we couldn't get back together,' he said without any prompting.

'Ah well, just a thought.'

CHAPTER 22

'I feel as though I'm putting myself through the mill,' said Jenifer, hovering about the dining table while Victor laid it for four.

'Cindy probably feels the same as you. Here,' he said handing her a handful of cutlery, 'finish laying the table while I open a bottle.'

'I don't know why I'm doing this!'

'Because you still love your dear old Dad even if he's jumped from one side of the law to the other,' he replied putting the opened bottle down and reaching for Jenifer's face between his hands and kissing her cheek. She smiled without looking at him and pushed her hair back and tensed up as she heard a car draw up.

'Hooray, she's here,' said Victor glancing at the clock on the oven.

'Hello Jenifer. Let me put these down first,' said Cindy, half swinging and half lifting the bags onto the kitchen top.

My goodness, thought Cindy, she is so good looking, but not warm enough for a kiss or a hug. She balanced the bags upright and reached for Jenifer's forearms and smiled at her.

'I'm glad you could come, Jenifer. Hi Victor,' she continued, glancing at him but not kissing him as normal.

'I've put the bathroom things away, Mum,' said Elly loudly, a second before entering the kitchen. 'Oops, sorry, I forgot,' she said, suddenly feeling desperate to look as serious as the three of them.

'Hello, I'm Elly. You're Susan's sister Jenifer, aren't you?' she said, holding out her hand. 'You're very tall like Susan. I hope I'm tall when I'm older.'

Jenifer couldn't hide her look of surprise as she took Elly's hand.

'I'm sure you will be,' said Jenifer.

Elly withdrew her hand once she'd completed the ritual Victor had taught her.

'Hello Victor,' said Elly, giving him a hug and holding her face up for a kiss on the cheek. 'Please can I play on your iPad?'

'I'm sure you can and you may,' replied Victor.

'OK. *May I*?' she said. 'I keep forgetting.'

'Have you done all your homework?'

'Not the maths, but you're helping me with that tomorrow after breakfast.'

'I haven't forgotten. Dinner will be ready in fifteen minutes.'

'What are we having?'

'Baked salmon with boiled potatoes and vegetables.'

'I'd sooner have fish fingers.'

'I'm sure you would.'

'Down in fifteen minutes,' Victor called after her.

'I won't have any wine yet,' said Cindy as Victor poured. 'I'll have sparkling water.'

'Cheers!' said Victor.

'Cheers!' said Cindy.

Jenifer nodded and sipped her wine.

'You two could leave me to cook,' said Victor.

'No,' said Jenifer and Cindy almost simultaneously, 'I'm happy in the kitchen,' said Cindy, 'we can sit and watch you slaving away.'

'I see the wash basket's gone upstairs,' said Jenifer.

'How's work, Jen?' asked Victor.

'That's the best thing about my life at the moment. It's going very well. I'm glad I completed my business studies before starting work,' she said glancing at Cindy. 'Or starting anything else for that matter.'

'Victor's not told me much about your work,' said Cindy.

'He's probably been too busy. I see the oven and the microwave now tell the same time. Somebody has magic fingers around here.'

'Were they different?' asked Cindy.

'Do you not notice things like that?'

'They've been in sync for over a year Jen,' said Victor.

'Children seem to have a knack with these things,' said Jenifer.

'They're not afraid to press buttons,' said Cindy. 'Ask any child to reset the TV equipment and it's done in a flash.'

'I can't be bothered with TV nowadays,' said Jenifer.

'I synchronised the oven and the microwave,' said Victor, looking directly at Jenifer without smiling, while Cindy glanced from one to the other.

'They've been out of sync for years. What spurred you on to change them?'

'Pass me the plates please. They're in the top oven and probably hot.'

Jenifer took an oven glove from a hook on the wall, retrieved the plates and spread them out on the counter.

'Thanks, Jen. Please call Elly. She'll be in the large spare bedroom.'

'I'll call her,' said Cindy making for the door.

'Dinner's ready,' called Cindy from the hall before shutting herself in the bathroom.

Victor put cooking pans on wood boards while Jenifer needlessly looked through her handbag in silence.

'It's self-service tonight,' said Victor to Elly as she came into the room.

'I feel tons better,' said Cindy, returning, having washed her face (in cold water) and vigorously brushed her hair. 'Don't worry, Victor, I'll help myself thanks. I'll have some wine now,' she said taking the bottle from the counter. 'Anybody want a top-up?' she asked glancing at Jenifer who made no response.

'Thanks,' said Victor, pushing his glass forward.

Cindy topped Victor's glass to half way and without waiting for an answer poured the rest into Jenifer's glass.

'What sort of work do you do?' asked Cindy.

'I'm the regional director for a leasing company,' Jenifer replied with tones of officialdom before putting a fork of fish in her mouth.

Cindy ate while Jenifer silently took a second mouthful, then a third.

'How does regional directing in a leasing company work?'

Jenifer slowly chewed and swallowed before wiping her mouth with a serviette. 'We approve or reject loans based upon the lessee's ability to pay,' replied Jenifer, in a manner that suggested she'd been reminded of an important message. She reached into her bag and retrieved her phone. The screen glowed for a few seconds after she pressed a button. She switched it off, put it next to her plate and carried on eating.

'That's what the company does. I'm more interested in you. What does a regional director do?' asked Cindy leaning back and looking directly at Jenifer.

'It certainly keeps me busy. There's lots of staff,' replied Jenifer, without looking up and becoming more interested in her food.

'Are you responsible for achieving local targets based upon defined KBRs, and do you then send the results to senior directors based somewhere else?'

'Well, eh, yes,' replied Jenifer picking up her phone and returning it to her bag.

'Do your senior directors report to a foreign office or is it a small UK based company?'

Victor felt his stomach muscles relax when Elly interrupted. 'What's a KBR?'

Cindy put a forkful in her mouth and slowly chewed while Elly looked at her, then at Jenifer, who was also chewing. Cindy swallowed, sipped some wine and after a few more seconds of silence said: 'It's an acronym for Key Business Ratios Elly. The answers tell managers of businesses if something is getting better or worse when compared with itself over time, or better or worse when compared with another region or a similar company.'

'Like what?' asked Elly.

'How much profit they're making per person for each region, administration cost per Pound of sales; all sorts of things the senior directors regard as key to the success of the company.'

'Victor said there were too many TLAs,' said Elly grinning.

'Three Letter Acronyms,' said Victor.

'I hear the old Volvo's been replaced with an Audi estate, but I didn't see it in the drive.'

'I had to stop to change the radio channel when I first got it. I think Elly knows how all the gadgets work though, don't you?' Victor said looking at Elly.

'Victor gives up if things don't work first time. Then he tells me about it and I show him. Mum drives it as she finds it.'

'Don't you find it a big change from your car?' asked Jenifer.

'I haven't scratched it yet. And my old Renault gets used every day, but now that Elly goes to your old school, she's desperate to be like the others and won't be seen dead in it,' said Cindy reaching across the table to Elly and smiling. Elly put her hand in Cindy's palm. 'It's very shallow thinking and Elly knows it,' she said squeezing her hand and smiling at her. 'But why not? She's young and enjoying it and if you can't get it out of your system at her age, when can you do it?' she said looking directly at Jenifer. 'And Victor's getting to grips with the idiosyncrasies of my rusty old Renault. You haven't had to push start it yet, have you?' she asked smiling at Victor.

'I'm opening another bottle if there are any takers,' said Victor.

'No thanks,' said Cindy.

'I could open a dessert wine if you would prefer. Might go well with the apple crumble.'

'I'm OK thanks,' said Cindy.

'I'm driving,' said Jenifer looking at her empty glass.

'Jenifer?' asked Elly.

'Yes?'

'Do you use makeup? I can't see any.'

'Why do you ask?'

'I want to be beautiful when I'm as old as you.'

'I use cream every morning to protect my skin against the sun,' said Jenifer quickly reaching for her bag. 'Excuse me, I'll be back in a moment.'

'Is Jenifer alright?' asked Elly, looking from Cindy to Victor.

'She's fine,' answered Victor. 'Are you ready for apple crumble?' he questioned while clearing the dinner plates from the table.

Cindy collected bowls from the cupboard, leaving Elly alone and feeling worried. Jenifer returned and smiled at her. Elly's face lit up.

They had nearly finished the dessert when Elly spoke. 'Jenifer?' she asked. 'My name isn't really Elly. Would you like to be the first person to call me by my real name?'

'That would be a privilege,' said Jenifer. 'What is it?'

'Emma. Emma Oosthuizen.'

'Pleased to meet you Emma,' said Jenifer holding out her hand and shaking Emma's.

'May I leave the table?' asked Elly, sliding off the chair without waiting for an answer.

Victor turned to receive Elly's kiss on the cheek. He kissed her roughly on the neck in return, making her squeal, while Jenifer looked on and was instantly taken back ten years when she experienced that same kiss.

'Good night, Elly. Sleep well,' said Cindy as they exchanged kisses.

'Good night, Jenifer,' said Elly giving a little wave from the door.

'Good night, Emma,' she replied waving back.

'I've got an early start tomorrow. Thanks for a lovely meal but I must go,' said Jenifer moving her chair back.

'Tea or coffee?' asked Victor.

'No. I really must go.'

'We'll come to the car,' said Victor when Jenifer attempted her goodbyes at the front door.

Cindy kissed Jenifer's cheek while Jenifer kissed the air next to Cindy before lowering herself into her BMW while Victor held the door open.

'She's certainly good looking,' said Cindy in reply to Victor's 'what did you think of the evening?'

Cindy locked the front door from the inside while Victor stood watching her locate the keyhole in the semi-lit entrance area.

'She doesn't like me,' she said as she stood up.

'Give her time. She may be jealous,' said Victor.

'Oh yes? Of what?'

'You, Elly, lots of things.'

'What about me?'

'She's not going home to anyone for one thing and, of course, I'm not available at the drop of a hat like I used to be.'

'How do you feel about that?'

'This house is buzzing again, and when she's ready she'll join in, I know that.'

'You've asked her to come back here if she wanted? You did, didn't you?'

'Of course I did, and told her that her bedroom is still here if she feels like the odd night away as well. But she knows that.'

Cindy didn't immediately respond to Victor's embrace in the entrance hall but they remained together for a while before she kissed him, giving him an extra squeeze before releasing herself.

CHAPTER 23

'I thought I was OK with the evening but it's been on my mind ever since and I can't shake it off,' said Jenifer to Sylvia over the phone. 'Sorry Aunt Sylve. Oh my God! I really did call you Aunt Sylve. Sorry. I feel so angry. The more rational I try to be the worse it is. That bloody woman has taken up residence and my Dad is falling for it. Sorry, but that's how I feel. He's making a complete fool of himself.'

'I keep hearing sorry. What's that all about?'

'Sorry, didn't mean it like that.'

'I'm not chastising you, Jen, my darling girl. You don't need to apologise for being angry. I'm asking you why you feel you should say sorry. What's that about?'

'Figure of speech, that's all.'

'Worked up is what I can hear,' said Sylvia.

'OK. Worked up then,' said Jenifer feeling thwarted at having to be specific.

'Don't you feel a bit upset with him?' asked Jenifer. 'Don't you miss him?' she added before Sylvia could answer.

'Your Dad and I had a lovely lunch together last Monday,' said Sylvia. 'Lasted nearly three hours.'

'Oh well, it seems like I'm the one that's out of kilter. Did Cindy know?'

'If your Dad wants to talk about Cindy he does. I don't pry and I have no idea if she knew or not. And Jen, you're not out of kilter, my love. A lot of things have happened recently which you can't control and it doesn't matter whether it's for the best or not. It's de-stabilising you.'

'You mean you've seen a lot of him?'

'Jen, we've known each other, your Dad and me, since dinosaurs clambered over the Cotswolds. We're hardly likely not to keep in contact.'

'That's precisely what I'm on about. He's old enough to be her father.'

'He would've had to have been a very young father,' said Sylvia. 'Perhaps he's going to be an old father,' she added mischievously.

'Oh god no! What's he said?' Jenifer almost shouted down the phone.

'Nothing,' said Sylvia laughing.

'It's no laughing matter,' said Jenifer. 'It gave me a jolt when I saw a box of Tampax in the bathroom cabinet.'

'Jen, I know what you said about being free of David, but it's still a huge loss and I'm very much aware of your feeling of loss for your mother. Nothing diminishes that and I'm not making light of any of it. I'm expressing my own feelings. I love your Dad. I don't want him hurt. I want him full of life, and I have to admit he's certainly that at the moment.'

'You sound like Susan with her love this and love that. Where's the meaning any more?'

'Jen, we started this conversation with me inviting you for lunch on Sunday and it got lost somewhere along the line.

Please come. There's the usual crowd, none will stay late so we can have a chat afterwards and make an evening of it. What do you say?'

'Dad won't be there with Cindy, will he?'

'No he won't.'

'Thanks. What time should I be there? Can I bring something?' she asked and then thought of the word 'can' and got annoyed with herself.

'Bring yourself,' said Sylvia.

Jenifer felt increasingly depressed as the week progressed, but managed to make an unscheduled appointment with Helen, her counsellor, for the Thursday evening, which she later considered a waste of time. She was on the verge of pulling out of the lunch when Sylvia phoned.

'Is it OK if I invite Mark? He's been in touch with Matthew.'

'It's a long time since I saw Mark. There's nothing to worry about but thanks for considering me. No. It would be good to see him.'

'Well, he might not be able to make it, but I thought I'd better ask you first.'

*

Jenifer alighted from her taxi into the hubbub of lunch on the warmest May Sunday for years, having psyched herself up to attend. Aware of her possible fragility, Sylvia, alert to her arrival, stopped what she was doing and got to Jenifer first.

'You don't have to worry, Jen. Cindy and your Dad won't suddenly turn up. So take that worried look off your face.'

'I've seen Susan already and I did wonder for a moment, but you were so sensitive about Mark. I guess I'm feeling vulnerable. This is really lovely of you Aunt Sylve. Where's Mark?'

'Before you run off, let me look at you,' said Sylvia holding Jenifer by both shoulders.

'You look stunning my lovely Jenifer,' she said looking up at Jenifer's six feet one, in medium heels, and complementary long light blue lace skirt and white blouse. 'If someone whisks you away from here, we'll meet up another time. Don't stay for my sake.'

'Don't get ideas of Mark and me, Aunt Sylve. It won't happen. I know he doesn't have a partner here because I spoke to Susan in the week and she's very excited about the possibility, but I am so resolved about my life and I'm really happy with work and home. The only fly in the ointment is 'you-know-who' and her wily ways, but on a day like today even that can fade.'

'Bitterness doesn't suit you, Jen.'

'OK, where is he?'

'I saw him pouring drinks in the garden. Now go and say hello.'

'Where's my drink then?' asked Jenifer to Mark's back as he held forth about small businesses carrying the highest proportion of costs to a group of three men and one woman.

'Wow!' he said turning to look at her. 'Give me the biggest hug you can.'

Mark kissed her on both cheeks, to which she responded with only slightly less enthusiasm.

'No. Don't go,' she said to the group that looked as if it was about to take the opportunity to disperse. 'I'm sorry. It's only that we haven't seen each other for ages. I'll get a glass and have some of that white wine you're carefully protecting.'

'Where was I?' he said, as he and two of the others watched her walk to a table covered in upturned glasses.

Jenifer had steeled herself to make her opening gambit with Mark and to her it felt false, but having done so, she relaxed into a role she enjoyed but hardly recognised.

Much later that afternoon a couple finished clearing the dishes they'd brought with them, and by the time they'd said their goodbyes, the kitchen was a hive of activity with people preparing to go home. Mark, Jenifer, Susan, Susan's latest partner Simon, remained with Sylvia until the house was tidied up.

'I'm off,' said Mark.

There was a chorus of 'you can't go now' from nearly all the remaining guests while he moved amongst them with handshakes, hugs and kisses, including one for Jenifer, indicating nothing of their arranged dinner for later in the week.

CHAPTER 24

Andy was so absorbed with the inside of a computer cabinet that he didn't notice Mark standing next to him.

'Hi, Andy. Leave that for a moment. I'd like to chat. Let's go to the office.'

'I'll just finish this and I'll be with you.'

'No, I've only got a few minutes.'

Andy straightened himself up and followed Mark, feeling unsettled by their lack of normal chitchat.

'What's up, Mark?' he asked pulling a chair out from under Mark's large old desk.

Mark shut the glass door, pulled out another chair and sat the same side of the desk as Andy.

'I'm hoping you can help me, Andy.'

Andy's shoulders sagged back down while Mark outlined the story of computers being recycled back into the market place.

'How do you think this is happening?'

'Perhaps one of the staff is nicking stuff,' said Andy calmly.

'Stealing unrecorded returns? It's possible, but it doesn't totally add up.'

Half an hour passed with Mark and Andy playing roles as joint problem solvers, each surreptitiously studying the other before they strolled back to the workshop discussing the merits of improved documentation, record-keeping and stocktaking.

'OK. Let's get the office staff and take a complete inventory now,' said Mark.

'I can't. I've got installations to do for the rest of the day.'

'OK. We'll do it soon.'

Mark leaned against the workbench watching Andy put the computer he'd been disassembling onto a shelf along with some of its components.

'OK. See you tomorrow,' said Andy, picking up his tool kit.

It had gone midnight when Mark returned to the neat well-lit industrial estate with its wide roads and grass verges. He enjoyed sitting in his empty office with a coffee and a notepad, while the majority of the world slept. He never expressed to himself, or anybody else, the warm feeling he got from silently bonding with night shift workers and truck drivers at nearby factories. Tonight however, with only a pocket torch, he passed the offices along the central corridor to the workshop, listened carefully before unlocking the door and stepped carefully around cardboard boxes, searching the shelving and benches. He didn't expect anybody to be there, but nevertheless his own imagination nearly got the better of him and he was close to shouting before realising the torch beam was casting unfamiliar shadows. Breathing deeply, he switched on the lights, confirmed that the security of the building hadn't been compromised and that the computer Andy had been working on earlier had gone.

With his leather jacket over his head Mark hurried past rapidly filling puddles to his car, opened it and climbed in shaking the jacket outside and then throwing it onto the front passenger seat before settling down for a slow drive home.

*

Andy felt his mouth go dry when he saw Mark's BMW in its space at seven a.m. His stomach knotted knowing his plans for meeting the morning's delivery and being away by seven-thirty had been dashed.

'Hi Mark,' said Andy as he walked past Mark's office to the workshop.

'Hi Andy. Before you start, grab a coffee and come and join me.'

'OK, be with you now.'

'What did you get up to last night?' asked Mark.

Andy began to relax while drawing out details of meeting his mates and some girls at the Carpenter's Arms. Even laughing.

'You didn't come here after we left last night, did you?'

'No. Everything's all right, isn't it?'

'I was the last person to leave yesterday and the first person here this morning and nobody's been here since.'

'So, what's the problem?'

'A computer went missing during that time.'

'Well, you said the records weren't a hundred per cent. It mightn't have been here in the first place,' replied Andy.

'It's time to stop playing, Andy. The computer you were working on before you left yesterday is missing and before you start making up a story, nobody else knows about this apart from us. Either come clean now or I'll call the police and it'll be thoroughly investigated.'

'Come on, Mark. They're only scrap pieces. Nobody wants them.'

'Stop it, Andy. Don't make out you're stupid, and don't insult my intelligence by trivializing what's going on. I know what you're doing. I took a chance when I took you on and you've let me down. How would you like me to handle it?'

'Perhaps I should just fuck off then,' said Andy standing up and taking the van keys from his pocket and putting them on the desk.

'If you walk out I have no option but to call the police. I have to report a crime.'

'What the fuck do you want me to do then?'

'If you work with me to retrace all the replacements and get the books straight, in addition to your normal work, we'll see how it goes. I'm taking one hell of a big chance on you. I hope you understand.'

The veins in Andy's neck were visibly pulsing and dark patches at his armpits contrasted with his light blue tee shirt. 'I guess I have to,' he said through almost closed lips

'You don't fucking recognise what you've been offered,' shouted Mark.

'I'll do it. OK,' he shouted back.

'I've checked what you're working on today. Complete that and be back here at four-thirty. We'll need a couple of hours at least to go through things.'

'But I've got to be ----.'

'I don't give a fuck where you've got to be. Be here at four-thirty,' said Mark almost throwing the van's keys at him.

Mark watched Andy leave his office, thinking 'If he slams the door, I'll fire him and call the police'. However, feeling drained, Mark closed the door and fell back into his chair, put his elbows on the desk and rested his head in his hands.

CHAPTER 25

I must have been out of my mind thought Mark. What a change. Wow! She looked so fantastic at Sylvia's and the way she spoke out! I couldn't believe it. I still can't. It's only a catch-up meal for goodness sake, and besides, she chose the restaurant and booked it.

Feeling relieved and less committed, Mark bounced up the five steps to the restaurant door five minutes early.

'Hi. I'm early. Table for two booked under Jenifer ------. Oh dear, I can't remember her surname.'

'Miss Elliott?' questioned the young Polish woman, looking at the computer.

'Yes.'

Reverted to her maiden name already thought Mark. Good for her.

'This way sir.'

Jenifer pushed her chair back and stood watching Mark being ushered towards her.

Mark braced himself to look taller than his five feet ten against Jenifer's six-two. She oozed confidence, he thought, erect as usual and unafraid to sport three-inch heels. He kissed her on both cheeks and remained standing.

'I'll get really embarrassed if you carry on staring at me,' Jenifer commented.

'Yes. OK. I suddenly jumped backwards in time. You look wonderful.'

'I hope you don't dwell too much on your jump backwards.'

'I was thinking, I have an inside track to this beautiful woman, but I don't know her at all.'

'I don't recognise this charmer talking to me either. What's your name again?' she grinned. 'This is a lovely way to catch up, Mark. Thanks for inviting me. I hope you like my choice of restaurant.'

'It was great to see you the other day and I wanted to hear more. I hear you're a big shot in the finance world now?'

'Never trust rumours. Now, tell me what you've been up to.'

'I can't complain about work. Computer maintenance has changed since I started out, but clients have grown and we've grown with them. New clients are hard to come by but communication networks has led us to all sorts of new places and the maintenance contracts give us a good revenue, then there's the integration work and -----------.'

Jenifer had forgotten how she admired his enthusiasm, and the evenings together in his bachelor flat - he reading up on new things that he never considered as work, and she doing some coursework.

'Enough of work. Now confess about the women in your life,' she laughed.

'There's nobody special.'

'You must tell me the difference between special and the others sometime.'

Mark looked at the table, feeling and looking like he'd been caught with his paw in the honey.

'I'm teasing you, Mark. Take no notice of me.'

'I feel like I'm on a date with a married woman and shouldn't be.' *Why did I say that?* thought Mark. *I'm pouring my heart out to a stranger.*

'Technically I am, but I'm single in reality.'

'I'm sorry to hear about that not working out for you.'

'No need. Do you want to hear about it?'

'Only if you want to but yes, it goes no further regardless of whether we see each other again or not,' said Mark, feeling even more relieved at having made a statement of limitation, but then unexpectedly feeling empty. He couldn't hold back from qualifying it. 'We will though. I'm sure of that.'

Jenifer's voice wavered, 'Mother died soon after we split up. I don't know why I'm telling you this. She'd been ill for a long time as you know. Sorry I can't talk about her without crying.' She used the serviette to dab her eyes. 'Dad's taken up with the mother of a burglar who tried to rob our house. Can you imagine, mother's things could have gone forever. I don't want to talk about that, I get too worked up. Then there's David. No, I didn't come here for you to listen to a compressed file of four years of moaning. I'm stopping right now before you sneak off to the gents and don't come back.' She laughed, put her hand on top of his and studied his face. 'So, there's nobody special? I like ending on that note.'

'My car's this way,' said Jenifer, taking his arm. 'I'm being familiar but I don't care, and besides you might not want to meet up again, and this is a lovely evening even if it's a one-off. So there.'

'This is it,' she said, approaching her car. 'I'm really off this time,' she said again ten minutes later.

'Next week, same time, same place?' he whispered in her ear.

'I'm glad you asked first, but I'm definitely paying,' she said.

'We'll argue about payment later.'

'I'm so pleased we've made contact again. I hope you are,' she said through the open window while turning on the ignition. 'You've no idea the explaining I think I'm going to have to do.'

He wondered what she'd meant, and where he'd left his car.

CHAPTER 26

'Getting my big sister excited I hear on the grape vine.'

'And which grape vine is that then?'

'I'm teasing you, but I know you went somewhere posh for dinner. She told me.'

'It was great, but don't read too much into it. We just wanted to catch up. I really wanted to up-date you on Andy. I've given him another chance, Sue. He's worked solidly for two weeks, giving details of clients whose computers were removed, which people were involved in buying reconditioned units and he's managed to get the complete client list of some big suppliers. We're working on a few avenues at the same time to ensure we've stabilised the situation, then we can get back to normal. I think he enjoyed it once the initial pain was over.'

'Please be careful, Mark. If you haven't reported it and there are other companies involved, you could be exposed.'

'Wow! The embryonic lawyer is making noises inside its egg. Will it be like a crocodile and start biting immediately it hatches, or will it be a cute yellow chick and be excellent at appeals?'

'Mark, I'm serious. It might be better to get legal advice now before it's too late.'

'OK, Susan. Thanks for that. I'll give it some thought.'

'I know you, you'll hope it goes away.'

'No. Honest. I'll give it serious consideration. And thanks for your thoughts. I have one problem though: it's talking to Jenifer while keeping the secret of my involvement with Andy. I want to be honest and open with her and obviously questions will lead to questions and how come I got involved in the first place. I don't want to drop you in it but you can see my dilemma.'

'Mark, just tell her everything. Dad only knows a bit of the story, simply because he didn't want to dig any deeper and have the same problem. I'll handle it when she talks to me, which she will. The sooner you tell her the better. I'm sorry about Andy though.'

'Susan, you're a real gem.'

'I wish more people thought so.'

'They probably do but who's going to tell you in your competitive field?'

'Getting back to Andy though,' said Susan, 'she'll probably say I told you so when it comes to this latest upset.'

*

In spite of having had three dinners with Mark in five weeks and the promise of a fourth, Jenifer sat on the edge of her bed feeling vulnerable and tearful as she reflected on their break-up years back. She remembered saying 'if that's how you feel then you'd better go' and Mark, without a word, collected his things and left. She shivered remembering his shouting: 'I'm not here for you to control', then the clunking sound of keys hitting the metal dish by the door. *I must slow this down before we hit the rocks,* she thought.

'You're looking serious,' said Mark helping Jenifer with her (mother's) coat while the waiter hovered.

'Sorry, I had to rush. It seemed to take me ages to get ready.

'There's no need to be sorry.'

'That's what people keep telling me. Let's look at you. You're frowning. How's work?'

'Much better than expected and I want to discuss it with you but I'm a bit nervous.'

'You, nervous of me? That's a first.'

'You see, a few months back I employed Andy Oosthuizen,' he said looking dejected. 'He started as a driver but he was obviously bright and ---------.' Mark detected a faint smile on Jenifer's face and stopped. 'You're smiling,' he said.

'Yes,' she said leaning across the table and kissing his cheek while holding her blouse. He looked nonplussed while she smiled again. 'I knew he was working for you. You not telling me has been niggling at me but I didn't want to be the one to bring it up. I'm so relieved you came out with it, and I'm glad you suffered,' she said reaching for his hand. 'It doesn't change my opinion of him or his mother. I think he's a little shit and as for his mother – well, let's not go there.'

'How did you find out?'

'Oosthuizen isn't a common name, and I knew it was Cindy's surname so when an application with Andy's name on it came to my company for finance to purchase a van I wanted to know more, and there it was - age, employer, the lot.'

'And you kept it to yourself. Did he get the loan?'

'Not supposed to give personal details, but no, he didn't need it in the end. Apparently some goody, goody two shoes employer,' she said grinning at Mark, 'let him have the use of a company vehicle for personal use.'

This is not the Jenifer I knew he thought, still looking nonplussed.

'Penny for your thoughts, Mark.'

'A week ago,' he said after a long silence, 'I made a vow, which I intended to keep to myself. I'm almost afraid to tell you.'

'Go on, go on, tell me,' she implored.

'Well. I said to myself, I'll never hold back from telling you anything. It wasn't only about Andy. I thought about us when we were together. I remember driving back to my flat after that row… argument… call it what you like, feeling free but with an intense feeling of loss which I only shook off when I received an invitation to your wedding a year later. There, I've said it.'

'I don't know what to say. Nobody's made an impromptu declaration to me before. I'm really touched. You've blown my plans out the water.'

'Plans?' frowned Mark.

'It's nothing.'

'You're not going to tell me, are you?'

'No, sorry, they're now redundant.'

'You weren't intending to call it a day or going away or resigning from work or anything like that?'

'No. And stop questioning me, Mark Walters. This evening has magic attached to it,' she said holding her glass up to him, 'and I wish you good luck with Andy.'

Mark clinked his glass against hers and breathed deeply.

Jenifer leant back in the chair and thought about Helen, her counsellor, and her reply when she'd said through tears and nose blowing that she was through with men forever.

Live with that, Helen had replied. See how it goes and take whatever freedom it gives you, but don't use it as an objective or you may find it constrains you. I don't like using metaphors but you'd be painting yourself into a corner.

'Now it's my turn to ask a penny for your thoughts.'

'I'd be breaking client confidentiality,' she laughed. 'It's nice to be able to just be. Now you can tell me about all the women in your life and I don't care if I'm prying.'

'Three months ago I stopped seeing a woman after nearly a year. It hurt her badly, actually it hurt me badly as well, which I didn't expect, but we'd drifted into a routinely pathetic relationship. It was my fault. It was easier to carry on. She tried to spice up our lives by selecting weekends away, but my heart wasn't in it and the last trip felt like a chore. Sorry Jen, I've been going on and on.'

'I'm enjoying listening to you Mark, but we are just about the last ones here and I think we should go.'

'Tomorrow's Saturday,' said Jenifer opening her car door. 'What are you doing in the morning?'

'I'll be in the office at about eleven to prepare things. Then I'm having a quick meeting with Andy at twelve which will take about an hour and then I'm free for the day.'

'Would you like to follow me home and let me pamper you with an early breakfast? Otherwise, how about this place, next week, same time?'

Mark looked at her broadening smile before they buried their heads in each other's necks.

CHAPTER 27

Tring… tring… tring echoed the workshop phone, now incredibly loud without the background sound of people and machinery. Mark jolted upright from his relaxed position, spilling coffee on his jeans in his haste to get his feet off the desk and reach for the office extension. 'Not again,' he berated himself as he leapt to his feet and brushed his legs before the liquid had a chance to soak through. 'Switchdata. How may I help you?'

'Mark Walters please,' a mature, well-spoken man's voice asked.

'Mark speaking.'

'Lloyd Appleton here. I'm the finance director of MDC. Are you OK to talk on the phone about possible breaches of security affecting both our companies or would you prefer to meet up first?'

'I'm happy to talk on the phone.'

Lloyd outlined MDC's business of supplying software and hardware to its clients, and in the process, coming across hardware that appeared to come from Mark's company. He provided reference numbers, installation dates and specifications. They exchanged e-mail addresses with the promise of more comprehensive information from each other and a time for a meeting the following week.

'I must be as thick as pig shit trusting you!' shouted Mark. 'You weren't just selling the occasional reconditioned computer, you were in cahoots with your mates in other companies. For all I know there's a whole web of you people ripping us off.'

'It's stopped Mark, honest,' said Andy. 'I haven't done anything since that day you found out.'

'You said you reconditioned the odd computer and your mate was selling them for private use and that was that. Now I find you were building them to order and your mate was ripping off his employer and you were sharing the profits.'

Mark's construction of the fraud was part intuition, but his forceful verbal delivery took any wind out of Andy's sails that would have driven his imaginative stories forward with even the slightest air of credibility.

'So what's the fucking difference? I stopped didn't I?'

'Sometimes you seem incredibly bright, and sometimes you either pretend to be or you really are as thick as two short fucking planks. Be here at eight on Monday,' said Mark as he moved to the office door while Andy rose to his feet.

'What're you going to do?' asked Andy.

'I don't bloody know. Get out!' he shouted slamming the door.

Mark spent all of the following Monday and most of Tuesday gathering information from company records and Andy's memory in preparation for a meeting with Lloyd Appleton on Wednesday at eleven in the lounge of a large hotel on the outskirts of Oxford.

Wearing a dark blue suit, white shirt and an expensive silk tie, Mark arrived half an hour early to give himself time to relax and hone his story. However, the cheerful receptionist looked at her notes and pointed towards a settee where a slightly overweight and balding man of about fifty-five, wearing a blue shirt and red tie, was leaning over the Financial Times spread open on a large low table. His suit jacket was folded on the cushion next to him. Feeling out of place, Mark made his way between small conspiratorial groups seated around low tables.

'I kept glancing up at the desk,' said Lloyd, getting to his feet and reaching for Mark's hand. 'Somehow I missed you. I'm Lloyd Appleton.'

Mark matched Lloyd's affable smile, introduced himself and ordered a coffee from a waitress who appeared by his elbow within seconds.

'Got here early to read the paper,' said Lloyd folding it methodically and sliding it into an open briefcase half under the table.

'Glad you're early. Want to get to the office. Lots to do. Here's my card.'

Mark sat on a settee opposite.

'Mark. May I call you Mark? We have a problem. Lack of controls in your company has created a loss situation in mine. I wanted to discuss it with you before we take any action.'

Mark accepted a coffee from a tray held by the waitress, added milk and stirred it, said thanks and waited for Lloyd to continue while looking at his card thinking "Divisional Finance Director?" He's not the finance director of MDC after all. This man probably needs to constantly prove himself and doesn't have much discretional freedom.

'So,' said Lloyd, 'someone in your company has been supplying hardware through another party to one of our procurement people and sharing the spoils. They would have got away with it forever if they hadn't become greedy. What was happening at your end of this ruse?'

'Under contract, like you, we replace faulty computers we can't fix on site in a reasonable time. The faulty ones go to our workshop and either get fixed or go to scrap. It's within that process where something possibly went amiss,' Mark casually replied, feeling the cold light of explanation whittling at his credibility. 'We have a small trusted team, but have recently put tighter stock controls in place.'

'When was that and why did you do it?'

'I realised we couldn't continue to rely on trust for stock control and besides, the workshop needed serious rearranging to make better use of the space before we expand further.'

'We were quick to find the culprit inside MDC and the third party through the invoices, but they both gave us a cock and bull story about building the computers from spares and gave no names. The industry's full of technical geniuses with no common sense whatsoever. We thought it was all over until one of our guys visited a client on Friday morning and found disk drives we don't normally supply. A couple of phone calls later and we discovered that Switchdata purchased the drives. Confidence bred carelessness it appears. Then I phoned you with the serial numbers. It was pretty obvious there would be no profit in it unless he was getting the majority of the computer from somebody. Who was it in your company who was pilfering the stuff? Have you called the police?'

'Our controls for stock and tracking are well bedded in and we carry out regular physical checks.'

'I take it that's a "no" then? Pity, you could've got a police report and claimed on your insurance and we would've probably known about this earlier and saved some time and money. You also put us at risk. Have you anything to add?'

'No. I know MDC's business is mainly industrial software for quality control. You do a lot of consultancy for the automotive industry. Which division do you work for?'

'I work in all areas. Let's call it a day and I'll be in touch. You have my email if you think of anything else,' said Lloyd rummaging through his briefcase.

'Yes, thanks for the meeting,' said Mark, searching for Lloyd's eyes as he shook his hand while thinking: Lloyd's grip was not as strong as his introductory one.

'Cheerio. You'll need a car park token from reception to get out,' said Lloyd.

'I'm going to have to cancel our date tonight, my lovely Jenifer,' said Mark from his office.

'I love the "lovely" and I love the "my Jenifer", but I don't like the cancel bit. What's up?'

'There are a few things at the office I have to sort out.'

'You sound low, Mark. What time do you expect to leave? No. Forget I asked. Sorry,' she said suddenly conscious of her controlling side becoming exposed. 'Please let me help if I can. You know I want to see your downs as well as your ups.'

'You show me yours and I'll show you mine; sounds like a good start,' he said smiling for the first time that day. 'OK, I'm only going to sit here thinking and rethinking and getting nowhere.'

'Is it OK if you stay in your office and I bring a takeaway at about seven?'

'You really are wonderful,' he replied.

Mark stood and pulled the window blinds to one side on hearing a car. He watched her slam the driver's door and walk to the rear door where she stooped over pizza boxes on the back seat.

'Too busy looking to open the door I notice,' she said, kissing him.

'There we are,' said Mark after forty minutes of outlining the problems. 'Andy's helped as well as hindered, but on balance we're better off. It's just this thing with MDC that's hanging over me.'

'I'm not going to comment, Mark. I get too worked up. You must deal with it as you see fit.'

'Here's the letter from MDC's solicitor. It's not happy reading I'm afraid,' said Mark handing it to Jenifer.

'They want twenty-two thousand six hundred and eighteen pounds compensation for damages?' questioned Jenifer.

'Yes. They're saying if I'd reported it the moment I suspected something, the police would have revealed the extent of the goings-on earlier. What is not in the letter is the detailed breakdown of the costs. MDC have to show their insurance company they've done their best to recover the costs, regardless of how they've fabricated them. Lloyd's taking a chance because he's assuming we knew about it.'

'But you did.'

'I didn't tell him that.'

'I'll leave it to you Mark, but it's not the end of the world, even if you have to pay it.'

'It's a typical lawyer's letter and a distraction I can do without. And before you ask, Andy is still here. I know you think I'm mad but ---'

Before he could finish, Jenifer went to his side of the desk and held her forefinger to his lips.

'Come on, Mark. Finish your pizza. I know you'll feel better.'

'You're right. We can't let a thing like this get us down,' he said holding her waist and burying his head in her midriff.

*

Feeling impotent in the face of Mark's problems, Jenifer struggled to concentrate on her work and instead stared through the glass-panelled walls to the busyness of the large crowded open-plan office, hoping for inspiration or at least some distraction. No harm in looking at Andy's credit application again she thought, scrolling through the "Obsolete" folder. 'How long at your present address,' the form enquired. She scrawled the answer onto a notepad, tore the page off, folded it and wedged it in the outer pocket of her laptop bag. Later that evening after watching yet more disaster on the TV news, which she could do nothing about, and then washing dishes with amplified feelings of frustration, she threw the dried cutlery into a drawer and jumped aside as it bounced back out. 'Fuck him, fuck him, fuck him!' she screamed. Five minutes later, feeling desperate to get out, she pulled on her mother's coat over jeans and a cotton blouse to face the clear cold December night. She stepped into her casual shoes, hurried to her car and drove to the address without referring to her note, and parked nearby. After watching the apartments for about ten minutes, feeling futile and redundant and suddenly conscious of being cold, she switched the engine on, put the car in gear and waited for a vehicle to pass before pulling from the curb to go home.

"Switchdata Industrial Computer Services" was emblazoned on the van's rear doors above "my other van is white" written through the day's dirt onto the paint below.

Jenifer lost sight of the van when she reached the corner. However, seeing the open archway at the side of the apartment, she drove in. Andy stood by the van's open door and glanced at Jenifer's car. The gears crashed as Jenifer tried to reverse. They crashed again as she inched the car forward into a tight turn. The car stalled on the next attempted reverse and she leaped out leaving the door open.

'You're Andy Oosthuizen!' she blurted.

'Yeah, and who's asking?'

'You don't need to know. You little shit. I just wanted to see what a thieving-no-good looks like. I probably see trash like you every bloody day without knowing it.'

'I don't know what's got your knickers in a twist lady and I don't know what you're talking about,' said Andy closing the van door.

'That's right. Walk away. You don't care about people's lives.'

'Who the fuck are you?' shouted Andy.

'If you showed any interest in your mother's life with my father you'd know, but you only care about yourself. You selfish bastard.'

'I've had enough of your crap. I'm going,' said Andy turning away.

'Great. Go. And I hope you take your bitch of a mother with you.'

CHAPTER 28

Nurse James questioned Jenifer while she lay on a bed in the A&E department and a doctor studied details of her broken nose and the hairline fracture of her cheekbone on a computer screen. She said she didn't know how it happened, or how she got to the hospital. However, she clearly remembered the crashing blow, the feeling of her face caving in and the high pitch noise in her ears drowning out a possibly imagined scream. She didn't tell them about shouting 'help me, help me,' or holding her arms as if she was about to run into something, or about Andy putting a large ball of cloth into her hand and gently guiding her into the passenger seat of her car. She remembered the beep, beep, beep of her seat belt warning system and Andy repeating, 'Oh fuck! I'm so sorry. Oh fuck, I'm so sorry,' as he drove.

'Ow!' she cried as two men eased her from the car into a wheelchair.

'I'll move the car,' answered Andy to one of the orderlies who asked, 'How'd it happen?'

'Oh, Jesus Christ!' said Andy, panicking at the sight of blood in the car before throwing his leather jacket and polo-neck pullover on the ground and tearing off his shirt to mop it up. Satisfied but shaking, he grabbed Jenifer's bag from the back seat, shut the car and walked slowly to A&E with his jacket on his arm concealing his right hand and sodden shirt.

'This bag belongs to the woman who's just been admitted,' said Andy pushing it over the counter towards a reception nurse, whom he pretended not to hear when she asked his name.

'Her car's in the car park,' he said looking back over his shoulder.

Andy half ran, half walked back to the apartment. Twenty minutes later, he stood where Jenifer's car had been and was relieved to find no blood or anybody waiting for him. Later still, naked but calmer, Andy cleaned the floor, his shoes and the outside of the washing machine with his tee-shirt before stuffing it inside to join the rest of his clothes. Feeling reassured by the click of the inlet valve and the gushing of water, he showered, changed and bandaged his hand to avoid knocking it.

'We're going to keep you in,' said Doctor Jameson. 'You've had a small operation on your nose to help you breathe and straighten things out, but the swelling has a long way to go. The nurses will look after you and we'll see you tomorrow afternoon.'

A few minutes later Doctor Jameson returned, 'They tell me you were on your own when you signed the consent forms and you didn't want anyone to come to the hospital. Apparently you were caught up in a fight and somebody hit you in error. Forgive me for asking Miss Elliott, is there anybody you know who would harm you?'

The soporific effect of the medication enveloped her and the droning of Doctor Jameson seemed connected to a dream, requiring only a slow side-to-side movement of her head.

'We'd be happier if there was a friend or relative who knew you were here,' she persisted, leaning closer. 'Do you want us to call someone?'

'In the morning,' she whispered.

*

'Jen, you sound awful,' said Susan, holding her phone away to read the time. 'Have you got the dreaded lurgy? Oh my god, Jen. I'm coming now. No, I won't tell Dad or anybody. I'll ring for a taxi. I should be there in half an hour.'

Simon sleepily put one arm around Susan's waist, but hopes of a sexy start to the day diminished as he filtered the conversation through layers of lethargy.

'What's happened?'

'I've got to get to the hospital. My sister's had an accident.'

'Holy shit, is she OK?'

Too numb to be sarcastic, Susan went to the bathroom and brushed her teeth before scampering about the room drying her face and gathering clothes for herself and Jenifer.

'Come on, come on,' she shouted at the bathroom door, 'I'm ready to go.'

'What happened?' asked Simon while reversing out of the front garden.

'I don't know but she sounded awful. Leave me at the entrance. Don't go to the parking area, you'll never get out.'

Simon pulled up behind a row of taxis.

'Go!' she said. 'I've no idea how long I'll be. I'll give you a ring.'

Susan's talk with the nurse felt clinically simple and comforting, but failed to stop her putting a hand to her face and gasping when she saw Jenifer's closed puffy eyes peeking above a thick white dressing. She assumed Jenifer was asleep until her hand tightened around hers.

'I thought you were totally out. Oh Jen! Can you speak? What can I do for you?'

'You're here,' whispered Jenifer slowly moving her jaw as if testing its limits. 'Please let me have some water.'

Susan removed an up-ended glass from the top of a jug, half-filled it and put it into Jenifer's hand.

'Thanks. I can see if I strain my eyelids, but it's easier to just let them droop.'

'What happened? No Jen, tell me when you're ready. I must tell Dad you're here.'

Jenifer gripped Susan's wrist, 'No Sue, please.'

'OK Jen. Don't fret.'

'They're going to check on me at three and I'll be discharged sometime after that.'

'I'm moving in with you,' said Susan, 'unless you want Mark to look after you?'

'I said we should see each other, warts and all, but this is over the top. I don't want him to see me like this, and I don't know what I'm going to look like afterwards. He may hate it.'

Tears trickled from Jenifer's dark blue and red eyelids into the dressing. Susan pressed a tissue into Jenifer's hand and took another for herself.

'I'm so sorry, Susan, your big sister seems to need you more and more.'

'You'll soon be back to normal, Jen.'

'What's normal?'

'Your beautiful elegant self.'

'It was Andy,' Jenifer said gripping Susan's arm. 'Nobody else knows.'

Susan flinched, and Jenifer lay back against the pillows talking without moving, feeling protected by the surroundings and conserving her energy to speak.

'Did he come looking for you?'

'No. I went to the apartment. I know all about Andy and Mark. This is my fault. I provoked him. I couldn't stop myself. I've been putting the pieces together and it's coming back to me. I asked for it. He hit me and drove me to the hospital. I couldn't talk, but I could hear he was shocked. I could hear it.'

'Nobody knows it was Andy?'

'I didn't see Andy after I got here. I've no idea what he said but I know the people here don't know who he was. I made up a story of trying to stop a fight and being hit, but I can tell they didn't believe me. Now I'm absolutely finished. I must sleep. Please tell Mark and Dad I accidentally got mixed up in a fight. I'll sort it out later. And please phone my office.'

'I'll see you this afternoon. Sleep and don't worry.'

'There's nothing you can do at the moment. She'll be asleep anyway,' said Susan to Mark. 'The doctor said she'll be out this afternoon after a checkup. I'll report back at four and let you know.'

'I don't think I can work knowing she's there like that.'

'I can't stop you Mark, but she said she didn't want visitors. I'll phone you when I've seen her.'

'OK. Thanks, Sue.'

'Why didn't she phone me?'

'Dad, I don't know --- no, I can't tell you any more. She should be out this afternoon. I'll phone you when I know more.'

'There's more to this, but I won't push you. Jenifer in a fight? Pull the other one.'

Jenifer was sleeping in a chair next to the bed when Susan stooped and gently took her hand.

'Hello, Sue. The nurse said she'll talk to you about medication, then we can go.'

Susan stood at the counter of the ward office feeling intrusive in the presence of the hustle and bustle of the collective objectivity until a nurse stopped loading a medicine trolley and smiled.

'You've come to collect Jenifer Elliott?'

'Hello. Yes.'

'Her medication is here so there's no need to go to the pharmacy,' she said, joining her for the walk back to Jenifer and handing over a sealed green bag. The doctor wants to have a few words. Probably wants to make sure your sister doesn't pick a fight with somebody,' she laughed. 'I'll go and find her.'

'Will Jenifer be OK?' Susan asked Doctor Bhatia.

'There's medication there for the next two days,' she said indicating to the plastic bag, 'and she has an outpatient's appointment for Wednesday at two-thirty for a change of dressing. It looks good. The swelling will start to go down in a few days, but the colour will spread further and be with her much longer, so she shouldn't worry about that. She's healthy and fit and there's no permanent damage. Her left eye will need the drops,' she said pointing at the green bag. 'It looks bad, but the eye itself will recover rapidly. She's quite lucky in many respects. We're pleased she's not on her own,' she said holding out her hand.

'Thanks for everything.'

'No permanent damage and they're confident about your nose and eye. I spoke to Doctor Bhatia.'

'I'm lucky is what she told me, but I don't feel lucky at the moment.'

'I had trouble holding Dad and Mark at bay. They both wanted to drop everything and come here.'

'Let's go home. They can see us both then. Thanks for everything, Sue. Please stop at Marks and Sparks and get something to eat for everybody.'

Jenifer stood up, holding one hand over her face and the other on Susan's arm. They slowly made their way to a chair in the open reception area where Jenifer waited while Susan shopped in the hospital's M&S and retrieved the car.

'I was so over the top, Sue. I said dreadful things to Andy about his mother. I know Dad is happier than he's been for years. But Sue, I couldn't stop. I've jeopardized Dad's happiness. He's going to hate me.'

'He'll never hate you Jen, you know that. Now stop it.'

'But what about Cindy? What will she do when she finds out?'

'Let's see. Come on, Jen.'

'You think she'll leave Dad? I couldn't bear it. What do you think Dad will do when he knows it's her son who hit me? This is horrible.'

'I hate to say this Jen, but you wanted her out of the family.'

It was already ten past five and Mark was still thirty miles away when Susan, sounding more cheerful than he'd expected, phoned. 'Jenifer says she wants to see you but she's not sure you can cope with the results of warfare. We're on our way to her apartment. She says come at six-thirty for a snack. Dad will come over at about seven-fifteen, but I don't know how long she'll be up. She said I must throw everybody out at eight-thirty.'

'I'm really scared,' said Jenifer, 'I think I was buoyed up by the medication when I suggested they come here this evening.'

'You know deep down that the sooner you tell them the better.'

'Yes, but what do I tell them?'

'Just tell them the truth Jen,' said Susan looking at her watch. 'If you keep imagining what they'll say and think, you'll be a wreck by the time they get here.'

'They'll want to know, especially Dad, about what made me go to Cindy's and I can't tell him what I said to Andy about Cindy. It was awful.'

'You're sorry you said it now, aren't you?'

'I'm desperately sorry Sue,' she said sobbing.

'Then that's it. Tell the truth, all of it. Let them make of it what they will and don't be afraid of the answers. You'll soon have your confidence back.'

'I'll get it,' said Susan, moving to the control button to release the front door of the apartment building.

'You're early Mark,' said Susan, kissing him on both cheeks, 'Jen's nearly ready. Would you like a drink?'

'Thanks. I'd love a tea with milk and one sugar,' he said, following Susan into the large open-space dining room and lounge with a high imitation marble counter top dividing off the gadget-laden kitchen.

'Is Jenifer lying down?' asked Mark, pulling out one of four matching white leather and chrome barstools.

'No, she had a brief rest when we got home. She'll be out shortly. I think she's attending to her new facial fashion statement.'

Bare-footed and wearing blue and white winter pajamas, Jenifer was already half- way into the room before Mark saw her.

'Sorry,' she rasped, her right palm facing Mark, 'the thought of anybody coming close to my face frightens me.'

'My goodness Jen,' said Mark, taking her hand, 'it looks painful. I can't see your eyes. Can you see?'

'I can see,' she said holding his hand tightly, 'but it's an effort to keep my eyelids up, but the doctor says it'll be OK. Please don't look so worried. I'm going to be fine. Warts 'n all I said - remember?'

Mark kissed Jenifer's hand and held it to his face.

'Thanks Mark, but I don't think you'll like what I'm going to I tell you.'

Mark pulled out the other barstool for Jenifer.

'No. Sorry Mark. I have to sit in a lounge chair with a blanket over my shoulders. I can't put a pullover on. I feel absolutely drugged and I could easily fall asleep. If I do,' she said turning to Susan, 'wake me. I don't want either of you seeing me with my mouth hanging open, as it's difficult to breathe through my nose.'

Mark put the barstools back and sat down in a lounge chair, leaving the couch for Susan, who was making space on the coffee table for a tray.

'Let me help you,' said Mark.

'You sit and chat. Dad will be here shortly, and don't eat too many snacks. There's a meal soon.'

'Sue said you were caught up in a fight and somebody hit you. Where on earth were you?'

'Have you seen Andy today?' asked Jenifer.

'Don't tell me Andy's involved,' said Mark.

'I won't blame you if you're furious with me,' slurred Jenifer, 'It was my fault. It really was. I provoked him. I'm ashamed of the things I said to him, but I couldn't stop myself.'

Finding it difficult to hear and anxious not to miss any words Mark, not wanting to ask her to repeat anything or speak more clearly, moved closer.

'You mean it was just you and Andy?'

Susan, who had heard every word, busied herself in the kitchen.

'Yes. I went to Cindy's apartment and saw Andy in the driveway. I said horrible things to him and he hit me in the face. I deserved it. I said things I didn't know I was capable of saying. I'm so ashamed. Have you spoken to him?'

'Andy hasn't been at work.'

'Have you spoken to him?'

'No. He won't answer his phone and he left his keys in the office post box before anybody got to work today. His van was in the building.'

'I'm so sorry, Mark. I've made things worse for you. I don't know what Cindy will do when she finds out and Dad will hate me for this.'

'Stop it,' said Mark, hitting the table with the flat of his hand.

'Oww,' said Jenifer, jumping, first at the sound of Mark's hand on the table and then again as Susan dropped a pot in the sink.

'I'm sorry, Jen. I didn't mean to shout. You've no idea how much you're loved and going back into yourself won't help any of us. I love you, your Dad loves you and we, all of us, are going to see this through together.'

'Uh, uh, uh,' was the only sound Jenifer made as her shoulders heaved with short intakes of breath. She took a tissue from a box on the table and dabbed her eyes, while Mark pulled his chair to face her. He took her hand and waited.

'I've no idea why I went there. I couldn't not go.'

'Do you think he thought you were going to drive at him?'

'No. I tried to get out of there as soon as I realised I was trapped, but I got flustered and stalled the car, and then I saw him smiling at me through the windscreen. It was a smile, not a smirk. And then I lost it. I called his mother a no-good bitch. Then I said he should go and take her with him. I didn't know I could say things like that. I'm so ashamed. What have I done? I'm so sorry.'

Her chest shuddered as she breathed and cried. 'Be angry with me but don't ask me any more questions. I'm feeling sick with exhaustion.' Just then, the doorbell rang.

'It'll be Dad. You two carry on,' said Susan. 'We'll be back in about half an hour.'

'Please tell Dad, Sue. I can't bear the thought of going over it all again.'

'What's going on?' said Victor after a brief hello to Susan as she joined him in the corridor still struggling with her coat.

'Jen will tell you all about it, but she's having a tricky conversation with Mark at the moment and I think it's important for them to carry on without us.'

'I'm feeling like an intruder in my own family. What's going on for god's sake?'

'Jen's feeling really low because she feels responsible for what happened and the medication's making her drowsy and emotional. Let's walk for a while, or sit in the car.'

'I just knew I was being spun a line about being caught up in some accidental attack. Do you know the real story?'

'It was Andy who did it, but she's convinced she provoked him. Jen is sick with worry.'

'What? How did they meet? Where was it? What time?'

'She'll tell you all about it, but she needs time, and Mark is doing his best to calm her down.'

'How bad is the injury, Sue?'

'I spoke to the doctor when I collected her and she's confident of a total recovery. It will take a week or so before it starts to come right, and she has an out-patient's appointment in a couple of days.'

'So. The very guy we're trying to help has beaten her up?'

'He didn't beat her up. He hit her once and then took her to the hospital. Jen says he immediately regretted it. Please Dad, wait for her to tell you, otherwise it will be confusing, but please don't give her the third degree. She's not up to it.'

'Don't tell me how to talk to my own daughter. Has anyone spoken to Andy? What did Mark say?'

'Nobody's heard from Andy. He's not answering his phone. The hospital only has the story of her being caught up with strangers in a fight, but Jenifer refused to get the police involved. They suspect it was someone she knows, like a boyfriend or somebody. She keeps saying how sorry she is.'

'What has she got to feel sorry about, apart from her own injuries?'

'You'll have to get it from her, but please don't question her too much tonight.'

'I don't need a bloody lecture on how to treat either of you.'

Susan held Victor's arm tight and they silently walked another two hundred yards along the wide, well-lit pavement towards the ring road.

'In your opinion, what is she so sorry about?'

'She said terrible things to him and he couldn't defend himself with words so he hit her.'

'Are you going to tell me or not?'

'She's worried about spoiling your relationship with Cindy. And before you answer Dad, she's sick with worry about it.'

'She wanted that to end anyway.'

'Dad, please don't. She's really upset about it.'

'I'm afraid I find that difficult to believe. Perhaps I should have killed the bastard when I had the chance.'

'Stop it, Dad. You know you couldn't, so stop it.'

'Sorry, Sue. I need to calm down before we go back. Let's walk a bit further.'

'If Andy hadn't tried to rob the house you wouldn't have met Cindy.'

'OK. OK. I know, but Cindy's got a strong mind and may very well leave as a result of this. Jenifer really doesn't like her and she makes no effort to bloody well hide it. She behaved abominably at dinner a few weeks back. It was a side of her I hadn't seen before and it's been on my mind ever since. It shocked me more than I can say. Cindy seemed to give as good as she got and made every effort to bring the evening to a happy end, but Jenifer succeeded in sowing seeds of discontent in Cindy and it's disturbed our relationship. What's happened now is just an extension of her will to get Cindy out of our lives.'

'No, Dad. Just listen to her. She's in a real state at the moment.'

'You have to understand, Susan, you and Jenifer come first before anybody and I'm desperate for Jenifer at the moment and I don't need a lecture on how to handle her. Come on, let's turn back. I want to know how badly injured she really is.'

In spite of having a key, Susan rang the doorbell.

'Hello Victor,' said Mark, 'Jenifer's lying down for a bit.'

'What do you make of all this, Mark?'

'I don't know, and I don't think Jenifer does either, but it sounds like she and Andy were both pent up. She won't be asleep. She wanted to talk to you the moment you got back. Sue and I will get the dinner ready.'

'Hello, Jen, my darling,' whispered Victor.

Jenifer slowly turned to face him. 'Hello, Dad. My head's spinning. I can't sleep.'

'Not the prettiest I've seen you, but I understand you're going to be fine. How do you feel?'

'Did Sue tell you I taunted Andy into doing this?'

'Relax, Jen. I only want to know about your injuries and to make sure you're getting the best treatment. You can tell me the rest when you're ready.'

'Both doctors said I only need time and the outpatient's appointments. I'm so sorry, Dad. I've really thrown a spanner in the works, and don't tell me I haven't spoilt things with you and Cindy because I know I have and I'm so, so sorry.'

'We'll talk about it in good time. You need all the rest you can get.'

'No, Dad,' she said, pushing herself into a sitting position, 'I need to talk now. Please don't leave it like this.'

'All relationships get tested, Jen. It's part of life. Nobody's died, and I don't want to talk about my relationship with Cindy at the moment. You may say things you'll regret later. Please relax. The most important thing at the moment is your health.'

'No. Please Dad, don't. I've been horrible,' she said putting both hands over her face and crying uncontrollably while Victor, feeling numb, sat on a small bedside chair pulling a chain of tissues from a box for her. He waited until Jenifer's gasps subsided then put the bundle of tissues in her hand.

'Oh Dad, what have I done?'

'Got yourself punched in the face by Andy. Beyond that, I don't know. It hurts me to see you suffer, and I'm relieved to hear you'll be fine. You don't have to tell me the details. Do you want something to eat or drink?'

'Help me, Dad, please. You sound cold and logical.'

'You relax and get better. We'll have all the time in the world to talk without any encumbrances after all this is over,' he said kissing the top of her head. 'Susan said be ready to eat in about five minutes. See how you feel, but I'd have it in bed if I were you.'

'Dad, wait, please!'

Victor stood a minute by the door wiping his cheeks with the back of his hand.

'Is she eating with us?'

'You ask her, Sue. She was very upset and didn't reply when I asked her.'

'Would you like a drink, Victor?' asked Mark.

'A large red wine please. I brought a bottle with me, and I've taken it for a long walk, so it should be itching to be drunk by now.'

Mark filled three glasses as Victor settled himself at the counter. 'Has Andy been in contact yet?'

'Nobody's heard from him since ----.'

'Let's all call it "the attack on Jenifer",' said Victor. 'Is that correct?'

'I guess so,' said Susan.

'It isn't a guess though, is it? It's a fact. And if we want to establish the facts we need an admission of guilt or a witness.'

'Dad, it's not to be pursued. Anyway, Jenifer wouldn't testify.'

'Maybe she should be persuaded to face up to her actions. I still don't know what happened, when it occurred or the circumstances. Will somebody please fill me in?'

'Andy's left his company van at the office along with all the office keys. No note, just gone.'

'I'm trying to piece the attack together. If either of you know what happened in chronological order, please let me hear it. Starting off with how and where they met.'

'She drove to Cindy's apartment, but couldn't tell me why,' said Susan.

'And I still can't tell you,' said Jenifer, having shuffled into the room unnoticed.

All three turned from the countertop as Jenifer, wrapped in a blanket, lowered herself into an armchair.

'Let me get you something,' said Mark.

'A weak lime juice with water from the bottle in the fridge please.'

'We'll eat from the coffee table,' said Susan, handing Victor a pile of placemats. 'Please put the two big ones in the middle. I'll serve from there.'

'A very small amount for me please,' said Jenifer.

'Let's leave the attack for another time. You must be exhausted,' interrupted Victor.

'I am, but I've had a rest and I won't be able to sleep until I've told you.'

At first, each thought Jenifer was stringing the story out, but they soon realised she was unable to talk without lisping or suffering pain. However, from her perspective behind closed eyes, she felt protected, insular and content with her deliberation. They occasionally winced as she struggled.

'And I'm not invoking action against Andy and that's that,' she concluded.

'But ---' Victor interjected before Jenifer stopped him with a raised hand.

'Andy's not a danger to the public and you would definitely lose Cindy if I brought any action against him. I feel terrible about Cindy and you, Dad.'

'I'm not going to argue with you Jen, and it's inappropriate with you being on medication and injured as you are. I'll simply make the statement that you've made on many occasions - that you don't like Cindy. You may want to make amends while you feel like you do now, but you'll probably regret it when you're better.'

'Please don't say that, Dad.'

'Perhaps I should leave while you're talking,' said Mark. 'I'll see you tomorrow evening.'

'Please stay, Mark,' replied Jenifer.

'I'm also conscious of you avoiding me when I'm with her,' continued Victor. 'Your welfare and your relationship with me are sacrosanct. So let's not beat about the bush. It's probably already too late. I anticipate Cindy leaving when she knows what Andy's done. It's fortunate she's not here. I invited her but she said she was sorry not to be able to come, and ironically wanted me to convey her concerns but thought it was more important for you to be with family. I suggest you put thoughts of repairing the relationship between Cindy and me aside and concentrate on getting better.'

Jenifer grabbed her serviette and held it to her eyes, and although wobbly, fended off help as she went to her bedroom.

'That was horrible and unnecessary, Dad,' said Susan. 'She's sorry. Just accept it.'

'I'm not going to justify myself. We both know the truth,' said Victor, throwing back the last of his wine and planting the glass firmly on the table. 'I'll pop in and say good night.'

'OK. I'm off,' said Victor into the dimly lit bedroom.

'Wait Dad,' said Susan.

'No,' he replied, leaning over and gently kissing Jenifer's head. He tried to kiss Susan, but she pulled away.

'Relax both of you,' said Victor. 'The air's been cleared tonight. Have a good night's sleep and I'll see you tomorrow.' He put on his coat and left.

'That didn't go according to plan, did it?' said Susan, joining Mark in the kitchen.

'How's Jen?'

'Asleep. She took her tablets. What did you think?'

Mark looked thoughtfully at Susan. 'I don't have any answers. Jen has been so laid back since I've re-met her. Her fight with Andy is out of character.'

'If anyone was out of character, it was Dad. He's correct about Jenifer's feeling for Cindy though. I find that so sad.'

'You're not entirely correct, Sue. She's been quiet about Cindy lately and I think it's because she wants to accept her but doesn't know how.'

'Come on Mark, you're making it up.'

'No. Over the last few weeks she has said more than once how happy your Dad is. She knows it's all down to Cindy. I think she may be jealous.'

'You may be correct. Cindy makes him happy and Jen doesn't.'

'I feel bad talking about Jen behind her back but she's a different person from the one I knew years back. I think she's found that it's not all bad when she drops her guard. It's given her a new perspective.'

'You're guessing.'

'Maybe, but many weeks ago she went to dinner at your Dad's place. She said she was horrid towards Cindy. Those were her words not mine. She cried and wished she'd had the courage to apologise. I suggested she phone, but I think she let it go and she's now paying for it.'

'You may be right. Poor Jen. She was twenty when Mum died. She tried to be mother, wife, organiser and social secretary.'

'Life's too complicated for my little brain,' said Mark looking at his watch. 'Let's clear up and I'll be off.'

'Wakey wakey, Jen!' whispered Susan stroking Jenifer's arm.

'What time is it?'

'Eye-drop time.'

'I have to phone Cindy.'

'You mean now? It's gone eleven-thirty. Dad might not have told her yet.'

'Oh Sue,' she sobbed, 'what have I done? I've got to tell her everything. I'm feeling sick with worry.'

CHAPTER 29

'I've told you all I know. I can't tell you any more. I don't think I've missed anything,' said Victor watching Cindy from across the coffee table. She sat forward in the armchair, dropped her head into her hands and her elbows onto her knees, letting her long hair fall forward over her green and blue silk dressing gown and remained frozen. Victor pulled the table to one side, knelt in front of her and took her forearms.

'I'm not going to pretend this is not a major blow, Cindy, but we'll get through it,' he said, gently lifting her chin.

She put her arms over Victor's head and rested herself against him.

'I've heard nothing from Andy and you say Mark's heard nothing. I'm going to see if he's at home,' she said getting to her feet. 'I don't know what to say.'

'It doesn't change us,' said Victor.

'Jenifer doesn't like me and now my son has beaten her up. Ask yourself, Victor, how can it work for us? I wanted to get to know Jenifer, and I feel like going to her because she's hurt, but I can't. You can. She loves you and you love her. I'm so sorry. It was a dream; she's out of my class. You're out of my class. I'm in a bloody nightmare. I must go,' she said sweeping her hair from her face.

Victor held her arm but she pulled away. 'Don't follow me, Victor. I'm on the edge and I could explode and it would be horrible.'

Five minutes later, dressed and ready, Cindy met Victor at the bottom of the stairs.

'Don't try and stop me, Victor. It's humiliating enough as it is.'

'At least talk for a few minutes,' he said gently, touching her elbow.

She pulled away and opened the door as he stood aside.

Victor waited twenty minutes before walking to the shops to use the pay-phone at the all-night supermarket.

'Please don't cut me off,' he said listening to the phone being handled for half a minute after she'd heard his voice. 'I'm so unhappy, Victor. I can hardly speak.'

'It's OK to be unhappy, but please don't make decisions while you're like this. You're a *joyful* person,' he said. 'We'll work through this.'

Victor hardly breathed during the following twenty seconds of silence.

'I need to be on my own and think things through. Elly's staying overnight at Mandy's and they're both going out with Susan after school tomorrow before going home - I mean to your place. Oh God, I'm calling your place home.'

'You did and you're correct.'

'So I'll have to be there after work anyway. Oh God, how did I get into this mess?'

'You know what's best for Elly.'

'Don't blackmail me, Victor. I don't need it on top of what I'm going through.'

'If that's what it takes to get you back then so be it.'

'Leave me be,' she said putting the phone down.

Cindy, feeling powerless and alone after leaving two messages on Andy's phone, poured herself a large glass of wine and sipped it while leaning against the sink. The sight of a small mark on the kitchen floor galvanized her into action. If I have to move back she thought, I want it perfect. She tipped the wine down the drain and, in spite of it being nearly one in the morning, set about cleaning the apartment. Andy phoned an hour later.

'Hello, love.'

'I suppose you know I hit the bitch. She deserved it.'

'Are you interested in how she is?'

'Are you interested in how I am?'

'How are you?'

'I knew this call was a waste of time. I suppose Jenifer, whatever her fucking name is, has reported it to the police.'

Cindy remained silent.

'I fucking knew it,' he said. 'You stay with that old man and I hope you're fucking happy.'

The phone went dead before Cindy could reply. She called him back. It rang twice and went dead. She didn't leave a message.

*

'Sorry to wake you. I know it's six o'clock.'

'I was awake anyway,' said Susan, 'and Jen's still sleeping. What's happened?'

'I thought you'd want to know. Cindy did leave last night.'

'What did she say?'

Victor felt like a teenager with Susan's words of warning of broken hearts ringing in his ears while he described the previous evening.

'You thought she might, but it's not the end of the world, Dad. She needs her own space for a while. I don't think she'll talk to Elly until they're face to face and Elly will be with me after school. Mark should be with Jen from about three this afternoon. Leave it with me, Dad. Please.'

'I've run out of ideas anyway.'

Cindy picked up the phone after two rings without looking at the name of the caller and remained silent.

'You have to congratulate me,' said Susan.

'How's Jenifer? Is she OK?'

'She's going to be fine. Now you can congratulate me.'

'It's good to hear you, Sue, but I'm not up to this at the moment.'

'I got up really early to phone you before you leave for work. That's a first and I need lots of strokes, so you have to congratulate me.'

'Congratulations,' said Cindy smiling.

'I'm taking Elly and her mate out after school today. Can you get off early and come with us? It's normally Elly and me but I know she's suffering from split loyalties and wants to be with her mate and me, but not at the same time. If you could come as well it would be really great.'

'You want to talk to me about the mess my son has created, don't you?'

'Of course I do. I want to talk to you before you blow

it up into something unwieldy. Please come and talk to me, Cindy. Pretty please.'

'This is so difficult for me, Susan.'

'Pretty please. You might not come to the answer I want if you go it alone.'

'What about what I want?'

'Great. Let's discuss what you want this afternoon.'

'I think I can manage it, but I'll need to phone you in about two hours.'

'Chat later, and here's a kiss for the day,' said Susan kissing into the phone.

The reflection in the wardrobe mirror told Cindy she looked OK for the office. Then she recalled her change in attitude with her change of clothes when she first met Victor. She changed and looked again. She hadn't changed her shoes but couldn't recall stooping slightly to get a full view of herself. She placed a pair of expensive high heels in a carry bag and went downstairs.

*

'You look stunning,' said Susan when Cindy removed her coat.

'If I look stunning, how do I describe you?' said Cindy, holding out her hands to Susan and admiring her high heels embedded with silver studs, tight black jeans and loose-fitting, see-through blue blouse.

'Elly and Mandy will be here in about twenty minutes. I hope you like my choice of café. I know you come here with Elly and my Dad sometimes.'

'I hope he won't suddenly turn up.'

'If he does, it'd be pure coincidence.'

'I spoke to Andy last night. I felt empty and ashamed afterwards. He was so abusive and selfish. I felt as if I wanted nothing more to do with him ever again, but then I thought of him as a little boy watching his mother being verbally and physically abused and I just wanted to cry out. He's seen me being hit; not only by his father. I haven't told you any of this before because it hurts to think of it. Your Dad's the only person I've ever told. He's given Andy a chance, Mark's given him a chance and Jenifer didn't report him to the police. Where does it all end?'

'Why do you blame yourself? I haven't had a child so I'm not qualified to advise, but it strikes me that you were a victim, and now you're blaming yourself for being one.'

'It's so easy for people who haven't been abused to be amazed at the amount of abuse someone will put up with,' said Cindy, thinking of Victor's words and moving the subject from the particular to the general. 'But it's only when you look back that you realise how damaging it is to kids who witness abuse because you couldn't, or worse, wouldn't stop it. Kids know if you can't defend yourself, you can't defend them. That's the guilt, Sue. I don't know if your Dad told you of our first meeting when Andy burgled your house, but boy oh boy, did he lay it on the line to me about my bringing up of Andy. He pulled no punches.'

'A lot of things have happened since then.'

'Oh yes. Victor said Andy's been given chances and if he can't find his way through life after all the help he's been given then it's time to move on with or without him. Your Dad's hard about that. He says life's not a dress rehearsal. When it's over it's over he said, and believing in the afterlife is a fictitious get-out card for those who fail to use the life they've got, especially as they don't recognise they've been given the gift of imagination. To expect a life hereafter is the ultimate in greed in his opinion.'

'He's made an impression on you,' said Susan. 'He can be quite the lecturer when he wants.'

'I was silly to run away last night but I felt so ashamed. Thanks for the rescue.'

'It's self-interest. Dad obviously told me about you leaving the house when you heard about Jenifer and it's easy to know why, but you mustn't think of staying away. I've got my real Dad back because of you and I'm frightened of losing him.'

Susan reached for Cindy's hand, and to the surprise of both of them, Susan became tearful and unable to continue. 'Put it down to lack of sleep,' she said holding a serviette to her lower eyelids.

'It must be catching,' said Cindy, dabbing her own lower lids with a tissue.

'I can see Elly and Mandy. I'll be back in a moment,' said Susan.

'Hello you two! Oh yes, I owe you this, Elly,' said Susan, handing over a twenty pound note as part of the ritual of an outing with Elly who always put the change in the dish in the hall for collection by Susan later. 'Your Mum's with me. We're sitting over there, come and join us. We've kept two seats.'

Elly gave Mandy a pleading glance as Cindy approached.

'Is it OK if we sit upstairs?' asked Mandy.

Embarrassed by Cindy's extra affectionate hug, Elly turned towards the stairs. 'Please phone when it's time to go.'

'Where do they get these ideas from?' said Cindy.

'The humiliation would be the equivalent of a public flogging if we went up and called them in person,' said Susan.

Cindy and Susan sat watching people passing the window for a few moments.

'Jenifer said she deserved it,' said Susan.

'Why she went to the apartment is beyond me,' said Cindy.

'Put it down to idle curiosity. She said she couldn't rationalise it herself. Anyway, apparently she said some really dreadful things, but she wouldn't tell me more. I don't think she can remember the details.'

'How is Jenifer? That's the most important thing. Is she going to be totally OK like Victor said? I can't stop thinking about her, and I can't go to her. I know she finds me unacceptable.'

'She's going to be OK. I spoke to the doctor before I took her home and she assured me all was going to be OK. The bruises will take time, but that's only to be expected.'

'I really hope so. I'm so sorry.'

'You aren't responsible for Andy's actions, just like I'm not for my sister's and neither is Dad.'

'I don't like talking about Jenifer to you. It doesn't feel right. It doesn't feel right talking to you about your Dad either, but we both love him so it feels different. Please understand my position, Susan. If I stay I have to accept her dislike of me and I now know I can't live with that. It'll eventually make me ill. It's all very well having jousting competitions with her at the dinner table but it's unpleasant for your Dad, and I find it very stressful. I've put up with a lot in my life and I thought I could look forward to a happy future with your Dad, but I think I've been naïve and this terrible thing has brought it home with a jolt. Our backgrounds are very different and one day there will be a major blow up, and I know I need to be totally self-sufficient. I don't want to hurt your Dad, but I'm not sacrificing part of myself at this stage in my life. Not after what I've been through. I learned that from your Dad. I'll be telling him this evening.'

'Before you carry on, I must tell you something, Cindy-----.'

'Sorry to stop you, Susan, but I've reached a conclusion and I hope to get Victor's support. I'll live in my apartment with Elly and Andy. I hope Victor will continue to help with school fees. I will still see your Dad and hopefully spend a lot of time with him, and go out for meals just as Sylvia does. I would hate to lose contact with you, Susan, and I know Elly will miss you at home so please let's meet up frequently. What do you think?'

Susan turned to face the window, feeling a knot in her stomach growing. It was the same knot that had been relieved nearly nine years previously by holding her mother tight and crying while looking into Jenifer's austere face.

'Are you OK, Susan?'

Susan felt trapped. Her face reddened, she turned further from Cindy and saw nothing through hot tears. Cindy tapped her arm and pushed a packet of tissues into her hand but Susan continued to sit without acknowledging it.

Susan heard nothing from Cindy during the few minutes it took her to gain some semblance of rationality. She dabbed her cheeks and eyes, blew her nose and faced Cindy. 'I've made such a fool of myself. I'm sorry. I think I should go.' She looked at Cindy across the seventeen-year age gap and felt she'd been thrown into the cold reality of adult life. Feeling numb, she stood without looking at Cindy and reached for her coat.

'Please say cheerio to Elly for me. I have to go. I'm sorry. I've made a huge mistake. I'm out of my depth. I don't trust myself.'

Cindy hurried to her feet and was mechanically kissed by an expressionless Susan. And I'm supposed to become a lawyer, and here I am completely misreading the situation and falling down at the first hurdle she thought. Cindy called after her as she left the café but Susan seemed not to hear.

'Wait, Susan, please wait,' she said, running up and touching her arm. 'Please let's talk some more. Don't leave like this.'

'I have to go to Jenifer. Perhaps she's made a mistake as well.'

*

'I'm on my way to your place with Elly,' said Cindy. 'Elly says you're going through her homework tonight.'

'I'm glad to hear it. Have you spoken to Susan?'

'Yes.'

'And?'

'She and I met at Starbucks, but unfortunately she got very upset and left in a hurry to attend to Jenifer.'

'Susan got upset? What on earth happened?'

'I was discussing a proposed plan for the future, which I'll tell you about, when she suddenly stood up to go. I think the last two days have been a bit much for her. I think it's been too much for all of us.'

'She left Jen with Mark at a quarter to three. I spoke to him a few minutes ago and he'll be going to his office after they've eaten.'

'In that case, she probably wanted some fresh air and has gone shopping. I'll be at your place in a few minutes.'

'What's happening, Mum?' asked Elly.

'I have to sort a few things out with Victor before we go home tonight.'

'Am I sleeping at the apartment tonight?' asked Elly, frowning as her anxiety grew during the ensuing silence.

'Don't worry, Elly. I'll tell you everything later when I've talked things through. It's a bit complex.'

Cindy parked her car and Elly took the house keys from Cindy's bag as normal and went to the front door as Victor opened it. He greeted her with a firm kiss on each deadpan cheek. She handed him the keys and went to her room.

Victor and Cindy hugged each other at the door. He pushed her hair to one side and kissed her. She gave him a tight squeeze and carried on into the house.

'A glass of wine, Victor? Go into the front room. I'll bring it.'

Victor looked at the keys in his hand with the elephant fob, pushed open one of the pair of doors, went in and sat in the middle of the sofa looking out over the table to the opposite chair and the window beyond. He felt apprehensive.

Neither spoke while Cindy poured two glasses of wine. They clinked them together and sat facing each other.

'Susan was upset because she didn't like my plan for the future. I gave my reasons first but I'm not sure she fully accepted them. She was silent after that, which disturbed me. I tried to talk to her but she looked right through me. That's when she said she had to go to Jenifer's. Has she phoned since we spoke?'

'No. She probably needs some space if she's unhappy with your plan, or she's shopping before going to Jenifer's.'

'I'll tell you as I told it to Susan, but before I do I must tell you I don't hold any grudge towards Jenifer. In fact I now feel released from her completely, but I feel sick every time I think about Andy's attack on her, and as I said yesterday I want to go to her and try and comfort her but I'm feeling so crippled by being held away. It hurts.'

'Jenifer won't hold you away.'

'I'm sorry, Victor, the undercurrent of her rejection has been dragging me down long enough. I can't and I won't take it any more, especially after this.'

'You need to-----.'

'Sorry to stop you,' said Cindy raising her voice slightly and flexing her wrists to show the palms of her hands to Victor, 'I know what I need for my own sanity.'

Victor carried on looking down through his glass of wine to the table while supporting his chin in his hands unaware of his right heel rising and falling to the beat of subconscious music.

'I know if I carry on living as your partner in your house, I have to accept Jenifer's dislike of me. Eventually it'll lead to a terrible blow-up, or one of us will become ill, or both. Better to have a plan now while we're both fit. What has happened has made me think of other things. She's never said so, but I can see Lizzy's not comfortable when she's here. I think I've seen her here six times in eight months, and only twice without her boyfriend. I love you and always will, Victor.' After a long silence she added, 'Please say something.'

Apart from keeping time to the beat in his head, Victor didn't move.

'I thought I could look forward to a happy future here with you and we both thought we could ignore the flaw in this wonderful bubble we were creating for ourselves, and now I know we can't. I've come between you and Jenifer. It's horrible and I'm very sorry. I've done enough damage through my son hurting Jenifer and you have to help her. I can't.'

'And your plan?' asked Victor without looking up.

'I'll live at my apartment with Elly and Andy, when he's there that is. I hope we'll see each other frequently. I can't get my head around any loss of Susan though. I love her so much, and there's Elly and you and Elly and Susan, but I'm hoping the move will not mean a break. I'm going to continue with Elly's education, come hell or high water.'

CHAPTER 30

'Let me take the bags,' said Mark.

'How's my sister?'

'Sleeping like a baby. I said I'd wake her as soon as you got home. She's dying to know how you got on with Cindy.'

'Don't wake her. It didn't go well. I thought we'd have stir-fry chicken followed by fruit salad and ice-cream. I'll start preparing it now. It's gone six-fifteen. Please lay the table Mark,' said Susan ignoring Mark's quizzical look.

'Are you OK, Sue?'

'No, I'm not.'

'It didn't go well?'

'No.'

'Do you want to talk about it?'

'No. I'm sorry, Mark. Open some red wine and let's just be for a while.'

'What's happened?' Jenifer quietly asked, while tying the towelling belt of her white dressing gown as she came into the room with nothing on her feet.

'How are you feeling, Jen?' asked Susan.

'Drugged but OK.'

'How does stir-fry chicken followed by fruit salad and ice-cream sound?'

'Who would like a drink?' asked Mark.

'Nothing for me,' rasped Jenifer, trying to clear her throat and straining to look at Susan.

'It's something serious, Susan. What is it?'

'I left Cindy and Elly about four-thirty and I haven't been able to make sense of what she said. I'm shocked. I thought she loved Dad and me, but I don't know any more. It's as though she's built a wall around herself and there's no way in.'

'Please tell me what happened,' said Jenifer lowering herself onto the sofa. 'Did you tell Cindy it was my fault? Did you tell her how sorry I am?'

'There was no way into her Jen. She wouldn't listen. She stopped me dead. She'd made up her mind. She's leaving Dad's house,' she replied, went back to the kitchen, turned on Radio Two loudly and busied herself leaving Mark and Jenifer sharing an awkward silence opposite each other across the low coffee table.

'You won't have to think about her being with Dad any more,' said Susan across the counter-top. 'We should drink a toast and take a leaf out of Cindy's book for being strong and living with it.'

'You should have let me phone her last night,' croaked Jenifer.

'I refuse to accept any blame. I'm sorry, Jen. Let's stop this conversation. I feel upset for you, I'm feeling very sorry for myself and I'm feeling desperate for Dad. Elly's like you - she's tough. Nobody really knows what goes on in her head and she'll be so loyal to her Mum, she'll be out of our lives before you can say Jack Robinson and we can all forget we ever met her. Sorry to drag you into this, Mark.'

Susan turned to the sink and stared at the wall for a moment before returning to the counter to cut up chicken pieces.

'Where are they now?' asked Mark.

'My guess,' said Susan getting busier and noisier, 'is they're with Victor. Cindy will be delivering her rehearsed speech in the same measured terms she did with me, Elly will probably be packing and Dad will possibly even cry, then Aunty Sylve will turn up and help him get over it. And we'll all live happily ever fucking after,' she shouted.

'OK, OK,' said Mark going to the kitchen.

'Don't touch me, Mark.'

Mark held his upturned hand on the kitchen top next to Susan and watched while she blindly cut the top off a packet of stir-fry vegetables. She tipped the contents into a wok, screwed the packet up and put it into Mark's hand, letting him close his hand over hers. She turned to him, put her arms about his neck and howled while Jenifer looked at the back of Mark's head and Susan's face, feeling as numb as she had felt when her mother held Susan many years before.

Jenifer returned to her bedroom and closed the door.

CHAPTER 31

The phone rang six times.

'I'm sorry there's nobody here to take your call. Please leave your number and one of us will get back to you as soon as possible,' replied Elly's well-rehearsed speech.

Having heard the phone ring six times again, Victor glanced at Cindy's face and then at his watch. Seven o'clock.

'It could be for you. It could be for Elly, but she obviously doesn't want to pick it up. Does she know your plan?'

'She knows she'll be sleeping at the apartment, she knows Jenifer's been hurt and she heard me talking to you from the car. We'll talk later.'

'I'm going to finish preparing dinner then I'm going through Elly's homework with her,' said Victor coldly. 'I suggest you stay here and think your plan through again and we'll talk after we've eaten.'

'I've been through it and through it since last night, Victor. I'm exhausted.'

'Then please stay where you are and relax and think on the words: synergy, sacrifice, compromise and compassion.'

'I'm not a child, Victor.'

'Then stop behaving like one. The black and white view of the world sounds grown up coming from politicians and it's a good starting point in the mind of a child,' said Victor ignoring the ringing of his mobile phone on the table between them, 'but it's idealistic, and idealists are a danger to themselves and everybody else.'

It rang again as he finished talking.

'Hello,' he said without looking at the screen. 'Speak up,' he continued brusquely, 'I can hardly hear you. What do you want? --- Sorry, Jen. I can hardly hear you. I didn't expect to hear from you, what with the dressing on your face and everybody there.'

'I want to speak to Cindy.'

'It's for you,' he said handing the phone to Cindy and leaving the room.

'I can't speak loudly. Can you hear me?'

'Everybody keeps telling me you're going to be perfectly OK. Please tell me it's true. I'm sick with worry and I'm so sorry you were hurt, Jenifer.'

'I'll be fine. It's just a matter of time, but I want you to know I'm really sorry for all that happened,' she said choking back tears and failing to continue.

'Thanks, Jenifer, but you have nothing to be sorry about. We are different people that's all. Andy did a terrible thing and regardless of what others say, I'm his mother and I feel responsible. Susan has obviously told you I'm moving back to my place. I feel a weight has been lifted off me by this phone call. Thank you so much. We're bound to bump into each other and I'm so relieved to know you'll make a full recovery. I wish you all the best and thanks again for the call. It means a lot to me.'

Cindy stared at the phone on the table, weighing up Jenifer's way of terminating their relationship. Feeling sad but relieved, she joined Victor in the kitchen.

'Jenifer phoned to say goodbye. I didn't expect that.'

Victor looked from the stove to Cindy as she laid the table for three.

'What did she say?'

'She said she was sorry about all that has happened.'

'Anything else?'

'Yes. She confirmed she'll be fine. She found it difficult to talk though.'

'Did she mention that she was sorry to have thrown a spanner in the works? Did she tell you she thought it was her fault that she was attacked?'

'Of course not, that would be ridiculous. No, she's sorry it's come to this. I think she's relieved that everybody can return to the world according to Jenifer. I'm pleased she called, it feels like a loose end has been tidied up and we can all move on.'

'Then there has been a major shift in her thinking since last evening.'

'Oh! And what was that then?'

'I'm afraid that has to come from Jenifer. Did you give her a chance to talk or were you too obsessed with your plans of self-destruction?'

Cindy continued laying the table, lost in thought.

'Come on, Victor, tell me what Jenifer said. You told me they had a terrible argument but that's no excuse for what he did. If anyone should know about being beaten up during an argument, it's me. Don't tell me she really did think being hit in the face was her fault? Because that's not feasible.'

'Ring her back and ask her. Be patient. She's finding it difficult.'

'She'll think I've gone mad. We've just said our goodbyes.'

'Better to feel foolish and gain understanding than to ponder in ignorance. That's for soap operas not intelligent life forms.'

'Oh! We are on our high horse,' said Cindy picking up Victor's phone.

'Hello, Jenifer. Sorry to phone back,' she said waiting for acknowledgment. 'Are you there?'

Cindy could hear indistinguishable voices and, thinking she'd inadvertently intercepted a call, was about to cancel it when Susan's voice came through.

'Hi, Dad! Please phone back in about ten minutes. Jenifer's so distraught she's not making any sense whatsoever.'

Cindy's neck tingled and her mouth dried as she closed the call.

'Is everything OK? You've gone pale,' said Victor.

'I don't know. Susan said to phone back in ten minutes because Jenifer's too distraught.'

'Sounds like there's a lot going on over there. Relax. Call Elly. Dinner's ready.'

They both heard creaking from the stairs.

'She's been listening to every word,' said Cindy.

'If my future was in the balance I'd do the same,' said Victor opening the door and calling Elly for dinner. 'Phone again after dinner.'

Elly sat at the dinner table glancing from Cindy to Victor.

'Have they found out what happened to Jenifer yet?'

'She got caught up in an argument and got hit in the face, but she's going to be fine,' said Victor.

'Where was it?'

'In town.'

'Were they drunk?'

'I don't know.'

'Am I sleeping here tonight?'

'Yes. And it's homework time immediately after dinner,' said Victor.

'Can - oops - may I speak to Jenifer?'

'Yes. When we've cleared away, but not for long. She's very tired and finds it painful to talk,' said Victor.

'I'm sorry. I can't eat,' said Cindy, pushing her plate to one side. 'I'll have it later.'

They cleared the table in silence. Elly finished putting things in the fridge, grabbed Victor's phone and hurried from the kitchen to her room.

'I don't think she should phone,' said Cindy 'and I don't think you should have said yes to her without me.'

'Are you trying to protect Elly or is there something else?'

'She might be hurt by what she's told.'

'Let's stop trying to manipulate the situation and allow it to find its own level. If Elly gets hurt, we'll help her through it. That's what we're here for and she'll grow up the stronger for it. I think Elly's innocence will prevail where sophistication will gum up the works. However, you could have a hidden agenda.'

'What are you talking about? What hidden agenda?'

'You could be protecting your plan to leave because you've set your mind on it and you don't want to consider any alternatives.'

Cindy sat down again and put her head in her hands.

'Let this thing, whatever it is, play itself out,' said Victor.

'Hello Dad,' whispered Jenifer.

'It's Emma.'

'Hello, Emma. Sorry about my voice.'

'You will be alright, won't you?'

Jenifer choked back tears.

'Yes. Sorry about my voice, it's the plasters on my face.'

'I hope you get better soon. Please can I come and see you? May I?'

'Soon, when I'm a little bit better.'

'I can walk there after school. I know where you live. Will you tell Victor when I can come?'

'Yes I will,' said Jenifer holding a serviette to her mouth.

'Mum wants to talk to you. I'll go and get her. Bye-bye Jenifer.'

Jenifer steeled herself to talk more, but by the time she'd taken a few deep breaths, she heard Elly handing the phone to Cindy.

'Hello, Jenifer.'

'Hello, Cindy. Please let me talk slowly. I'm really struggling.'

'Sorry, take your time. I'm in the front room on my own.'

Elly joined Victor in the kitchen with her schoolbooks, and with far more enthusiasm than normal.

'That only took thirty minutes. Your homework wasn't as difficult as you thought. Now get ready for bed. I'm going to see what your Mum's up to. We'll come up and say good night shortly.'

Victor found Cindy sitting in the middle of the front room sofa with her arms folded, staring into space. He pulled the curtains closed.

'Can people change so much?' asked Cindy without moving. 'She told me she behaved like a real bitch to Andy and hates herself for it. I've been on the phone the whole time. She was so upset, it took ages for her to tell me. She kept saying she was sorry and then I found myself talking to Susan. What's happening?'

'It's better you talk it through with her.'

'Give me some idea, Victor. You know her better than anybody.'

'I don't know what goes on in her head.'

'You must have some clue.'

'I can only guess. She's possibly more aware of her own shortcomings. I don't know, I'm guessing. I imagine Mark has something to do with it.'

'Do you think she's afraid she might lose you in some way if we separate and she really hasn't changed her feelings about me at all?'

'I've no idea. All I know is it takes a significant event to change a person's paradigm. And let's face it, being hit in the face and suddenly realising one really is responsible for a chain of events over which one has no control, is a rude awakening for anybody.'

'I'm taking her to the hospital tomorrow afternoon. Susan suggested it, and according to her, Jenifer was over the moon about it. It's not my afternoon off but I'm taking it anyway.'

'That's good, isn't it?'

'I don't know any more. I'm completely drained. Let's say goodnight to Elly then I'm going home for the night. I'm hoping to speak to Andy and finish tidying up. I'll be back in the morning before you take Elly to school. I'll get the groceries and something for dinner tomorrow.'

'You're going to your apartment, not home.'

'OK, OK. Let's say goodnight to Elly.'

CHAPTER 32

"This will see them off forever," Mark read from a yellow Post-It stuck to a covering letter from his lawyer, attached to a copy of a rebuttal letter to MDC. Feeling relieved he leaned back in his office chair with his feet up and cradled a mug of coffee to reflect on the fraught evening when the phone rang.

'Hello. Mark here, hang on a sec.' He stood and brushed coffee off his jeans. 'Sorry about that.'

'It's Cindy, Andy's mother. I'm glad you're there. This is the only number I have for you. Sorry to disturb you so late. Are you free to talk?'

'Hi, Cindy.'

'I'm so sorry about Andy. I seem to have caused problems for you and Victor's family.'

'Look Cindy, it didn't work out with Andy, but I can tell you honestly he contributed well to this company. It's only a pity it didn't carry on that way.'

'I'm so sorry,' said Cindy.

'We're all adults, Cindy. Please don't apologise for Andy.'

'I feel responsible for what he's done to you and Jenifer. I was hoping he'd be at home so I could talk to him but he's not here and I'm really worried.'

'I understand your worry, but don't let it spoil your life. You and Andy are separate people with separate lives and it's not your fault.'

Cindy felt she was listening to Victor regurgitating words for her benefit and reflected on his accusations during their first meeting.

'Thanks, Mark, but I did bring him up.'

'I may sound brutal, but if you've managed to get Andy to the point where he can strike out on his own with values you've imparted then you've done a good job. If he disregards those values that's hardly your fault.'

'Thanks. Have a good night.'

'Sleep well yourself.'

Feeling wide-awake in spite of the late hour, Cindy dragged the vacuum cleaner into Andy's room (normally a no-go area) to complete her grand clear-up, and sensed its emptiness even before switching the light on. Feeling numb and needing to be doing something while assembling her thoughts, she stripped the bed, bundled the bed-linen with Andy's remaining clothes ready for washing and fastidiously cleaned the room with increasing alarm until, at near bursting point, she dumped the bundle in the washer, switched it on and squashed the vacuum cleaner into its cupboard, ignoring the uncontrollable tube as it snaked onto the floor as she shut the door.

'He's gone!' said Cindy. 'I'm going mad. One minute I know exactly where I'm going, the next, I haven't a bloody clue, then I phone Mark to apologise and end up getting a lecture. I've come here to get my sanity back and find my son has gone without leaving a note and he won't answer his bloody phone. Life never used to be like this and I don't know where to ----------.'

'OK,' said Victor. 'I'm coming over.'

'It's nearly twelve. You can't leave Elly.'

'I'll be there in twenty minutes.'

Cindy ran alongside Victor, tucking Elly's duvet about her as he carried her from the car to Cindy's bed.

'Come and look at his room.'

'The bed's made up.'

'I've stripped it, turned the mattress and put fresh things on it. Don't ask me why. It's pretty bloody obvious he's not coming back.'

'Have you checked to see if anything is missing?'

'No.'

Victor sat on Cindy's bed while she rummaged through the bottom of the wardrobe.

'The door was open and I know it wasn't me,' she said pulling shoeboxes of papers out from amongst the shoes. 'Just papers,' she said, but then with urgency, carried one box to the kitchen.

'His passport's gone,' she said spreading the contents over the table. 'He's skipped the country.'

'Let's not get carried away. He may have taken his passport just to be independent. Come on, let's go home.'

'I am home.'

'Come on, let's go,' said Victor sliding his arms under Elly and her duvet.

'I am going to live with you, Victor, aren't I?' whispered Elly in a dreamy state with her eyes closed.

'Ask your mother.'

Elly battled against an urge to sleep but managed to open her eyes a little as she was being carried to the car. 'Are we going to live with Victor, Mum?'

'Yes, Elly.'

Elly suddenly felt heavier as she fell into a deep sleep.

*

Victor gradually surfaced and could hear the muffled sound of Cindy's voice from somewhere downstairs. He struggled to read six-fifteen on his watch and reluctantly got up.

'Whoever you were talking to gets up early.'

'They're two hours in front at the moment, and besides they get up very early,' she replied.

'You've lost me.'

'I bet he's planning to go to his Ouma's. The rest of us get a Christmas card from her but Andy gets his own with the same words every year inviting him to go and visit her when he's grown up. She's living in the past. She thinks he's a little boy.'

'And has he contacted her?'

'No. I told her he's thinking of travelling a bit and might visit her,' she said, looking at a fully dressed Victor before glancing down at her short nighty over matching pants. 'You leapt off the starting blocks. I left you pushing out the zeds and was going to bring you tea. Now you look all bushy-tailed and ready to take on the world.'

'Tell me what you want for breakfast and I'll get it,' said Victor, holding her against him and vigorously rubbing her bare back under her nighty.

'You can carry on doing that and skip breakfast if you like.'

'No you can't,' said a bare-footed Elly in yellow pajamas from the kitchen doorway. 'I'd like egg, bacon and mushrooms with white toast. Victor's taking me to school in his car, isn't he?'

'Yes, don't worry, the little angels you mix with won't have to look at my rusty old Renault.'

'I could drive you in Mum's car if you really insist.'

Elly gave Victor one of her 'don't-mess-with-me' looks through half-closed eyes before retreating to her room.

'Ready in five minutes,' shouted Victor.

'Egg and bacon would be great,' said Cindy.

At a quarter past eight Cindy kissed them both, apologised for leaving them to clear up and rushed for the front door. Ten seconds later she returned. 'Keys… keys keys… where are my keys?'

'On *your* desk,' answered Victor.

CHAPTER 33

Feeling nervous and a bit overdressed for a hospital visit, Cindy pressed the doorbell. Jenifer opened the door within seconds and regardless of what she'd been told, Cindy still got a shock when she saw Jenifer's face.

'It really does look worse than it is,' said Jenifer holding out both hands to Cindy. 'I can't tell you how relieved I am that you're here. Come in, I'll only be a few minutes. I'm glad you're early.'

'Oh Jenifer!' she said searching for her eyes in the midst of blue puffiness, 'I'm so sorry.'

'I'm feeling a bit sorry for myself, but I'm going to be all right and the pain has settled down. I'll get my things,' she said going to her bedroom.

Jenifer sat on her bed gathering her thoughts as though considering her prospective conversation with Cindy as terms-of-engagement and yet, even while these were percolating she felt nothing of the confrontation she'd previously felt with Cindy. Plus, seeing Cindy's look of concern, and sensing her feeling of sorrow, abolished what possible dregs of conflict remained. She stayed seated for a while, recovering from giving herself up to the situation and accepting her own vulnerability before picking up her (mother's) coat and bag and joining Cindy in the lounge.

Cindy had been deflecting her feelings of self-consciousness and being alone in the open plan area of Jenifer's apartment with its full length widows by concentrating on various framed family photographs taking prize position on what little wall space remained. She'd seen Anne's face looking back at her from photographs in Victor's house many times, but then suddenly realised she'd not seen so many of them recently, and certainly not in their bedroom. She'd not objected to them, or said anything to Victor, because she'd not only accepted them as a valuable part of his past but also embraced them as part of her life with him. It must have happened with the change in furniture he'd organised she thought. And the pictures would now be securely stored away or given to the girls. Or had she seen this one before in a different place?

'We look like real riders,' said Jenifer making Cindy visibly jump, 'but those horses did what they wanted. We just sat there being carted about. It was great until they were going home and started galloping. You should have heard my mother scream.'

'Where was the picture taken?'

'In your home country.'

'South Africa seems like a blur now.'

'I've got a lot to learn. I'm ready, let's go.'

Cindy took Jenifer's arm when she saw her hesitate at the top of the stairs.

'Thanks. It's my first trip out. I can't see over the edge of the dressing and it hurts when I put my head forward.'

'Take your time,' said Cindy as they descended two flights of carpeted stairs to the tiled floor hall with neatly positioned pot plants on the one side and mirrors on the other, which reflected the low winter sun through the glass doors.

'Keep your arm clear. I have to slam the passenger door really hard,' said Cindy, after helping Jenifer into the seat.

'Where's Dad's car?'

'He's giving tutorials this afternoon and needs it, and besides, I feel comfortable driving this. It's more me, but Elly had the choice of being delivered to school by your Dad in this or his car, or being collected tonight from Mandy's house with this one; but she couldn't have both trips in the same car. So you see we're being dictated to by a thirteen-year-old, going on twenty.'

'All sounds too complicated for me,' said Jenifer pulling the safety belt far out in front before securing it. 'Before we go, I have to say something. Please forgive me for the way I've been, Cindy. It's not easy for me to talk to you. It's to do with my mother. I've not been able to talk about her without crying and I can start any second without warning.'

Jenifer had rehearsed and had steeled herself for the conversation but felt shocked by its bluntness. She feigned a cough and quietly rummaged through her bag while Cindy overcame an urge to touch Jenifer's arm by exaggerating her need to concentrate as she pulled away from the curb.

It wasn't that they didn't want to talk during the ten-minute ride to the hospital; it was more like each felt they needed the silence to process their feelings of being together. Cindy slipped her arm into Jenifer's for the walk to the entrance and Jenifer responded by squeezing Cindy's hand between her body and elbow.

'How can I help?' asked the reception nurse, looking directly at Cindy from behind the glass screen.

'We've an appointment for Jenifer Ell---.' Cindy hesitated, unable to remember Jenifer's surname.

'Elliott – er! No. Long – er! No. Elliott. Sorry,' said Jenifer starting to laugh.

Cindy looked at Jenifer, and catching Jenifer's nervous laugh, only just managed to stifle her own. The nurse's eyes darted back and forth between them while tapping at her keyboard. By the time she'd checked Jenifer in and had asked them to take a seat, both were chuckling for no apparent reason.

A nurse, ignoring Jenifer, came to Cindy and checked Jenifer's details before ushering them both to a cubical where they looked at each other and started to laugh again the moment the curtain was pulled around them.

'Your eyes are starting to look like mine,' said Jenifer as Cindy yet again failed to hold a straight face.

'Sorry about this,' said Cindy to the nurse on her return ' but something just tickled us.'

'It's nice to see mothers and daughters laughing together. We need more of that around here,' said Nurse Gonzales, before leaving a medical trolley by the bed and swishing the curtain closed behind her.

Tears ran down Cindy's face while Jenifer choked back further laughs with tissues against her mouth to ease the pain.

'Do you want me to stay while they change the dressing?' asked Cindy, mopping her eyes.

'Please.'

The curtain swished back and forth and Nurse Gonzales suddenly appeared inside the closed cubical with them. She chatted without expecting answers (or allowing time for a reply), while settling Jenifer on the bed and her head against a pillow. She removed the dressing and gently cleaned Jenifer's face with cotton wool from a dish of strong smelling liquid. 'There we are. Looks good to me,' she said turning to Cindy. 'The doctor will be here shortly.'

A swish of the curtain and Nurse Gonzales, together with the trolley, disappeared. A further swish and they were left alone within the curtained cubical. Cindy sat on the edge of the bed and studied Jenifer's face, and as Jenifer was about to explore her nose and face with her fingers, Cindy instinctively took her hand to prevent possible contamination as she would have done at some time or another with her own children. Jenifer held Cindy's hand as she felt Cindy lessen her grasp and they sat in silence looking at their joined hands until the curtain was pulled to one side by a young woman with a stethoscope hanging from her neck.

'I'm Doctor Kavita Chetty,' she said, holding out her hand to Cindy. 'How is the patient today?'

'I feel a lot better,' said Jenifer.

'Fortunately your cheek took most of the punishment and that will heal nicely. Your nose will not require further work and will return to normal, but it will take a few weeks before the bruising goes away completely. I'm going to prescribe something for the pain and a nasal decongestant. Carry on with the eye drops for another five days and we'll see you again in ten days. Have you any questions?'

'Thanks,' said Jenifer. 'Do I need to make the appointment?'

'No. We'll send that to you. The nurse will dress it now, for your confidence and protection more than anything else. We'll see you in ten days,' said the doctor as she slipped through the curtain.

It had been a clear blue winter sky when they arrived. Now the sliding doors opened to a cold and artificially lit car park. Cindy was about to drive away but then switched off the ignition and turned to Jenifer, 'Nobody can replace your mother,' she said.

'It's taken this,' said Jenifer moving her hand in front of her face, 'to make me see things differently. Helen, I'll tell you about her later if you'll let me, has worked with me on my issues for over two years and I guess somehow, somewhere, I've stored up er… not advice exactly, she doesn't give advice, she's prompted my thinking with her questions. I felt I couldn't move on for fear of losing my mother.'

Jenifer cried quietly at first and then howled while Cindy held her forearm. 'I'm sorry,' she spluttered.

'We have all the time you need, Jenifer.'

'I've been a real bitch. It's taken all this time for me to accept that Dad's happiness with you is not a betrayal of my mother,' she said staring into her lap.

Cindy took Jenifer's hand and held it against her face.

CHAPTER 34

'She's dead to the world, Mark. She knows I'm going out but she thinks I'll be back shortly. I didn't tell her you'd be babysitting her,' said Susan. 'I think she'll be delighted to find you there, that's if she wakes up. I should be back at about eight.'

'I'll be there shortly. You can't afford to take any more time out.'

Mark sat next to Jenifer's bed reading the Financial Times, sipping from a mug and occasionally glancing at the mound of white duvet. An hour later, after his second cup, he watched Jenifer slowly move. She held out her arm to look at her watch, gently coughed and turned over taking the duvet with her.

'How long have you been there?' she asked sleepily.

'I nearly made for the door,' he said. 'I've only seen polar bears coming out from under huge mounds of white on TV.'

Jenifer smiled and adjusted her head on the pillow to face him.

'When did you get here?'

'I've been here long enough to have two cups of tea, read the whole of the business section, and I'm half-way through the rest.'

'Two minutes then,' she said quietly. 'I hope I wasn't snoring.'

'Purring,' he replied sliding his hand under the duvet to touch her arm.

Jenifer let her eyes close and continued to talk.

'Is Susan here?'

'Susan called it babysitting. I said I wanted to be here, so she's taken the opportunity to go to the law library. She'll be back in an hour or so.'

'I'm glad,' she said smiling.

'The new dressing looks better. I can see more of the colour scheme.'

'I need to get up and go to the loo,' she said sliding her legs off the bed.

Her nightdress had gathered almost to her waist and Mark felt guilty looking at her, knowing she couldn't see him through closed eyes.

'And it's time for another tablet,' said Mark on her return.

'Perhaps I should skip this one. It's only a painkiller and I'm OK at the moment.'

At Mark's insistence Jenifer swallowed the tablet with the remainder of the water and got back into bed.

'When did you say Susan would be here?'

'In about an hour. Do you want something to eat?'

'Later,' she said, lowering herself into the pillow.

Mark tucked the duvet around the back of Jenifer's neck after kissing it.

'Thanks,' she whispered.

'I bet she was pleased to find you here,' commented Susan, removing her coat.

'She was so drugged up, she spent most of the time sleeping,' said Mark.

'I'll wake her,' said Susan. 'She should get up and eat something. I'm sure she'll feel much better going to bed again after that.'

'OK. I'll make omelettes,' said Mark.

'No wonder she loves you,' said Susan.

'Do you think she does?' replied Mark.

'I'll ignore that.'

Jenifer, looking almost like a zombie, having combed her hair over half her face, came into the lounge in a light dressing gown.

'Well, what do I look like to you two? I had to force my eyelids open to look in the mirror. I thought I looked like one of those monkeys with hideous frowns and staring eyes.'

'Shall we tell her?' said Susan, looking at Mark. 'From the back nobody would notice and Mark hasn't run away.'

'He was too busy looking at my legs this afternoon when he thought I couldn't see.'

'OK you two, sit down. The omelettes will be ready shortly,' said Mark.

'Come on, Jen, what happened with you and Cindy?' asked Susan.

'I can't tell you how relieved I am. She was so easy to be with. We had a fit of the giggles and cried. We couldn't stop. I still can't believe it.'

Jenifer, helped by the medication, talked and talked until she sat back in the armchair and sighed.

'Time for bed,' said Susan, touching Jenifer's hand before heading for the bathroom.

Mark rose from his chair.

'Do you have to go now?'
'I'll wait 'till you're in bed.'
'Stay the night if you want, but be careful of my face.'

CHAPTER 35

'Yes, he's been here for two days,' said Esther Oosthuizen from her dark flat in Newlands near Cape Town. 'He's out at the moment. Do you want me to call when he gets back?'

'You haven't told him I phoned, have you?'

'No, Pet. You said I mustn't.'

'I thought you were going to phone if he got to your place.'

'I was going to Pet, but we've been so busy.'

'Please don't tell him I've phoned. I don't want him to know. I just want to know he's OK. I don't want him to think I'm checking up on him.'

'But you are my pet,' said Esther innocently.

'What's he been doing with his time?'

'We've cleared out the spare room. It took all day. I found an old photograph album I'd forgotten about. There's a picture of you with Koos. You looked happy together, but I knew the real story. Do you remember ---------------?'

Feeling frustrated, anxious about being late for work and needing to go to the loo, Cindy hovered from one foot to the other.

'Please phone me this evening when Andy's not there. I have to go to work now.'

'What work do you do, Pet?'

'Mom, I have to go or I'll be late.'

'I loved it when you called me Mom.'

'I really must go. Bye bye.'

'You said I must phone you.'

'Yes, please phone me.'

'What time must I phone?'

'Only when Andy's not there. Evening would be best.'

'Oh, he's not here in the evenings.'

'Don't forget your time is later than here by two hours. Now I must go.'

'I won't forget. Bye bye, Pet.'

The first few calls from Esther seemed cheerful enough, but although they were frequent and despite Cindy's probing, she felt less comfortable about Esther's wellbeing until after five weeks Esther's resolve crumbled.

'I don't know these people he brings home. They're skelms, I know they are and sometimes they stay the whole night talking. I'm too frightened to tell them to voetsak. Frightened in my own flat. He hardly says anything to me and he won't tell me who they are. He just laughs and closes the door. He used to think he could get around me with his smarmy marmies but now he doesn't bother. He's so rude.'

'I'm so sorry, Esther. I know you had high hopes for Andy. I'll talk to Victor. We'll sort something out; don't worry.'

'I told him I'd phone you if he carried on. I can't repeat what he said to me. It was horrible.'

'She's not a happy person.'

'What do you want to happen?' asked Victor.

'He's probably gone there because he thinks the police are on to him and he'll be charged with assault or something if he comes back. I could phone him and tell him it's OK to come back. There's nothing for him there without qualifications, and he's definitely up to no good.'

'Can you remember telling me about the last call you had with him?'

'Please don't nag. I was upset.'

'More than upset. You couldn't believe he could be so callous towards you and Jenifer, and what's more he still hasn't bothered to find out if she had brain damage, a slightly bloody nose or will be disfigured for life. Do you really want to go through that again?'

'OK. If you've got a better idea, let's have it.'

'I'll phone him. Perhaps I can get him to listen, that's if he doesn't slam the phone down,' said Victor.

'Thank you, thank you, Victor. You're doing so much for me when you should be concentrating on your work. I'm sorry to put this on you. You don't deserve it after all you've been through.'

'Cindy,' he said taking her head between his hands, 'Andy is why we're together and in an indirect way, Andy is why I'm on top of my university work. We just have to deal with this distraction as logically and as quickly as possible. Please stop feeling responsible for his actions.'

'Every time I see one of those bumper stickers that says "a pet is for life not just for Christmas", I immediately think the word should be "child" not "pet".'

Cindy made a list of things for Victor to get across to Andy in the hope of catching him before he went out the following day.

'You'll phone me as soon as you can, won't you?' she said soon after switching her bedside light off, kissing him and turning to face the same direction.

He pulled her towards his cupped body and kissed the back of her neck.

'Wakey, wakey!' said Cindy, holding two mugs of tea. 'Andy's asleep and probably won't wake up 'till mid-day according to Esther. He's been talking with some guys who only left at three this morning.'

Victor wriggled back from the edge of the bed to make space for Cindy to sit.

'See-through nighties don't allow me to make any sense of the world,' said Victor, eye level with the top of her legs.

'Move over more,' she said.

'OK. I'll phone about twelve, but I thought you weren't going to phone. You took a chance. Andy could have picked it up,' said Victor pushing himself into a sitting position.

'I wanted to be sure he was there and warn Esther about your call. It dawned on me that if she says it's you on the line he mightn't accept it, but if he thinks it's one of his mates, he will. Poor Esther. She didn't know what she was letting herself in for.'

'Good thinking batgirl,' said Victor.

'You're in one of your playful moods and I've got things to do,' said Cindy, handing him a mug.

'OK,' said Victor, kissing her arm.

*

Victor switched his phone alarm off at eleven, locked his office door and reviewed his notes.

'Hello, it's Victor here.'

Esther spoke so quietly without a preamble that Victor could hardly decipher her words.

'He's in his room and I know he's awake. I've heard him on his cell. I'll call him.'

Victor heard Esther knocking on a door. 'I don't know,' he heard her say.

'Yeah, who's this?' asked Andy.

'Just wanted to make sure you're OK,' said Victor.

'Not you as well. Ouma's just like the rest of you. Can't keep her mouth shut.'

'Your grandmother didn't tell us. Your mother worked it out.'

'Now she's with you she's become a fucking detective as well.'

'Jenifer had to explain to the hospital how she was injured and ---.'

'She can go fuck herself.'

'Please put your grandmother back on.' The phone went dead.

Victor sat on the edge of his desk and looked at the bare winter trees on the banks of the brook. He felt impotent and angry, then murderous, before finally calming down sufficiently to call Cindy. Five thousand miles away, Esther had locked herself in her bedroom and, ignoring the bright summer's day, had watched her tears darken an area of her old floral bedspread. She looked much older than her seventy-one years, and older than she did a month ago when she'd stood on tiptoe to kiss Andy. Now she felt crushed by foolish expectations, and much smaller than her five feet. She was already small enough to make her dark bedroom, with its single window look large, but now her dark dress and small lined face beneath her short grey hair blended with the surroundings, and apart from her blue eyes and the pink bobbles on her slippers, she appeared to be no longer there.

'What did he say?'

'We have to go for plan B I'm afraid. I don't know the details of how he spoke to you, but if it was anything like I had to put up with, then no wonder you were in a state. He had total disregard for Esther or Jenifer. I had no expectations for myself and I couldn't get a word in edgeways anyway. Phone Esther and send a letter to Andy as planned. Please don't mention Jenifer not reporting the incident. I think that's all we can do for now.'

'Why can't I mention Jenifer not bringing charges against him? He may come back if he knows that.'

Victor sighed and glanced at the list of unanswered questions.

'You don't want him back, do you?'

'We've been through this time and time again. If you want to mention it, then do so. The last thing I want is to tell you what to do, but I'd rather he made even a small gesture of an inquiry into Jenifer's wellbeing first; otherwise it's another example of how we keep pandering to him. He's nearly twenty-three for goodness sake.'

'Stop nagging me, Victor. Your phone call achieved nothing. I'll phone Esther now and I'll see you tonight.'

'Love you,' said Victor.

'Love you too,' she said absent-mindedly.

*

'I was just about to go shopping,' said Esther. 'No, he left an hour ago without saying a thing. I'm all right now. I just wish he wasn't here. Yes, write a letter to him.'

'I'm sorry he's gone to you, Esther.'

'He's just like his Dad, but I don't need to tell you that. Shame Cindy, my skat, you've put up with a lot. I hope your man, what's-his-name --- yes Victor, that's right Victor. I hope Victor's a good man. He sounds like a good man.'

'We have our ups and downs.'

'So long as there's more ups than downs, Pet, we shouldn't complain.'

Immediately after supper on Sunday Cindy typed a letter to Andy setting out her wishes for him including, as agreed with Victor, an allowance for further education, the use of the apartment and assistance in sorting out a possible future for him. She also described Jenifer's improving condition and her discretion in not reporting the "accident" to the police. Cindy reread the two pages, considered the content too structured and logical and rewrote it, not typed it, couching it in more loving terms. She left out the non-reporting of the 'accident', but added her wishes for him to be kind to his grandmother. After sealing the envelope she typed a one-page letter to Esther expressing sympathy for her situation, printed it out, read it and added two handwritten pages of random notes, which she thought Esther would find interesting. She felt she'd achieved something positive as she folded the pages together with a fifty-pound note.

Writing to Esther became a Sunday evening ritual, and Esther became blotting paper for Cindy's thoughts. Instead of replying by letter Esther relied on their regular Friday phone chat for all the news. However, after six weeks, Cindy saved her letters without sending them. Unaware that years later, even after Esther's death, she would continue writing a weekly "Letter to Esther", but for now she became totally engrossed in her writing each Sunday to the exclusion of all else.

Friday's weekly call to Esther always raised Cindy's anxiety at the start of the weekend. Esther had nothing new to say and her response was repetitious and never failed to illustrate how isolated she felt in her own apartment, and her increasing concern for "Andy's ways" and his "skelm friends." Esther once asked Andy to phone his mother. Only once.

Esther reluctantly confessed to Cindy that her letters to Andy remained unopened on the table next to the phone and that she'd found a couple in the bin, torn through while still in their envelopes. 'Yes,' she said, 'he'd possibly read one or two.'

Cindy became increasingly preoccupied with perceived activities in Cape Town at the expense of attention to real activities at home, and it took a long time and much soul searching before Victor admitted, but only to himself, that he was feeling increasingly resentful. It seemed to him that the more he supported and pampered Cindy, the stronger she felt to focus her attentions elsewhere.

'I've been putting off an invitation to Stellenbosch University. The funding's in place and if it's OK with you, I'll make some calls once I've cleared it with the department. I was hoping to make a bit of a holiday of it with you and Elly, but I think that can wait. If you're happy, I'll visit Esther and try and see Andy.'

'That'd be wonderful, Victor,' she said hugging him. 'How long will you be gone?'

'One full week with a weekend at each end should be enough for Stellenbosch. Then I don't know, maybe another week, maybe more. I'm guessing.'

Cindy wrote a toned-down version of her original list of things she wanted to get across to Andy which, with the help of Victor, whittled down to: a) ensure Andy knew there was no case against him; b) to be happy wherever he chose to live; c) to please let her know wherever he was; d) to please be kind to people – especially his Ouma; e) to be able to pay his way – and she and Victor would help with any education; f) make sure he stayed healthy and he could always call if he needed help and g) please communicate with his sisters – especially Elly who misses him terribly.

'I see you've put the word "please" in your list,' said Victor smiling.

'Stop it,' said Cindy, on the verge of being cross.

'Come. Let's not take it too seriously. We're making plans to communicate with him. Lighten up a bit.'

'It wouldn't worry you if Andy disappeared completely.'

'Oh it would,' said Victor. 'If it worries you it worries me.'

Victor hugged her, received as chilly a response as he'd expected, kissed the top of her head and returned to his study feeling more than a little despondent. Two hours later Cindy, with two mugs of tea, joined Victor on the sofa and rather than taking her normal adjacent seat to watch the news on TV, sat across from him.

'Sorry I'm being bitchy,' she said.

Cindy became increasingly preoccupied with her letters and although he was preoccupied with his preparations for South Africa, Victor had a nagging feeling of loss of Cindy. However, his spirits began to rise as she drove through light springtime drizzle to Heathrow, five hours before take-off.

'I could have easily caught the bus. Thanks a lot but you shouldn't have taken the afternoon off. No, don't go to the short-term car park. Drop me at the drop-off point, otherwise you'll get caught in the afternoon traffic.'

She changed lanes without a word, double-parked and pressed the tailgate release button.

Victor moved his things to the curb while Cindy stayed seated.

'I'll go when I'm fucking ready,' she screamed through closed windows at the security man gesturing her car forward. He approached the driver's side but then turned his attention to another vehicle when he saw Cindy sobbing into her hands.

Victor could still taste her tears long after passing through security.

CHAPTER 36

Mrs. Marais' garden flat near Stellenbosch University Botanical Gardens was spacious, light and self-contained. It had its own lounge-cum-dining room, as well as a large double bedroom and the promise of three course dinners for up to six people with an early morning notice.

'Most people from the university have breakfast at a quarter to seven,' she said, alerting Victor to serious readjustments to his sleeping pattern.

'Thank you Mrs. Marais,' Victor replied, 'a good walk after breakfast before work would be good. Where would you recommend?'

'Please call me Angie, its short for Angela,' she replied beckoning him into the garden. 'Go along this street and, depending on how far you want to go, you can either go to the edge of the reserve and be back in about half an hour or, if you're feeling really energetic, carry on into the hills for a longer walk. It's beautiful up there. I sometimes go to the top myself in the late afternoon, but I always take the dog with me.'

Feeling more at ease having established the bare bones of a routine, he thanked Angie, agreed to join her for dinner, made contact with the law faculty professor to confirm the kick-off meeting for ten the following day and settled himself in.

'I'd rather not take the dog with me but thanks all the same,' he replied to Angie's offer, before setting out for the hills on his first morning. The routine suited him perfectly; the chilly start with over an hour to reconsider the previous evening's notes and to enjoy the rapid rise in temperature for the last fifteen minutes' walk before immersing himself in work.

Nearing the end of his stay, he'd collected enough porcupine quills to be more particular about their quality and size before discarding or adding them to an overfull jar on his office desk.

'What are you going to do with them all?' asked Cindy at the half jar point.

'They're your present.'

'Bring yourself back in one piece. That'll be my present.'

'Cindy, I find this so stimulating. I feel as though I've been missing out.'

'You will come back, won't you?'

Victor's lighthearted laugh only partly convinced her.

'Don't start thinking about suntanned women in flimsy summer dresses while you're away,' she continued, feeling she'd ignited sparks within him that could start fires.

'It's mid-April and I can assure you there are no summer dresses in autumn, at least not until mid-day if I'm lucky.'

'So, you've been looking then?'

'No time.'

'Good.'

'I did go to Franschhoek for lunch with the law professor and his wife. He wanted to show me the view over the town. It was truly fantastic from the mountain pass. The contrast of the vineyards and the wild mountain scenery must make this one of the most beautiful places on Earth.'

'So, you're not coming back then?' she laughed.

'I don't speak Afrikaans and the university has only just stopped giving lectures in Afrikaans, but it's still very much the everyday language here.'

'Sounds like you've been thinking about it.'

'I'll talk to you about the risks of living in paradise when I get home. All this ends on Saturday. They've arranged a dinner for me. I can't believe my visit is just about over.'

Buoyed up by the students' enthusiasm and the positive influence of his own research, Victor left his digs on Sunday and, ignoring his satnav, the sign for the A2 and the good-intentioned advice given him by all and sundry about the risks of breaking down on certain roads, he headed towards Baden Powell Drive en-route for Cape Town.

From the picture book scenes of long, lonely beaches and the rolling Atlantic on his left, Victor pondered upon the lives of the people within the townships on his right. The mass of houses nestling beneath a network of overhead power cables reminded him of ramshackled fisherman's huts with their nets hanging out to dry. Twenty minutes later he turned right towards Newlands.

'Hello Esther, it's Victor. Is it OK if I come to you before I go to my hotel?'

'Thank goodness you're here. Yes, please come. He's out. He won't come back 'till late.'

Deep mauve bougainvillea spilled over a head-high brick wall, forming the edge of the property running parallel to the road. Beyond that, and across a well-cut lawn, sat a two-storey block of flats, with nothing to redeem itself apart from the blue agapanthus and orange and purple strelitzias that surrounded its base. Only after failing to push open the tall metal gate hanging between brick pillars, did Victor notice a grey metal panel within reach through the gate's bars listing names against buttons. He pressed the button corresponding to Mrs. E. Ousthuizen and a lace curtain behind a window on the top floor quickly opened and closed, and the gate's lock clicked loudly. Victor pushed the gate open against its springs, walked in and tried to close it quietly, but it closed with a bang before he could get his hand on any of the gate's bars.

A cracked concrete path dividing the lawn, ended at the base of a short flight of wide, red, polished concrete stairs at one end of the building, leading to a wide corridor that ran the length of the building with a chest-high balcony overlooking the garden. On the immediate right of the corridor were further stairs leading to the top floor corridor which matched the one below, with six equally-spaced green front doors, each with an outer gate of metal bars set within a substantial metal frame. On the left of each door was a small burglar-proofed window. The whole building was constructed from face-brick and off-white painted concrete, with an equally pitched dark brown tiled roof about its centre which was squared off at the ends with blank walls and black bargeboards, giving the building a functional but unattractive appearance. Victor had the feeling of it being a light security prison, or a scaled-up Lego model made by a seven-year-old.

As Victor reached the top stairs, a gate covering an opened front door swung open into the corridor some twenty yards away, and an extremely slim five-foot woman with a small pale, round face below well-cut medium length steel grey hair came out and waited for him to reach her. In spite of it being the warm part of the day, she was wearing a grey knitted cardigan over a dark blue blouse, a medium length heavy brown wool skirt, black stockings and black open-backed slippers. Her smile increased as Victor got closer, and her blue eyes looked sharp and well-defined against the whites.

'I know you're Victor. Cindy, bless her heart, also phoned to say you might come today and I was to phone you,' said Esther, waving a piece of paper on which she'd written his number as if to confirm a link with them all. She then grasped his elbows and reached up to kiss him like a baby bird wanting to be fed.

'I'm so pleased you've come. It's such a weight off my mind. Come,' she said, almost dragging him into the flat by the one elbow to which she remained attached.

'It's good to meet you,' said Victor.

Esther pulled the handle-less gate closed and it automatically locked.

'I'll leave the door open, the wind has dropped and we could do with a little air in here.'

'I feel I know you,' said Victor. 'Cindy's told me so much about you.'

'Cindy, bless her, is a wonderful girl. Andy's just like his Dad, I tell you. I'm ashamed of him for what he did to Cindy. Ons het so 'n stryd gehad.'

'When did you last see Koos, Mrs. Oosthuizen?' asked Victor, ignoring and not understanding her last remark.

'Please don't call me that. It makes me feel old. He was going into a bank in Muizenberg when a lot of us from the church were on a coach trip.'

'When was that, Esther?' he asked while thinking of her age and apparent timorousness, as well as their nine-year age difference, which he found disconcerting.

'It must be at least six years ago. He was friendly enough and said he would call, but he never did. He'll probably turn up one day as though nothing's happened. Andy's just like him. He'll use anybody and everybody including his Mom. And to think I sent him Christmas cards for all those years. I feel such a fool.'

'When's he coming back?'

'Andy? Oh, once he's out the flat, he's out for the day. He mightn't come back, but he usually does. He's mixing with skelms. I know what they're up to with their fancy cars and money.'

'What do you think?'

'What do *you* think? Boys like that with money and time on their hands....'

'I don't want to put words in your mouth,' said Victor, 'but .....'

'Drugs,' she whispered, as though the room was bugged. 'I can see Andy being important to them with his brains. Oh yes, he's got brains that one. He'll have them eating out of his hands in the long run but the police'll get them eventually, unless they pay lots of money.'

'Are you sure you won't come out for a meal?' asked Victor after two hours.

'You're so kind Victor, but I've got things to do and there's no need for me to promise to say you've not been here. He'll say hello if I'm lucky, grunt more'n likely, make himself some coffee without offering me any and help himself to what's in the fridge.'

Victor kissed Esther goodbye and walked into the afternoon sun feeling a weight had been lifted from him. He'd hardly got accustomed to the bright light when he was startled by the yelling sound of a pair of hadeda ibis as they left the lawn immediately in front of him and flew over the bougainvillea, circled back to the apex of the roof of the block of flats and looked down at him. I'm in Africa he thought, as the gate lock clicked at his approach. He turned and waved to the lace-curtained window.

He confirmed his late arrival time with the hotel and then drove over the pass to Hout Bay where he strolled along the beach. He carried his shoes, socks and scrunched-up blue shirt, and ignored the odd splash of water on his light brown slacks.

'Can you hear the water? I'm feeling trampish and free and I'm going to find a restaurant later.'

'Don't feel too free. It's freezing here without you,' replied Cindy.

CHAPTER 37

The phone rang once and Victor heard it being lifted from its cradle, then silence. He waited a few seconds.

'Hello Esther, can you hear me?'

'I've just brought the phone into my room,' she whispered. 'I'm sure he's asleep. He got home after midnight and he'll probably go out after midday as usual. No, I didn't tell him you'd been here.'

'Is it still OK for me to come to your flat to talk to Andy?'

'I hope there's not going to be a lot of swearing and shouting.'

'I'll be there in about an hour. Would you like me to buy some things on the way?'

'Cindy's a lucky girl,' said Esther. 'You bring yourself.'

Victor was totally absorbed with searching the shelves of Pic 'n Pay for items that would probably be helpful for Esther, when he unconsciously turned for advice from Anne. A tingling sensation started in his neck and ran down his arms making him grip the handle of the supermarket trolley. He took a deep breath, pulled his shoulders back and stood to his full height and phoned Cindy.

'Are you OK?' she asked after a few seconds.

'Yes, but now I think about it, we covered everything last night. Is Elly up-to-date with her school work?'

'Nothing has changed in the last ten hours.'

'Sorry, that was silly.'

'You don't need an excuse to phone me. Tell me what you're up to.'

Victor pushed the trolley to a quiet area near the pool-cleaning equipment and stacks of kids' garden toys, and described his plan for talking with Andy, leaving out key elements he'd carefully constructed and refined overnight.

'I love you, Victor,' she said kissing into the phone.

Victor still felt un-nerved when he returned to his car. After unloading the shopping, he sat in the driver's seat and closed his eyes for a few minutes before turning on the headlights and driving through the dimly-lit car park into the brilliant sunlight.

'You shouldn't have,' said Esther quietly, while Victor placed two plastic bags on the kitchen table.

'I hope it's all OK.'

'I'm sure it is. I feel really spoilt. Cindy's a lucky girl, that's all I can say.'

'I don't know about that.'

'Do you want me to leave the flat while you talk to Andy?'

'It might be a good idea, but only if you want to.'

'I'll make you some tea, or would you like coffee? Then I'll go to Hettie's at number six. Hettie said I should get the police but it's easy for her, it's not her grandson.'

'Tea would be wonderful. What's Andy done with Cindy's letters? Do you know?'

'I think he's only read one or two. Most end up in the bin, torn in half, still in their envelopes. The rest of them are in that lot,' she said pointing to a pile of colourful advertising flyers, half hidden by a newspaper on a table near the front door.

'Did he ever tell you what she'd said?'

'Never, and I've never asked after he told me to mind my own business. I don't know why he came here unless he's in trouble, but Cindy said he wanted to get away for a while and travel. I can't see him moving on. He's up to no-good.'

Esther quickly put her cup down and picked up her bag when she heard Andy moving about. 'Number six,' she whispered as she closed the front door behind her.

Victor was part through tidying up the table when Andy came into the room carrying a mug of coffee.

'What the fuck are you doing here?'

'Protecting you from the British and South African police,' stated Victor forcefully, 'so you had better listen up and stop being aggressive or you'll be in serious trouble. I'm helping you. God only knows why.'

'I don't need your fucking help with the South African police.'

'I didn't want to talk in front of your grandmother. She's gone out. She'll be back shortly and if my plan to get you out of trouble fails, I don't want her involved. So I propose we finish here and go for a drive and a talk.'

Andy leaned against the doorjamb and sipped his coffee looking casual in last night's creased blue tee-shirt, crumpled jeans and bare feet.

'I'll fetch your grandmother while you get dressed, OK?'

'Do what you like.'

'If I did what I liked, the police would be here within the hour. Shall I do that?'

'That'd be the last time you fuck my mother.'

Victor stared expressionlessly through Andy's chest and beyond to the kitchen, waiting for the shock wave of Andy's statement to dissipate and quelling his urge to hit out.

'It's eleven-fifty-three,' said Victor, unnecessarily studying his watch. 'I'll give you twenty minutes to be across the road at the white Toyota Corolla. I'll tell your grandmother I'm finished here.'

Andy grunted and turned back towards the kitchen.

Victor sat on a low wall near his car looking at the newspaper, without seeing it, and didn't notice Andy until he was close by.

'OK. What have you come all this way to tell me?'

'All the way from Stellenbosch or all the way from England?' replied Victor.

'Oh! Here we go, playing fucking games again,' said Andy.

'I've been with students at Stellenbosch. Come sit for a bit,' said Victor patting the wall next to him.

'The police have fuck all on me, so you're wasting your time.'

'It's a bit more complicated than that. I don't know why so many people, including me, are going out of their way to protect you, but they, and me, for that matter, can only do so much without your co-operation. I think you're down to your last chance this time. Come sit.'

'I've got friends picking me up.'

'OK. See you here tomorrow. What time?'

'I'm doing things.'

'Tell your friends you're working on something big. Tell them you need the whole day. Tell them anything you bloody well like, but I strongly advise you to be here at eleven o'clock tomorrow at this wall.'

'Hmm,' grunted Andy.

'I'll take that grunt as a yes,' said Victor getting up.

'Take it how the fuck you want,' said Andy turning away.

Victor drove a few hundred yards to the shade of a tree, parked and phoned Cindy.

'What did he say?'

'We said enough to meet tomorrow,' said Victor, feeling all alone with plans he knew she wouldn't sanction, and guilty at not being totally honest with her. 'You'll have to leave it to me. I know going faster will only cause more confrontation and even less communication.'

'It couldn't be less,' said Cindy, not bothering to hide her disappointment. 'I do love you so much and I really appreciate what you're doing,' she added quickly.

'I miss you,' he said quietly.

Esther mustered all her strength to carry her deadpan expression into the kitchen with accusations from Andy following her.

'You fucking knew he'd be here!' he shouted at her silence before going into his room and slamming the door.

Andy lay on the bed wondering what hold, if any, Victor had over him; knowing deep down he had no choice but to meet him and find out. His mind wandered to the possibility of really doing something big instead of handling the three friends who sold stuff for him. *After all, I'm the one taking the big risks and negotiating with gangs,* he thought.

He picked up his phone, 'Pick me up in fifteen minutes, Josh… yes, same place. Cheers.'

Resisting the opportunity of being a tourist, Victor found a restaurant for lunch before returning to his hotel to round off his university work. It was twelve-thirty by the time he climbed into bed with clear thoughts about engaging with Andy the following day: that is if he turned up.

Victor was so engrossed in thinking of a plan to get Andy out of Esther's flat for good that he only became aware of him at the last second.

'Thanks for being early. I really appreciate it. Let's go to Kalk Bay and find a place for lunch.'

'I don't know why we have to go through this,' said Andy. 'You could spit it out here and now.'

'It's a bit more complicated than that and, besides, I want to get it across to you, face to face in a relaxed manner, and we could both probably do with lunch.'

'Don't tell me this is going to be a pally, pally meeting, because I'm not up for that.'

Victor walked along the road leaving Andy hovering for a few seconds.

'Don't tell me we're going to fucking walk there.'

'The car's in the next street.'

Victor was in awe of the views of the ocean from the mountain road while Andy, having glanced at the miles of Muizenberg's sandy beaches and the white and green housing development around the lake below, grumbled about the heat and fiddled with the air-conditioning.

Victor followed the traffic through the road works into Kalk Bay, glancing at the slowly passing restaurants.

'You choose.'

'Any one,' said Andy.

Victor handed a five Rand coin to a sunburnt man, in his late thirties, who had an alcohol-induced wiry figure and was wearing flip-flops, frayed denim baggies and a Billabong tee-shirt. He had beckoned the car into a space wide enough for three and had then held out his cupped hands for a tip, all the while looking down.

'This car park is the same as it was years ago. The parking people were black or coloured then, and he,' said Victor surreptitiously gesturing towards the would-be-surfer ushering in another car, 'would've been smoking pot and talking of waves he nearly caught, believing he could get a job at any time if he wanted it.'

'Looks like a fucking loser to me.'

'There but for the grace of God,' said Victor.

'Hmm,' replied Andy walking ahead to the main road, 'he'll spend it here,' he continued, gesturing towards the entrance to the wine shop at the corner.

'That's possible. The next town is a dry one.'

'What do you mean?'

'It's a town where no alcohol is allowed to be sold.'

'You've got to be fucking kidding!'

'Let's take a chance here,' said Victor, walking up half a dozen steps towards the smell of cooking, rough planking furniture and noisy conversations. 'It's a bit crowded but I think they'll all be full.'

'Table for two in less than five minutes,' said a cheerful young waitress, with long brown hair hanging over her small round face and "Arleen" boldly printed in pink on the front of her black tee-shirt. 'Drinks at the bar,' she added, before turning to take an order from a nearby table.

Victor was about to ask Andy what he would like when he was pre-empted by Andy asking for a Lion Lager. Victor ordered an orange and sparkling water in a large glass.

'Add that to table eleven,' Arleen called, as she swooped down on the drinks and walked off with them towards a window table followed by Victor and Andy.

'We couldn't have ordered a better spot,' said Victor.

Arleen returned and placed two heavy wooden menus on the table and told them what was not available. She pointed to a blackboard above the counter that listed the day's specials and said, with an air of authority, she'd be back in two minutes which, to the less confident patron, could have been interpreted as she'd have them turfed out if they weren't ready.

'Take your time,' she added.

Andy looked older than his twenty-three years thought Victor as he leaned back and watched him looking out onto the street below with the colourful, meandering tourists and the less colourful locals purposefully threading through them. He thought Andy looked fit and handsome in his light jacket over a powder-blue tee-shirt and blue jeans. And so did two girls eating snacks at the bar who kept returning his glances.

Victor and Andy ordered Kingklip, one with chips and the other with a salad, and handed the menus back to Arleen.

'I'll bring two more drinks?' she asked with eyebrows that converted the statement to a question. They both nodded.

'There's not much chance of being overheard in this place,' said Victor. 'I might as well get on with it. I'll tell you all I know and please ask questions along the way.'

Looking calmer, and for once directly at Victor, Andy didn't say anything.

'There are two issues: the one is your attack on my daughter Jenifer, and the other is whatever went on at Mark's company. I only know what I've been told, but as I understand it, there's enough evidence in both cases to initiate a case against you. In both cases neither wants to make an official complaint, which means you are free to do as you want.'

'You came *all* this way to tell me that?' said Andy. 'And how come you know Mark's business?'

'I know all sorts of things,' said Victor.

'All I know,' said Andy leaning towards Victor aggressively, 'is that you and your fucking family have been interfering in my life ever since ---.'

Victor slammed his hand over Andy's, crushing it into the table and holding it there.

'Ever since I prevented you from being arrested; or ever since you were given a chance to get a good job with Mark; or ever since I stopped your mother being your fucking slave; or ever since I agreed not to set the police on you for grievous bodily harm to my daughter. Which "ever since" is it, you ungrateful piece of shit.'

Andy withdrew his hand, ignoring the pain in one of his fingers and stared menacingly into Victor's serious face before self-consciously sitting back in his seat while Victor, with no qualms whatsoever, sat back in his, suppressing murderous feelings towards Andy. Andy had a sudden and sickening feeling that Victor really could curtail his activities if he set about it.

'Let's continue,' said Victor, as the surrounding tables resumed their conversations. 'There's an unexpected and unfortunate twist. Jenifer portrayed you as the good guy who rescued her when she was callously attacked in the street. She found it difficult to lie and the hospital didn't believe her and, what's more, your story has to be the same as hers if you're ever questioned.'

'That's it then, is it?' said Andy, perking up and swigging back his beer.

'Not quite. There's a survey into violent crimes associated with domestic and partner abuse. The local police authority, which has a newly-appointed commissioner, is championing this because she thinks it will save money in the long run by explaining people's rights and the places where they can go for help and protection. As part of the investigation, they are looking at past hospital admissions and scrutinizing those that look like domestic violence. Jenifer's name was on the list. She was asked in confidence if she would co-operate. She felt obliged to be involved, not fully realising where it would lead. She ended up telling them that a stranger attacked her and that you acted as the "Good Samaritan" and gave her assistance and took her to hospital. Their questioning may not stop. Jenifer feels stupid by being someone who is not willing to report an attack, and therefore by default, allowing an attacker to be loose within the community. She also feels like a liar in their eyes because it was obvious to her they didn't believe her. They know it was you at the hospital. You were picked up on CCTV. They were suspicious of your behaviour at the time, and apparently you're known to the police. They also know you left for South Africa a few days after the event, so when you return they will have some questions for you. You could phone Jenifer and agree the story with her,' said Victor.

'OK. I've got the picture.'

'Good,' said Victor.

'Now, is that it?' asked Andy.

'Your mother would like you to come back to the UK,' said Victor, 'but she said she'd be happy for you to be anywhere so long as you're happy. What she would like though, is some communication from you.'

'If I went back all I'd get is some poxy job where I'd work all fucking hours, taking orders from some cunt, and all for twenty K a year if I was lucky. It's easier to go on the dole and do bits on the side and I'm not doing that.'

'Mark said you were really good with computers and you picked up new software developments quickly. In fact he sung your praises. If you went back to the UK you could rise quickly in the computer business and you could, if you wanted, go into sales. There's good money in sales and with some recognised training, you could go a long way. Your mother and I would assist you with training costs, whether it's here or there.'

'I'm getting good money now,' said Andy.

'Sounds interesting. What are you doing?'

'Minding my own business,' said Andy.

'It's not in the computer business, is it?'

'It's not, and there's fuck-all money in computers. Listen, Mark paid top whack to his people but that wasn't great, and I know he wasn't making good money himself.'

'High starting income is just like high interest return,' said Victor. 'The higher the riskier, and that applies to legal and illegal activities.'

'I've told you. I'm earning good money now and I don't want people interfering in my life.'

'OK. I just hope you're not into something you can't get out of.'

'What the fuck are you trying to tell me?'

'If you are into illegal things with ruthless people here, then you are more valuable to them than all the money you're getting for yourself, and if you don't continually come up with the goods, you could find yourself in serious trouble.'

They remained silent, looking at the street for a few minutes while waiting for their food.

'Sorry for the delay,' said Arleen, looking from one to the other before placing the dishes in front of them. 'Can I get you something else?'

'Not for me thanks,' said Victor.

'Tomato sauce,' said Andy, without looking at her.

Arleen returned within a few seconds. 'Enjoy!' she said.

'How much of the country have you seen?' Victor asked.

'Not much.'

'You have the day off. I'd like to see if the seals are still in the harbour,' said Victor.

'If you want,' said Andy.

Victor ate slower than usual, while Andy had another beer and picked at an extra plate of chips.

'Come on Andy, let's have a dessert.'

They looked at the chalkboard above the counter that advertised home-made pies with different fruit fillings and the choice of ice cream or cream. Arleen appeared from nowhere, took the dishes from the table and turned in the direction of their gaze.

'We're out of Cape gooseberry but have all the others,' she said.

'Apple with vanilla ice cream,' said Victor.

'Same,' said Andy.

Andy's reticence melted somewhat as he watched some seals gliding back and forth near the harbour wall, while others lay on the concrete steps watching the fish- sellers with sticks ready to fend them off.

'Come, it's just gone two-thirty. I'll take you to Boulders. It's only thirty minutes from here.'

'What's Boulders?'

'Jackasses,' replied Victor. 'Come. I think you'll like it.'

Andy offered no resistance as they walked to the car where the once-had-been-surfer received a further tip from Victor.

Andy fell asleep within a mile or so and only came to when the car shuffled back and forth into a small space. They walked a few hundred yards to a sand dune with a clear view of the beach and a large flat rock where a couple of sunbathers were frustrating the attempts of a thieving penguin by holding their beach bags closed.

'I couldn't have set the scene better if I tried,' said Victor.

'Are they tame?'

'No, they're wild.'

'Wow!' said Andy, watching other penguins swimming around children in the shallows.

'Worth it just for that, eh?' said Victor as they walked along the boardwalk. 'The wild life here is wonderful. I can see you're interested. Great white sharks live within a mile of this beach. This country's full of interesting things. I'd love to show you.'

Andy was quiet as they drove along the coast.

'We're looking east over the sea here but if we drive over the mountain to Hout Bay we'll see the sunset, and I think the views will blow you away.'

Andy grunted.

Half an hour later Victor parked the car at a view site and watched Andy watching a family of baboons sitting on the crash barrier five yards from the car.

'It gets even better as we drop down into the Bay,' said Victor.

Neither spoke as the car followed the mountain road under overhanging rock and through tight curves hundreds of feet above the sea.

'A snack before I drop you back?'

'Yeah OK,' Andy replied as Victor turned into a parking area.

Victor dragged two chairs to one side of a table at the edge of the upper deck of a café where they viewed the dark red mountain they'd driven down, reflecting the last rays of the day.

'Make it two,' said Victor to a sun-tanned waiter in shorts and a "Hout Bay" tee-shirt who'd taken a beer order from Andy.

'Me and my mates watch it every night. Give me a wave when you're ready to order.'

'Thanks,' said Victor.

They watched in silence until the peaks turned black and the café's lights suddenly seemed to dominate.

'Penny for your thoughts.'

'Yeah, it's OK,' said Andy, sipping his beer.

'I enjoy working with students. I think for me it's the joy of sharing knowledge. It's one of the few things you can give and still keep. I find it exciting, but I nearly lost it when my wife became ill and died. Anyway, thanks to circumstances and to you I must add, I seem to have clambered out of the pit and have become re-energized.'

Victor carried on talking about his work, his role at Stellenbosch University, the students and how he saw the future, but stopped short of mentioning Cindy's name.

'Why are you telling me this?'

'I'm feeling relaxed and I'm happy just to talk to you. Though I have to admit I would like you to know a bit more about me. I would also like to know you better. Are you happy to let me ramble on?'

'Ramble on if it makes you happy.'

'Two more beers,' said Victor to the hovering waiter, 'and give us a few more minutes. Thanks.' He turned to Andy, 'Have you had a good day?'

'I could have been doing something.'

'Ah! But you wouldn't have seen the seals or the penguins, or the baboons for that matter.'

Andy sipped his beer and looked from the distance to the menu and raised his hand.

'What would you like?' asked the waiter.

'Hamburger and chips without salad.'

'A small chicken salad please,' said Victor.

'Bring me another beer,' said Andy.

'Water for me, thanks,' said Victor.

'Your mum would have been delighted to have seen you this afternoon. You looked happy. I felt happy watching you.'

'I'm never going back.'

'If there's one thing I've learned in my life, it's to never say never. Internalised commitments eventually cause pain.'

'Quite the fucking philosopher,' replied Andy, whose eyes were also fixed on the hidden mountain.

'Think about it, that's all. I think you're far more sensitive than you portray.'

'Maybe.'

'I've got a proposition for you,' said Victor. 'I'd like to show you more of the country before I go back to the UK. How about it?'

'Can't. I've got people to see.'

'Employment possibilities?' asked Victor.

'You could say that.'

'Like I suggested yesterday, tell them you're working on something really big. Tell them anything you like but give yourself a week's break. We can always cut it back if it doesn't work out. It'll be my treat.'

Andy rocked back and forth on the back legs of his chair and thought of Josh, Shane and Lungelo selling drugs without him, knowing he had to trust them for his plan for expansion to work.

'I'll think about it.'

'I'll ring you tomorrow morning, and if you say yes then we'll leave the following day or the day after if that suits you better,' said Victor as he waved to the waiter.

Puzzled by Andy's lack of questions, Victor began thinking about his trip, with or without Andy.

CHAPTER 38

By the time Andy had finished telling Josh to call the others and meet at ten-thirty the next day (and not to be late), he felt every part the man he hoped to be. His alarm went off at nine and thirty minutes later he was wearing his smartest casual clothes and sunglasses; he surprised Esther in the kitchen with his cheerfulness before downing a coffee and saying 'cheers' as he left.

Andy joined the others at their usual table outside the café where, to their surprise, he shook hands with each one before sitting down.

'Your usual?' asked the waiter.

'Not today Dee, orange for me.'

Andy ignored Shane's "quite the dude today" comment. The other two looked apprehensive while Dee took their orders.

'It's grown-up time. I want to know if you're OK with Josh in charge and if you can handle ten days supply without getting yourselves killed, robbed, or worse, losing the cash. If you have doubts say it now because the consequences could be really bad.'

They all felt insecure without Andy. Even though he didn't speak any of their languages, he'd been where they'd feared to tread and negotiated prices and territory. Now their livelihoods depended on him.

'I'm in,' said Josh without hesitation, having agreed beforehand.

'I'm in.'

'And I'm in.'

'OK. I'm trusting you with the sales and stock while I'm away.'

The three of them, all older than Andy, listened to his story of their future and wealth with hope, wishes and little else.

*

Andy, complete with rucksack and a bulging hold-all, had been sitting on a wall near Esther's flat for fifteen minutes when Victor arrived.

'Looks like you've got enough there for a month,' said Victor, walking to the back of the four-wheel drive Subaru estate.

'Got more'n that. I've got everything. Not going back there again, nosy bitch.'

'Come on, she's only got your interests at heart,' said Victor cheerfully. 'Where're you going to stay when you get back?'

'With a mate. Back the car up. I don't want her nosing out the window.'

Victor also wanted to avoid being seen and, having helped Andy load the car, reversed along the road before making a U-turn and driving to the Rhodes Memorial restaurant for breakfast.

Victor thought Andy looked distracted, but felt happy to see him listening with apparent interest while he described the route to the Kalahari.

'I'd like to get there by tomorrow afternoon. It's pushing it but if we end up taking three days, it's not the end of the world. I thought you'd like your own tent. It's cheap, but if you're careful it'll be OK. You can keep it. Actually, keep all the items I'm not taking back to the UK if you want. I got you a warm sleeping bag. It'll probably be over forty during the day, but it could be freezing at night. I think we've got everything. I hired a twelve-volt fridge, I borrowed an old shovel from the hotel and we've got plenty of water. Here're the keys, I'll see you at the car.'

After using the toilet, Victor phoned Esther without mentioning Andy.

'I don't know where he's gone,' said Esther. 'He left very early. He's taken all his things and left the place in a mess. I don't think he's coming back. I found the keys by the front door. I'm so relieved but what am I going to tell Cindy?'

'Tell her the truth. She'll understand and you've got my number if you need help. I'm going away for a few days and I might not see you when I get back but I'll phone.'

'Cindy's a lucky girl.'

Victor said goodbye and phoned Cindy.

'Hello, Victor. I'm really missing you.'

'Esther's just told me that Andy left this morning with all his belongings.'

'Where's he gone?'

'She doesn't know. I'm hoping he'll phone you. There's no point in getting upset.'

'I think I've resigned myself to the situation, especially after the brainwashing I got from Mark. If he's told me once, he's told me ten times that Andy has his own life and if he's brave enough to be independent then perhaps I've not done such a bad job. I think I'm beginning to believe it, but I still feel guilty. And Jenifer's been wonderful. I miss you, Victor. Come home soon, please. I'm feeling like the lady of the manor without you. Oh, and Elly is now officially Emma.'

'I'm going exploring a bit as I said I would.'

'I know you spoke to Elly, I mean Emma, last evening but she keeps asking me when you are coming home.'

'Tell her I love her more than you and I'll be home in about twelve days.'

'She already knows the first bit. Don't take chances.'

*

Andy had pushed an earphone into each ear, played with his phone for a few minutes, reclined his seat and had closed his eyes before they turned northeast on Table Bay Boulevard. Two and a half hours later they started to cross the northern Cederberg Mountains.

'This is fucking amazing,' said Andy.

'If you look behind you can see the Atlantic Ocean,' said Victor, glancing in the rearview mirror.

The rumbling of the tyres woke Andy an hour later as the car dropped off the tarmac onto a stony picnic spot shaded by a camelthorn tree. An inquisitive ostrich trotted up to the nearby fence as they got out of the car. While Victor loaded the concrete table with a cool-bag, Andy went over to the bird and looked up at its blinking eyes.

'What have we got to feed it with?' asked Andy, looking down the semi-desert valley to distant brown hills.

'Cut up an apple and give it half. I'm sure it'll eat it.'

Andy spent most of the short break feeding the ostrich as Victor, while eating a sandwich, studied Andy.

'OK, let's get the show on the road,' said Victor. 'There's no point in pushing ourselves. We'll stop at about four.'

'Yeah,' replied Andy.

The sign "Klein Heuwels" on the left at the junction of the main road and a narrow track indicated nothing of significance. However, a notice hanging below the sign advertising accommodation, caught Victor's attention. He glanced at the clock and eased up on the accelerator.

'Let's at least take a look.'

Andy pulled his earphones off and sat up as the car bumped off the road onto the gravel and then back onto the road as Victor did a U-turn. The sign appeared to have welcomed long-ago travellers and, had it not been swinging securely on heavy metal links, it would possibly have been uprooted by an unscrupulous tourist and be hanging in a manicured garden in Johannesburg.

'What do you think?'

'Probably a pile of stones at the end of the track,' replied Andy.

'If it is then we pitch camp. OK?'

Eleven kilometres later Victor also anticipated a pile of stones while listening to Andy saying: 'There's nothing, not even tyre tracks.' However, a few minutes later they rounded a small hill and in a valley, saw a cluster of buildings and a large water tank with a wind pump surrounded by green trees.

Hendrik Grobler ducked slightly as he came out of his front door, placed his brown bush-hat on his head and walked towards the spot outside the house where he anticipated Victor's dust-covered car would draw up.

'Welcome to Klein Heuwels,' he said, removing his hat for a moment with his left hand and shaking Victor's hand. 'I'm Hendrik Grobler. My wife saw your dust trail over the hills five minutes ago. Eyes like a vulture, my Mary. We don't get many visitors nowadays. Welcome,' he said raising his hat to Andy as he stepped out from the car. 'We're always glad of company. We can collect your things later if you like. Come on in. I'll lead the way.'

Victor felt that Hendrik was one of a few men who impressed others by his very being. He looked about sixty, relaxed and content within his skin. His 115 kilogram upright frame, his gentle voice, his rugged well-shaven face and clear blue eyes seemed to tell a story of inner confidence. His dark green sleeveless jacket with more pockets than could be counted in a single glance, rested unbuttoned on his brown long-sleeved shirt, giving him an appearance of smartness and functionality (and possibly the envy of other less self-possessed beings).

Andy and Victor followed Hendrik's unhurried steps to the house where only he needed to duck through the doorway.

'How many nights will you want to stay? If you want more than one, you could come with me tomorrow and I'll show you the whole place while I sort a few things out. It'll be a long drive but very beautiful. Mary will be here shortly. Make yourselves at home at the back there, out of the sun. Bathroom's on the right. I'll bring a jug of iced water. What will it be, tea or coffee?'

'Tea for me please,' said Victor. 'We're glad we found you. Thanks.'

Hendrik gave Andy a questioning look.

'Coffee,' said Andy.

Hendrik continued looking at Andy without moving until Andy looked up.

'Coffee, thanks,' said Andy.

'One tea, one coffee,' he said jovially. 'I know Mary'll have tea at this time of day. We'll join you outside.'

'Don't get up,' said Mary with a smile that automatically elicited smiles, as Victor started to rise to relieve her of a full tray. She was slim, five foot-four, slightly sinewy and young, and attractive enough for both Andy and Victor to inadvertently glimpse her shape through her light floral skirt. 'I'm Mary, Hendrik's wife,' she said, speaking quickly to overcome her embarrassment from having misjudged the looseness of her new blouse as she set down the tray before them. 'Welcome to Klein Heuwels, which means Little Hills.'

'I'm Victor and Andy's my stepson,' said Victor standing and taking Mary's offered hand and hoping not to be contradicted.

Hendrik came into the garden with a coffee pot just in time to see Andy with an odd look on his face shaking hands with Mary.

'I'm here on a visit to Stellenbosch University from England and Andy's taken a break from his job in Cape Town to spend a few days with me. We're heading for the Kalahari.'

'If you change your mind, stay for a while. There's plenty of wild life here if you know where to look for it,' Hendrik said with a tinge of hope in his voice.

'That would be lovely,' Mary added eagerly.

'Thanks for the offer but I think we'll push on tomorrow. Andy and I don't see each other often and we've lots to talk about.'

'I understand. I want to keep my boys here when they visit,' said Mary, looking a bit sad.

Conversation oscillated between the three of them while Andy watched, making no attempt to hide his boredom.

'Let me show you your rooms and I'll give you a hand with your things,' said Hendrik.

Victor and Andy were shown two small attic bedrooms with a common bathroom.

'Dinner will be at a quarter to seven. Come down any time you're ready.'

Andy glanced at Victor in the hope of guidance as Mary, on Andy's left, reached for his hand above the white embroidered tablecloth. Victor prayed for Andy to accept the ritual of saying grace before dinner, while Mary held Victor's right hand, and Hendrik, whose huge hands were evidence of forty years of heavy farming, grasped the whole of Andy's right hand and Victor's left without ceremony, as though holding the handlebars of a Harley Davidson at full tilt. With closed eyes and a voice that matched his hands, he invited the Lord to bless the food, their guests, his wife, his children and himself. 'Amen.'

Amicable conversation during dinner bounced along the tops of subjects from human rights law to university life, to life near the Kalahari, to two boys (now in Jo'burg). Although Victor delicately described Anne's passing, he carefully skated around his relationship with Cindy. Andy was spurred on by Hendrik into making a contribution to the party, and with a bit of prodding from Victor, described his work with software and hardware, leaving out where it took place.

'There's candles, matches and a torch in each of your rooms. The generator will shut down at ten and breakfast is at seven,' said Hendrik. 'I wish you both a good sleep.'

'Don't worry about clearing up,' said Mary, 'I know where everything goes. Have a good night.'

Unsure of the protocol, Victor and Andy shook hands with Mary and Hendrik, thanking them and wishing them both a good night.

'Oosthuizen,' said Hendrik at breakfast, 'I wouldn't have guessed, would you Mary?'

Mary and Hendrik tried to link Andy with the Oosthuizens of Mossel Bay and then of Kimberley, without much help from Andy before entering their private world in Afrikaans, which took them back to their own ancestors, the Boer War and the British concentration camps.

'More coffee?' asked Mary loudly, suddenly becoming conscious of Hendrik's and her own rudeness.

'Sorry,' said Hendrik, shrinking slightly at Mary's unspoken rebuke. 'Yes, thank you, Mary.'

'Sorry you're not staying longer. The farm looks sparse but it's very interesting.'

'Once Hendrik starts you won't stop him,' smiled Mary, as the redness of her embarrassment subsided.

'Yes, it's a great pity you're going. You could have come with me today. I'm checking out the sheep. We've got fat tails here, hardy as anything, but no defence against leopards. She took another one two days ago,' he said looking at Mary. 'Left me to finish a couple of others off. Provided a good meal last evening though. Proof that somebody's watching over us. I know where she's hiding. She left her spoor plain as day with the weight of that sheep. It was too close to nightfall to go after her, but with the help of The Lord and some luck, I'll get her today. She's on that small hill on the northwest border, Mary.'

Victor and Andy helped Hendrik load his old Ford F100 pickup.

'Thanks,' he said, while handling his two rifles as if made of balsawood. 'Come back this way. Be our guests and we'll have another dinner and I'll convince you to stay for a while.' He opened the passenger door, whistled once and a large brown beige ridgeback ran from an outbuilding and bounded onto the front seat and immediately looked through the windscreen. 'A pleasant drive to you both, drink lots of water and put plenty of salt on your food.'

All three watched as the truck slowly disappeared in a cloud of fine dust.

'There's nothing better than homemade bread,' said Mary, looking sad and a little awkward as she handed over a bag. She took a few steps back while Andy and Victor packed their car. 'Have a good trip,' she said hesitantly, then quickly turned and kissed them both before half running back to the house.

'I feel I'm in contact with the real world when I come across people like that,' said Victor. 'I know it's romantic, but when you see a man like Hendrik who's taken water, guns, a dog and a bag of god-knows-what in that beaten up truck, I feel something wonderful. If that truck were to break down, he wouldn't last a day without water. It's over thirty degrees and it's only twenty to nine.'

'What the fuck do they live on?'

'Sheep and ostriches to make money. Hendrik shoots for the pot and they grow their own vegetables and fruit. Wonderful life.'

'I think it sucks. She's at least twenty years younger than him and did you see the look on her face when we left? She didn't look happy to me.'

'I don't know what all that was about. It could've been anything.'

'Lack of money,' said Andy with conviction. 'Did you see any other car when you went for a walk with the old man?'

'I have to confess, I didn't.'

'She's not going to get far on that old tractor, and those horses look more dead than alive. The old man said he's taking a round trip of a hundred and forty kilometers and won't be back 'til dark. She's bloody stuck there with that smelly sheep-dog that's virtually blind after a fight with a ….. what did he call it?'

'Black-footed wild cat.'

'And all those chickens. Don't tell me she's happy. I don't fucking believe it. The only thing that would have brightened her day would have been if you'd stayed behind and given her a really good shagging.'

It was difficult to hear Andy above the drumming of the car on the rock-strewn road and, by the time they reached the gate, Andy had to be woken up to open and close it.

'How are you going to make really good money, as you called it the other day?' asked Victor an hour later.

'Work for myself.'

'Come on Andy, tell me more,' cajoled Victor.

'Not stealing, if that's what you're thinking.'

'But it's not exactly legal either?'

'Some arseholes make stupid laws that deserve to be broken. Like the place where there's no shops that sell alcohol. I could sell it from a flat or a car there, and if nobody found out, I could make a big profit from people who leave it too late to drive to someplace else.'

'You're too late for that one,' said Victor, 'more than likely someone's doing that right now. It's difficult to tell what makes some authorities ban things and others not. Marijuana is banned throughout most countries because it's dangerous.'

'Can't be. They're thinking of making it legal in the UK,' said Andy.

'Now we really are talking about arseholes.'

'What do you know about it anyway? I know guys who smoke marijuana all the time and they're OK.'

'Anecdotal evidence is always sufficient for those seeking the answers they want. Unfortunately it spawns ignorance not understanding. There's a lot of research which says that for every ten people that take marijuana to go on a trip, one never comes back, but the anecdotes that support that come from the inside of mental hospitals.'

'So fucking what,' said Andy.

'Somebody has to take responsibility,' said Victor. 'It's the state or charities, prisons or hospitals, or their parents. Lots kill themselves.'

'You're talking shit.'

'Wish I was. So you're getting Durban Poison or something stronger and selling it.'

'What are you going to do about it? Report me to the police?'

'No.'

'I'm still wondering why you're taking me on this trip.'

'I told you, I'm hoping we can have a better relationship and besides, we're going to experience wonderful things while you're free to live where you like and do what you want. I'm also hoping you'll feel less inclined to be bitter and possibly phone your mother and your sisters every so often.'

'To make your life easier,' said Andy.

'To make everybody's life easier. Why go about full of resentment? It doesn't do you or anybody else any good.'

Beyond the dry barren countryside near the horizon to their left and in front, a green tinge appeared, and within twenty minutes, they were driving east and parallel to the Orange River towards Upington.

'If we have time on the way back I'll take you to Augrabies Falls,' said Victor. 'It's spectacular and we could take the long way back to Cape Town via Pofadder. The name tells you something about what to expect. Make sure you've got everything you want, because this is the last town before the Kalahari.'

Victor's estate looked miniature among the sea of 4x4s with trailers outside the shopping complex.

'I'm going to make a call. It might be a good idea to make last-minute calls from here,' suggested Victor, hoping to nudge Andy into calling his mother. 'I'm not sure what the reception will be like later.'

'I can't stay in the car, I'll bloody die. I'm going for a drink over there,' said Andy, pointing to a café table under an awning.

Victor stood in the shade where he could see Andy and called Cindy.

'Victor, I'm so glad you phoned. You said Andy might phone after your chat but he hasn't.'

'You never know, he may phone soon.'

'I do hope so. Where are you?'

'I'm in Upington and I'm going north.'

'Wow, Victor! Please be careful, it's one of the hottest places on earth. I hope you have a reliable car. And please stay on main roads.'

'I think you may be exaggerating a trifle. Have you ever been here? And yes, I do have a reliable estate, and the hire company supplied some extra spares.'

'No, I've not been there. I wanted to go with Lizzy but Esther persuaded me against it. Soon after that I read the horror stories of the great trek and the Dorsland Trek and people dying, so I was glad I didn't.'

'It's not as wild as that today and it wouldn't have been when you were thinking about it. You'd have been more at risk of being run over by a tourist being distracted by kids.'

'Come home soon. I miss you, especially when I have to get into a cold bed. I love you, Victor. Don't take chances.'

'Well, how is she?' asked Andy, as Victor edged the car out into the traffic. 'It was her, wasn't it?'

'You're spot on. And she seems very well. She asked after you and was hoping you'd phone.'

'Did you give a report back on our little holiday together?' he said sarcastically.

'No. She's no idea you're with me. I was leaving it to you to tell her in your own time and give her a pleasant surprise.'

'Does she know where we are?'

'She knows where I am,' said Victor. 'She knew more about this area than I'd imagined. Did you know she wanted to come up this way before you were born but your Ouma persuaded her otherwise? So she stayed in Cape Town with your father for another two years before he left her the first time.'

'You seem to know a lot.'

'I'm building a picture from all sorts of things. When I'm really interested in someone it just happens. I tell her lots of things about my life and Anne, my wife, and your mum asks lots of questions. That's how a good relationship is built.'

'Yeah, yeah, yeah,' said Andy.

'Do you know lots of things about your friends in Cape Town?'

'I know enough to make good money with them.'

'Buying and selling drugs you mean?'

'Supply and demand, that's all it is. Everyone's a fucking adult and if they don't want it they don't have to buy it.'

'How about the addicts who want it, but can't pay?' asked Victor.

'They pay in the end, that's for sure. I'm not their mother, and I don't give a fuck about how they pay or where they get the money from. That's their fucking business.'

'And if they don't?'

'All I know is they do and that's that.'

'Don't you feel anything for the people who buy the stuff?'

'Why should I? I've just told you, I'm not their mother.'

Victor was struggling to stay calm while reflecting on the suicide of Angela, the daughter of a close friend. She had been bright and cheerful until being collected from a rock concert in an ambulance, and then became abusive to her parents for five years before tearing herself from her mother's grip and jumping in front of a Central Line tube train. He then thought about the many people who, on hearing the story, revealed similar painful stories of people they knew, and how the victims refused their medication when they started to feel well and then became psychotic without it. After the many up and down cycles, some took their own lives, while a few survived.

It took another sixty miles before Victor could shake off thoughts of parents he knew who'd changed from being enthusiastic nurturers to becoming carers for mentally sick offspring.

'You've been fucking quiet,' said Andy.

'You've been asleep for the last hour.'

'I'm awake now. The sweat's pouring off me and I'm sticking to the seat. How much further?'

'I think we should stop for ten minutes, have a break and then it's about two hours,' said Victor, 'and I'd like to carry on where we left off earlier.'

'Not still on about that, for fuck's sake!'

'Play along with me for a bit,' said Victor calmly. 'I want you to picture a young fit guy who takes some of your stuff just once and it renders him incapable of work for the rest of his life. I'm not asking you to answer or give an opinion now. Just think about his life and the rest of the family, and how their lives will end.'

Andy was about to say something.

'Please don't say anything now,' said Victor, raising his hand in a calming gesture. 'Try and imagine the story, and then please try and internalise it, own it. After that, I'd like to talk to you about it. Indulge me Andy, please. Don't just write it off.'

They withdrew into their own worlds, watching the narrow road hemmed in by rocky outcrops disappearing into the distance.

'That's a nest and a half,' said Andy.

Victor slowed the car down to a standstill and looked in the direction of Andy's finger, which was pointing towards a tree with a nest that completely covered it.

'They're lots of interwoven nests of social weavers. Pass the binoculars please. They're in the green rucksack. It's on the back seat. You'll be able to see the birds. I don't know what social weavers they are. Could be buffalo weavers, but they're too far away for me to be sure.'

'Let's get going,' said Andy, 'it's sweltering.'

'We'll be at the gate shortly. I don't know how much the entrance fee is.'

Andy reached over the back of the seat and started to sort through his large rucksack.

'There'll be plenty of time at the border office, no need to struggle now,' said Victor.

'I thought you'd be paying for everything anyway,' said Andy.

'I thought it would be symbolic if you paid this. I'll pay for everything else including pocket money, but believe it or not, you'll look back on this trip one day and have a sense of achievement and hopefully tell your kids about it.'

'How far to the border gate?'

'About ten kilometres.'

'I'll show you what I think of symbolism,' said Andy, searching for a place to hide before pulling a sleeping bag out of its sack.

'You can pay for yourself but I'm hiding. Tell them what you like but if you split on me, I'll make life hell for the rest of the fucking trip. I've had it up to here with your fucking lecturing.'

The border officer's enthusiastic and friendly nature quelled Victor's nervousness as he completed the admission and weapons control forms and accepted the area map on which crosses had been drawn where lions and gemsbok had been seen in the last few days. They shook hands and said their goodbyes. Victor walked back to the car carrying a folder of paperwork, while the officer shouldered his rifle and opened the barrier.

'Tell me when we're clear,' said Andy.

'Stay there for a few minutes. We're in but we have to think about how to get out when I hand over the papers at the exit. And how we go in and out of the campsites just in case.'

'Same way,' Andy cheerfully replied.

'You enjoyed that, didn't you?'

'Why shouldn't I? Best thing of the day so far.'

'I hope that officer doesn't drive into the park.'

'You fucking worry too much. It must be OK by now.'

'I guess so,' said Victor, glancing in the rear view mirror.

Andy struggled from under the luggage, sat up, tugged off his sweat-soaked tee-shirt and drank a bottle of water with hardly a pause.

'You could have turned the air con on,' said Andy.

'It's on full,' said Victor, gesturing to the controls. 'You're going to have to hide yourself again when we get close to the camp entrance. Even years ago it was busy with tourists, so once you're in the camping area where everybody looks after themselves, you can mingle and blend in, but don't do anything to attract attention.'

The campsite guard lifted the barrier and directed Victor to a camping area a kilometre away.

'There're showers and toilets here and more down at that campsite, and there's a washing-up room with hot water. The lights go out at ten,' he said saluting.

About two hundred metres away from their campsite down a gentle slope, a small lake fed by a slowly rotating wind pump, reflected the setting sun. Andy arose from his camping chair and went to the fridge in the back of the car and got a second beer, while Victor opened a folding chair for himself and joined Andy with a weak whiskey in a tall glass.

'Cheers, Andy!'

'Cheers!' Andy replied, as if mesmerised by the far-off trees, which suddenly looked taller as the sun silently slipped between their trunks to the ground.

A minute later it was dark.

'You shower now. I'll get supper ready then I'll shower and wash up. How's that?' asked Victor.

Without a word Andy got up, went to his tent and retrieved a towel and a bag, switched his torch on and, apart from a diminishing wobbly pool of light, disappeared along a path. By the time he returned Victor was half-way through conjuring up what he called a balanced meal. They silently stood with glasses in their hands, listening to the insects competing with the hiss of the gas lamp.

'Tell me how much you want,' asked Victor, dishing out food from one of the two pots on the table cooker.

'Thanks,' replied Andy taking the plate and returning to his chair.

They sat with their plates on their laps and ate while facing the lake, with the moon behind them making the lamp superfluous, and small moving shapes visible on the far side of the water.

'Give me your plate,' said Victor. 'Would you like another beer?' he added as he got up.

'No. I'll come with you,' replied Andy, picking up the pots to be washed, 'then I'm going to bed.'

*

The ablution block at six in the morning hummed like a beehive with friends chatting and others, like Victor, making the odd comment while, through the wall, there was a similar buzz from the women's facilities. Excited children ran around with newfound friends, while back at the tents, Andy had made two mugs of coffee and was gathering his things together.

'Coffee's made,' said Andy throwing a towel over his shoulder.

'Thanks. Looks good,' said Victor, taking a sip. 'What are you hoping to see today?'

'Lions,' said Andy.

'OK then. Breakfast'll be ready by the time you come back.'

The night insect noise began fading as the day shift took over, while Andy and Victor zipped up their tents.

'You may want to take your sleeping bag to cover up as we go in and out. The guard didn't look at the papers, but I'm sure they remember every face and I don't really want to explain how you got in.'

'OK, OK,' said Andy, showing signs of impatience and unzipping his tent.

The barrier went up as their car approached and the guard waved them through. At the junction Victor turned north towards the interior of the reserve.

'You can come out now,' said Victor.

By nine o'clock Victor, sensing that Andy was bored with watching 'not more springbok', was relieved to find some shade, and decided to take a break from the burning sun on his side of the car.

'Are you going to watch that bird all day?' asked Andy.

'I don't think he's going to last all day,' replied Victor.

'Neither am I in this heat,' said Andy.

'Shush,' said Victor, handing his binoculars to Andy and taking the camera.

Andy watched the drongo swoop and return to the same perch a few times before a cloud of black feathers burst above the pool.

'Missed it!' said Victor.

'What the fuck was that?' asked Andy.

'A bateleur eagle. I don't know how the drongo didn't see it coming. I thought I saw the bateleur as we drove up but I couldn't be sure.'

'Where's it gone?' asked Andy.

'Still flying,' said Victor pointing.

*

Apart from the "exploding bird" as he called it, Andy was obviously bored and later that evening said so. They'd seen four lions taking up the only shade available for miles. Only one of the lions bothered to look at them and that was because Andy banged on the side of the car, which started an argument between them when Victor told him to stop. Victor had taken a lot of pictures of a wide range of animals and birds, occasionally raising Andy's interest level to a point where he'd voluntarily made the odd comment, such as about the Kori Bustard that insisted on walking in front of the car in the middle of the road. Other than that, he'd either complained about the heat or had slept.

'Did you think about what we spoke about the other day?' asked Victor, while they sat clutching their respective drinks after an early supper.

'I told you. I'm going to make serious money. I'm quite capable of looking after myself and I get a buzz out of it, just like you get a buzz out of this,' said Andy, gesturing towards the lake from his chair and clutching his half-full beer bottle.

'And the other part of what we were talking about?'

'Oh, I know what you're on about; being responsible for the arseholes that buy the stuff.'

'Yes,' said Victor. 'The arseholes who think one try with drugs won't make any difference to their lives. Because you persuade them to buy it, they end up mentally disabled and needing care. They're the arseholes we're talking about. There's also the people that act as mules and die or, become imprisoned because they think they can make money. What about their mothers, fathers, wives, brothers and sisters? Can you picture all this or not?' continued Victor.

'I don't need a fucking lecture from you, OK?' said Andy.

'OK,' said Victor calmly, 'I'd like you to picture something else though.'

'OK, go ahead. You're going to anyway.'

'The other day there were two bright looking girls who couldn't take their eyes off you in the restaurant. I know you saw them.'

'Yeah, so what?'

'I want you to picture them as addicts and then tell me if they are as attractive to you as they seemed to be the other day.'

'If they're going to buy stuff, they're attractive and that's that. And I'll tell you something else Victor, and I know this for a fact, OK? There are lots of better looking girls who'd do anything, even for a small amount of the stuff. And I mean anything.'

'OK, we'll drop the subject for now,' said Victor.

'The trouble with you, Victor, you want the world to work as you like it and ignore what makes it really work.'

'You don't mind if people are damaged by you so long as you make serious money, as you call it, because you think the laws that try to prevent harm to kids are made by arseholes. Is that it?'

'You may think you're responsible for all the people in the world but I know you're not and neither am I.'

'If you extend that further, then everyone takes the law into their own hands and it's a free-for-all,' said Victor.

'OK, you're so fucking bright. What would you do?'

'As a punishment for dealing in drugs you mean?'

'Yeah.'

'Following your logic Andy, I should take the law into my own hands and dish out punishment in proportion to how strongly I feel. Therefore, if I felt strongly about something I should take extreme action and if I'm not worried about it, I should forget about it.'

'OK I'm still asking. What laws would you make?'

'I'll think about it and let's talk tomorrow.'

'I knew you'd chicken out. I'm going to bed.'

Andy lay on his back in his sleeping bag, consolidating thoughts for a running start for when he got back to Cape Town. Twenty feet away Victor lay in his sleeping bag, his hands behind his head staring at the green glow of the moon through the fabric of his tent and feeling sick with disdain for Andy. Neither slept much, and both woke to the call of an emerald-spotted wood-dove from a nearby tree prematurely heralding in the day.

Victor climbed out of his tent into the cold and dark as Andy's shadow appeared against the inside of his orange tent like a strange moving embryo in the torchlight. A few minutes later they gathered at the gas fire and waited for the kettle to boil.

'How long to get back?' asked Andy.

'You eager to get back?'

'Yeah.'

'I'd like to go north, then west to Keetmanshoop. We could be back in Cape Town the day after tomorrow.'

Five minutes before the official time of raising the barrier Victor, from all appearances, patiently sat alone in the car while Andy snoozed under a sleeping bag where he remained until the sun came up ten minutes and four kilometers later.

'Are you sure you want to get back so soon? Wouldn't you like to spend another night in the northern part? Then we could take a more leisurely drive.'

'I want to get back.'

'I hope nobody's threatening you.'

'Those guys need me more than I need them.'

'I'm just concerned, that's all.'

'They know I can pick and choose. They're small-time guys, and I'm working with really good guys who can pull strings and make things happen with no pressure because I'm increasing sales without being on their turf. It's what you might call strategic marketing in your world.'

'I get the drift,' said Victor. 'You're heading up a small-time group and buying from the big guys and giving them sales they wouldn't have had if you hadn't got involved.'

'Well done, Victor.'

'What happens if you fail to pay the big guys?'

'I don't. My guys will get paid cash.'

'And if they don't, for some reason?'

'They'll get the cash. That's for sure.'

'You mean they'll threaten.'

'They'll do more than fucking threaten.'

'And if you're caught, say after a year?'

'I'm fucking careful,' replied Andy.

'If you're caught, what would you expect as a sentence?'

'We pay the right people so it's not going to happen. A year from now I'll have a hell of a lot of cash. You should see your face, Victor, that's the best look of disapproval I've ever seen. Come on mister lawmaker, what would you make the sentence for a first timer? You chickened out last night.'

'A first time dealer in cocaine or crystal?' asked Victor, exploring Andy's face.

'Yeah, you didn't answer yesterday, so come on, let's hear it.'

'How about death?' said Victor.

'You're fucking mad!'

'As mad as the Indonesian government?' asked Victor.

'Now what the fuck are you talking about?'

'Any person trading drugs in Bali is tried and possibly executed. They give plenty of warnings though.'

'They're as mad as you are,' said Andy dismissively.

'Are they? Or are they trying to protect their citizens and the thousands of young people who go there every year? They probably realise a single trader could ruin many lives and be a drain on their economy. Until something can stop it, like mass education for example, I tend to go along with them.'

'You're all fucking mad,' said Andy reclining his seat as far as possible.

'Drink and something to eat?' asked Victor when they'd been on the road for nearly three hours.

'Can't stop here, we'd fucking bake,' said Andy, sitting up.

'I didn't mean skid to a standstill. I meant as soon as we see some shade.'

Perched side by side on the floor of the rear of the estate, beneath the open tailgate with a towel over its window for shade and their feet on the ground, they drank a two-litre bottle of water between them within a few minutes.

'Be honest with me, Andy. I know we've been over it before, but pretend for a minute you could start all over again with your mum and me paying for further education and helping you out with accommodation. What would you really like to do with your life? And don't forget about Elly. She loves you and is always asking after you.'

'You don't fucking believe me. You just want to control me. I get a buzz from my work, my men and my contacts. I'll grow that business into something really big. I'm not a fucking loser like my dad.'

'If your Dad had been different, you wouldn't be doing this. Is that what you're saying?'

'He did me a favour. He moved out. Then I did what I wanted.'

'Isn't that what he did? He did what he wanted and now you think he's a loser.'

'He had kids. I don't.'

'OK. Don't answer immediately because it's extremely important for me. You're over twenty-one and consider yourself an adult. Yes?'

'Too fucking right.'

'If you think breaking the law is OK because the law is made by arseholes, as you say, then people like you and me should make our own judgment and do whatever we see fit. Yes?'

Andy remained silent for half a minute before saying, 'Yeah, natural justice, it wins in the end anyway. Yeah, natural justice.'

'You could be right. Fits in better with survival of the fittest, but where does compassion fit in?' asked Victor.

'What is this, a fucking quiz?'

'Please bear with me for a bit. It's extremely important for me.'

'Compassion is a weakness,' said Andy. 'Like you said, survival of the fittest.'

'What about when people have shown you compassion? Where does that fit?'

'I'd have got by. I've always bought and sold stuff. I'd have collected my dole money and I'd more'n likely have used my contacts better had you and your fucking family not interfered. And I wouldn't be at the other end of the fucking world.'

'So that I don't put words in your mouth and again, please bear with me, tell me what you're going to do with your life in Cape Town.'

'This is stupid,' said Andy.

'Please, just tell me. I feel it's important for you to say it. It's like owning something or, possibly being able to look at it from a different angle. You're young, you're fit, you're a good-looking guy and you're quite entitled to change your mind. Go on, Andy, indulge me. You've heard my reasoning over the last couple of days. Let me hear yours.'

'You hoped to convert me like some priest by bringing me to this place. Well, it didn't fucking work.'

Victor remained still and silent for over a minute while Andy stared at the ground.

'When I get back to Cape Town, I'm going to concentrate on an area with my men to ensure we keep the territory. It's not been farmed properly, so there's nobody there that's making good money. My mates and me are, and because I'm proving myself and making lots of money for some really big guys, I get assistance when I need it to keep others out; plus, I've got other areas lined up already where I can leave guys to look after them. OK, is that good enough for you? Because if it's not, it's too fucking bad.'

'Who's buying the stuff?' asked Victor casually.

'Young guys like you said. They buy any shit once they know where to get it.'

'Fair enough,' said Victor. 'No second thoughts then.'

'You've got to be fucking joking,' said Andy getting to his feet.

'OK. Let's get going,' said Victor.

Only the dust cloud streaming from the car was visible to Victor in the rear view mirror, like a light brown comet's trail against darker brown earth and ahead, the shimmering desert road and its watery reflection maintaining a constant distance below the vast blueness.

'We're outside the reserve. You can relax now.'

'I've been relaxed all along,' said Andy, clutching a bottle of water and leaning back in the seat to hone his plans for Cape Town. However, thoughts of Hendrik making him say thanks when he asked for a coffee came to the surface, making him flinch. Fuck 'em all he thought, feeling niggled. He thought of his father filling the doorway as Hendrick had done and of Hendrick's non-threatening hands engulfing his own at dinner and breakfast, and the sound of Hendrick's voice almost a whisper, automatically commanding attention. He thought of Mary and her youthful figure and remembered glancing down her blouse and seeing her breasts and protruding nipples hanging in a loose-fitting bra as she put the tray down in front of them. He winced when he remembered telling

Victor that the only thing that would have brightened Mary's day would have been if Victor had stayed behind and given her a really good shagging. His face twitched as he failed to recall his mother's image. He thought of Kirsten ditching him soon after she met Victor, using language she'd not used before – *accepting abuse or something* – she'd said, after he'd called her a slag for talking to an older man at a party. He felt his mother moving out of reach as he thought of the many weekly letters she'd sent him. He clenched his back muscles, readjusted his seat and thought of the guys waiting for him in Cape Town, and imagined the money he'd soon be making and how he'd spend it. Then thoughts of Elly popped up. He could hear her pleading with their mother – *please, please, please let me wake him before I go to school* - then she'd hug him while he pretended to be asleep or he'd hold her wrist with his eyes still closed while she laughed and struggled. He quickly returned to thoughts of Cape Town, the money, his mates and his plans, but these were eclipsed by further thoughts of Mary; in horror, he involuntarily turned his head towards the car door to fend off an image of his mother kneeling on the floor of his bedroom, as Kirsten had often done, and being fucked by Victor. But then a vivid image of his real father replaced Victor and he clearly heard his father's voice – *how long have you been there you little prick* – he'd been seven years old. He remembered his mother crying on the other side of the slammed door and he, crying and banging on the door, thinking his mother was in pain, the door being opened and his father hitting him across the face with the flat of his hand, and how he'd rushed into the bedroom and been hugged and almost smothered in her dressing gown with the sound of the front door slamming shut.

'Are you OK?' asked Victor.

Andy groped under the seat for a fresh bottle and savoured the excess water running down his chin to his tee-shirt and his black shorts. He turned towards the door, closed his eyes and fitfully slept for nearly an hour before being woken by a change in road noise. Looking ahead, he saw the road had narrowed to little more than a track that stretched to the horizon. He looked past Victor's profile to the north and saw the road they'd been on disappearing behind the car.

'This is not only quicker, but if you look out your side in an hour or so, you'll see beautiful rocky outcrops.'

Andy unfolded a map and, with Victor's help, located Keetmanshoop, but the vast light brown open spaces spread over his lap only amplified his feeling of disconnection, making him feel slightly sick. He quickly folded it and closed his eyes.

In spite of the heat, a cold shiver ran down Victor's spine and goose bumps formed on his arms. He fumbled for the bottle of water jammed in the shelf under the steering wheel, and with his elbows on the wheel, undid the cap, took a long drink and poured the remainder over his head. The distance to the rocky outcrops Anne and he had climbed during their South African trip alluded him, but the memory of them making love near the top remained vivid; perhaps under an hour he thought. He'd started rehearsing the story he'd tell of his trip, with Andy airbrushed out, when he felt the car's engine falter; he was only partly relieved to discover his right heel rising and falling nervously, almost vibrating the accelerator. He put his foot down and blocked out all noise, apart from the drumming tyres which gave him the feeling of being propelled by some angry powerful animal beneath the car as it rose above the stones. A deep flat twenty-kilometre wide stony bay, surrounded by high rocks, jolted his memory. He turned and slowed the car for the eight kilometre drive over soft ground to the back of the bay.

Beads of sweat ran down Andy's face, and salt outlined previously dried areas of his black tee-shirt. The silence woke him.

'Can't stop here, there's no bloody shade. Where are we? All I can see is rocks and sand. Where's the road?'

'What about that beautiful outcrop of rocks on your left? You can see the colours change with the height. Look at the shadows where the overhangs are. It's like a live Pierneef painting.'

'You're sightseeing. Can't we just keep driving? I've had enough. Where are we?'

'We've travelled about seventy kilometres from the turn-off where you picked up the map and I think there's about fifty to the next main road. Keetmanshoop is about two hundred from there. The track we were on is about fifteen kilometres over there,' said Victor, gesturing to the right.

'Don't tell me we're going to drive across the desert. We'll get stuck and fucking die.'

'We probably could drive but we won't. It's only a thin layer of sand on rock. The trick is to roll to a standstill in neutral, with no brakes and then pull away with as little traction as possible. Besides, I've got a shovel and mats if we get stuck.'

'Glad you're so confident. Why've we stopped?'

'I've been in this area before and it's as beautiful as I remember. The girls stayed behind with friends while Anne and I went exploring, so I'm going to take a few pictures and then I'm going to find a crevice in the rocks up on that far ridge of sandstone,' he said pointing to a shaded overhang, 'and I'm going to leave something there.'

Andy shook his head and breathed an exaggerated sigh of exasperation, opened the door and got out. Victor also got out and rummaged through the cooler box at the back of the car.

'Here, have one of these,' said Victor, rubbing an apple against his shirt.

'You have it. If we're going, let's go,' said Andy, getting back in the car and holding a fresh cold bottle of water against his chest. 'I can't hang about in this heat.'

Victor's hands were shaking as he rummaged through his rucksack for a small box.

'Come on, let's get going,' said Andy, without any intonation of malice.

Victor's mouth was too dry to reply immediately and he motioned to Andy to throw him the water bottle.

'We can't get closer to the hills with the car,' stated Victor, putting on socks and walking boots. 'The sand inclines towards the hills. It'll be too deep.'

'Don't tell me you're going to fucking walk.'

'Yes. It looks a long way but it's less than two kilometres and it won't take long to climb to that ridge. You can see the way up quite clearly. Have a look through the binoculars.'

'How long is this going to take? It's already a quarter to twelve.'

'Twenty minutes there, say fifteen minutes up, ten down and twenty back. That's twenty, thirty-five - an hour and a bit,' replied Victor feeling calmer.

'I know you, Victor, that's going to be one-thirty at the earliest. And that's not counting the time you'll be looking at this, that and the other. What're you expecting to see when you get there for Christ's sake?'

'I'm not sure,' said Victor, putting two bottles of water in his shoulder bag.

'What's that?' asked Andy, looking at the box Victor was about to push into the bag.

'I'm going to leave this up there. It's just something I have to do.'

'Give me the fucking thing, whatever it is. I'll go. I'll be back in less than an hour and then we leave for Keet-whatever the fucking place is called.'

'Keetmanshoop,' said Victor.

'Whatever. Give it to me.'

'I promised Jenifer I'd leave it in the wilderness in a secure position away from the weather and sun, that's all.'

Did Andy really flinch at Jenifer's name thought Victor?

'There's plenty of places up there. Don't you worry. I'll find a place for it. What is it?'

'It's something for posterity. Everybody has some foible or another. Can I trust you to find a secure dry place on that ridge?' he asked, pointing to the shadow of an overhang.

'I'll do it. OK.'

'Perhaps I'll get some really good shots of you with the telephoto lens.'

'Whatever,' said Andy putting on his trainers.

'Here,' said Victor handing over the box.

Andy took it with hardly a glance and shoved it into his shoulder bag along with half a bottle of water.

'It's better to wear your boots. The heat from the sand will be too much for those. And put a lot of suntan lotion on and take another bottle. It's well over forty. And make a noise on the way up; don't want you accidentally cornering a leopard or something.' Why am I telling him all this thought Victor? I don't give a shit about him.

Andy went through the pocket of his bag, found the suntan lotion, squeezed out far more than necessary in order to make a point, carelessly smeared it over his face and neck and went off towards the rocks without a word, his boots or additional water.

CHAPTER 39

Only the Groblers on their remote farm could honestly say that they'd seen him and Andy together thought Victor, while picking at the detail of his plan for Andy for the umpteenth time since flirting with the idea twenty-four hours ago. However, Andy's intervention of taking the box from him and volunteering to place it up in the hills, virtually pre-empted the major part of the plan, where Victor intended to construct a reason for Andy to leave the car for a moment or two, check the rear tyre, make sure the tailgate was closed or some such thing, and then drive away without him, knowing full well he'd last no more than ten hours at the most.

Victor could picture himself saying casually to Cindy: *'who knows, he may call you out of the blue at any time. His Dad did exactly the same with his mother.'* In fact he'd silently rehearsed it a number of times while driving during the morning and was now convinced that the whole project was just about risk-free and do-able, including facing the interrogation he anticipated from Cindy and Jenifer, and the barrage of more subtle questions from Susan. The only misgivings, which now started to amplify themselves, were his thoughts about the box and the demise of Andy and his fear of recalling them at some future time as a single event. He tossed this about in his mind for a few minutes, then steeled himself into accepting it, along with blocking out of all feelings for Andy. Yet again, his mind went back to his plan. He had no trouble justifying it to himself from a socially responsible point of view, which he believed to be the single and paramount reason anyway. He considered the personal benefits, such as removing an irritant from Cindy and Esther to be a byproduct, a sideshow, an incidental benefit, a bonus (he actually thought of it as cream on the top before self-censuring). And good for Andy he concluded, as he envisaged him failing to satisfy his masters and being tortured to death as an example to some other would-be trader who thought he could bite off more and still be allowed to chew it.

If only I'd done as I'd intended and left the box in some secluded place yesterday he thought, while focusing the telephoto lens on Andy who was walking towards the base of the rocks. He readjusted the tripod and looked at the rock shelf below the overhanging rock, a hundred metres above and about two and a half kilometres away. However, the cave created by the overhang was too deep to see anything, let alone any ledge that Andy might find within it. *Why on earth did I leave it to him?* he thought. *I could have said no and insisted I go myself. At least that would have separated my thinking about Andy and the box. Jenifer will question: where, when, how, what time? She's the one with a serious investment in the box. I don't even know why I'm putting myself through this* he thought; *I could have just thrown it away. Nobody would have been any the wiser.*

Jenifer, never far from Victor's thoughts, had rehabilitated herself in his mind and the thought of her being hurt by Andy had left a deep scar in his psyche, which only Andy could have repaired with some conciliatory word or action. The fact that nothing had been forthcoming from him increasingly riled Victor and now, as he watched him arrogantly walking into the distance without any regret for his malicious attack on her, or even an enquiry regarding the damage she suffered, or her welfare, he felt he could burst. He then thought of the two girls in the restaurant as though they were his daughters, becoming sexually depraved in order to support their drug dependency because of the likes of Andy. One thought led to another until he felt he could take it no more. 'You worthless piece of shit!' he shouted at the top of his voice.

*

Two kilometres away Andy could only hear the noise of his unrestrained heavy breathing while he clawed his way upwards through the baking-hot rocks. He stopped a third of the way up and looked back at the small, silver car, then saw a dark shape bobbing up and over the rocks as it rapidly closed in on him. He almost cried out as the shadow of a very large, inquisitive bird passed over him. Badly shaken, feeling vulnerable and alone, he immediately and subconsciously sought Victor's company and was relieved to see his shimmering image through the waves of hot air standing near the car. He sat for a moment and thought about Victor's expression and strange mannerisms as he had handed the box to him. *Victor looked OK while he was preparing to go up the rocky outcrop by himself* he thought, *but then looked like he was going to die, couldn't even speak properly, and his hand was shaking while he fiddled with his bag for the box. I wonder if he's really ill* he thought, *I've heard of old buggers like him suddenly getting ill and dying.* Then Andy felt his shoulder muscles relax as he remembered Victor perking up a bit when he told him he'd find a secure place for whatever it is in that box.

Andy looked up towards the overhanging rocks and reassessed his capability and pace under the relentless sun and, with less enthusiasm and a nagging feeling, he resumed his climb. Fifteen minutes later, after throwing his bag onto the rocky shelf, he heaved himself onto it and stood shaking and sweating profusely below the overhang. He pulled at the backpack's drawstring to get at the water bottle, causing it to knot, which he impatiently fiddled with before losing his temper and snapping it by tearing the top open. He looked at the bottle, thought of Victor advising him to take more water, mumbled 'fuck it' and slowly drank most of the water before carefully resealing the bottle and putting it back in his pack.

Andy's eyes became accustomed to the dark after a few minutes, enabling him to make out the cave's details and take tentative steps towards its inner wall. 'Victor!' he cried out (but was never able to recall using Victor's name) as he heard the scraping of claws on rocks all about him. He stared open-eyed, but couldn't see the six or seven well-camouflaged rabbit-sized creatures scamper past him. He spun around as if to run, just in time to see the silhouettes of the Rock Hyraxes before they disappeared over the lip of the ledge. His heart was pounding while he walked along, close to the wall in the eerie silence, over the cushion of hundreds of years of accumulated dung, in search of a suitable deep ledge for the box among the many shallow ones. Impatient and trembling too much to get the square box, together with his hand, through the small round opening in his pack, he shook the contents on to the floor. He picked the box up, unwrapped it and felt its solid gloss-smooth finish and pebble embossing before holding it to his ear and shaking it. Hearing nothing, he took it into the light near the front of the cave and read: *Olay Anti-Wrinkle Pro-Vital Anti-ageing Moisturiser Day Cream;* prised the lid open, tearing it from its sellotaped edge. He pulled out a plain glass jar by its silver top, spilling its foam packing. Finding nothing written on the jar and failing to unscrew the lid, which appeared to be sealed with some sort of lumpy resin, he returned to the ledge, stretched up and pushed the jar in as far as his fingers could reach. Then he bent down, put his sun-cream container and other things back in the backpack, put it over one shoulder and carried his near-empty water bottle back to the edge of the overhang where the sun beat down on the rocky ground. Still shaken, he returned to the ledge, dropped his backpack and water bottle and tried to retrieve the jar. It moved further back into the ledge with each touch. He jumped up while gripping the ledge with one hand and dived for the jar with the other but his middle finger jabbed the rock above, bending the nail back before hitting the jar and sending it further back. 'Fuck it,' he said, shaking his damaged hand and looking about for something to stand on. Outside, he found a rock, too heavy to carry, but easy enough to roll. He balanced on it and grabbed the jar, hopped off and returned to the light with it. With his left hand he picked at the sealant holding the silver screw cap, while blood from his throbbing finger coated the jar making it difficult to grip. He then gently tapped the cap in several places against a rock to break the seal. It opened easily. He looked inside at the whitish granules, held the jar to his nose and sniffed. Sensing nothing, he eased the paper liner out of the jar and read: *Anne Elliott, Oxford, UK. May 16th 2010.*

*

Victor sat in the car with his feet on the ground outside and anguished over his own incompetence at not foreseeing the actions of the disposal of Anne's ashes and the demise of Andy as a single event before handing them to Andy. *I've no feeling for ashes. I'm not interested in bloody symbols and there's probably nothing of Anne in there anyway* he thought. *Serves me bloody right for being so eager to take advantage of Andy's offer, but it was probably what I needed to kick-start the plan. What a bloody shock I got when he said he'd go - completely threw me. She let this ashes thing drag on and on* he thought. 'Leave these in South Africa,' Jenifer said, '--- the rest can go in the Thames when you get back and we're all together.' 'Shit,' he said aloud, clenching the hair on the side of his head and banging his elbows on his knees. *I could have told them to come to the river when I found the container during the renovation, but no.... I listened to Jenifer, and now this fuck up: leaving everything to the last minute as usual. I could come back in a few days and look for it* he thought. 'Stop it, stop it, stop it!' he shouted, throwing the tripod into the back of the car and slamming the tailgate.

Victor returned to his position on the passenger seat, unaware his left heel was dancing up and down until he tried to focus the binoculars on Andy. Even then he could hardly make him out through the haze. One second he appeared lanky, the next he seemed to be severely distorted and floating in the air. He put the binoculars on his knees as angry thoughts of retribution pervaded his very being and invoked memories of Anne's memorial service: the black dresses, the dark suits and the solemn looks. *Was I the only one who knew she'd have hated this* he thought. *And that bloody crematorium, the ceremony with its smells and noises and pathetic, pious, presumptuous words and me, numb to it all.* He remembered the embarrassment, which he now relived, of being unable to talk and using some innate ridiculous smile to fend off soundless mouths opening and closing in front of him. *And if that hadn't been bad enough,* he thought, *there was Jenifer asking me to visit the crematorium a few days later with Sylvia and then she cried and became non-communicative when I said no for the umpteenth time, and bugger me, if she didn't come back bearing the container like a trophy.* He remembered Jenifer's unflinching look when he'd suggested that perhaps he should rub the ashes into his skin with a Brillo pad to make sure he really hurt.

'As though the pain hadn't been sufficient, and now this,' he shouted, throwing the binoculars into the back of the car. He took one of the plastic bottles from the foot-well of the passenger seat, unscrewed its top, leaned forward and slowly poured water over his neck, letting it seep through his hair and drip onto his knees. He threw the un-capped empty bottle back into the foot-well and vigorously rubbed his wet face with both hands. He got up, slammed the passenger door, went to the driver's side and lowered himself into the seat. 'You're way beyond salvation,' he murmured, glancing in the direction of Andy through the windscreen while he carefully eased the bulk of the car forward from its sandy, settled indentation. Half a minute later, and relieved to hear the drumming of the tyres travelling fast over the stony surface, away from the hazards of sand and oppressive heat, Victor opened his window and the rear window on the opposite side of the car and let the air flow over his sweat-soaked shirt. He pushed thoughts of Andy away and concentrated on the night's accommodation, but within seconds, his thoughts turned to the construction of plausible stories he'd need for his return home: his loss of communication with Andy -- *he said he'd be there and didn't turn up; never did give me his mobile number and then he walked out of Esther's place without a trace. No, I didn't find out where he normally went.* His failure to coerce Andy to join him -- *he enjoyed his day out with me looking at seals, penguins and baboons but he wouldn't come away for a few days. Yes, I did my best to persuade him.* Placing the ashes in the rocks -- *long walk through burning sand to some isolated rocks – yes, I did find a cool dry place; no, the silver lid will not corrode. The view was wonderful from the top.* All these and other well-rehearsed phrases to parry anticipated, penetrating questions. However, he was aware of his reddening face while thinking through potential questions about the ashes: *did you cover the container? Will baboons be able to get at it and play with it 'till it breaks? I'd hate to thinks of Mum's ashes harming some wild animal, that would be horrid, and she'd be horrified. If it's the only metal item in the hills will lightning strike it in* a *storm? Oh, I do hope you put it in a secure place. Was it sandy or rocky? You said you jammed it in, but if it was sandy was the rock crumbling? Did Andy know you were going to dispose of mum's ashes? Do you think that's why he wouldn't go with you?*

'I don't care about fucking ashes,' he screamed, hitting the steering wheel with his fist.

Suddenly he felt frightened as his vision of Anne disappeared from his mind leaving only her disapproval. Andy deserves to die of sunstroke he argued; better than being knifed or tortured in some back street. He imagined Andy coming down from the rocky outcrop and wandering into the desert looking for the car. He'd think he'd come down the wrong way and panic. He probably wouldn't even find the car's tracks. So what if he did? He'd possibly make five miles at the most before sunset, and then if he was lucky, find a cave for the night. The cold would get to him wherever he'd be and he'd sleep, possibly for the last time. *Would it be the last time* thought Victor? *Perhaps he'd wake up with a hyena sniffing about. He might even drive it away by screaming and swinging his bag at it, but then it would skulk off to a safe distance into the dark and yelp, yelp, yelp until it was joined by others. Then it would return with them and they'd surround him and size him up while he screamed, threw stones, perhaps put some in his bag, before swinging it about. Then one would rush in and grab it, making him fall. The others would move their heads from side to side watching him adopt a foetal position before tentatively snapping at his body.* Victor saw all this clearly in his mind's eye: the bloody furry heads and Andy's flaying stumps.

*

Jesus Christ, fucking ashes! thought Andy, involuntarily jerking the jar from under his nose thinking he could smell something unpleasant. Then he brought it slowly back and, while keeping it at waist height, he peeped in from one side as if something would leap out. His shaking hands tried to get the paper back in the jar. 'Fuck it!' he shouted, tipping the ashes away from him and stepping back. He replaced the paper in the jar, scooped some sand off the ground with it, screwed the top back on, ignoring the cross threading and strode back to the rear wall of the cave. He jammed the jar in the nearest crevice and ran into the sunlight near the edge of the ledge where he stopped and cleaned his hands against his shorts. He stood shaking and moaning with thoughts of his Oupa's funeral; thoughts that were so close to the surface of his consciousness that he could almost smell the loss of him. He recalled the church service as though it had happened that day and remembered the noise of his own sobbing while his father looked down at him – *Stop making a fool of yourself, Prick.* Humiliation welled up within him as it did that day, and tears filled his eyes as for the first time in his life, he pictured himself as a little boy.

He pulled his tee-shirt to his face and roughly wiped his eyes and face.

Unbearable haze filled his vision as he tried to search for Victor with his eyes stinging with sun cream. Having no intention of returning to the shade of the cave, he sat on a rock, leaned over his knees and let his nose run and tears flow while he sobbed. No longer feeling anxious or rushed, he waited fifteen minutes before getting up.

Half climbing, half sliding on his bottom, Andy reached the bottom of the rocky outcrop and stood shaking, thinking of Victor's loss and inability to dispose of the ashes. *And yet he trusted me,* he thought.

Making no attempt to dry his face or construct a story, Andy walked the last three hundred metres, watching Victor walking towards him with a full bottle of water.

'You couldn't do it, could you, Victor?' said Andy.

'You're correct, Andy. I couldn't.'

If you would like to find out about more books from this author, please get in touch at:

heroffeyauthor@gmail.com

Printed in Great Britain
by Amazon

24143604R00179